"Grea

"It's brandy! It's to take the edge from your hunger! And if you think I'm trying to make you boskey, you were never more out in your life!"

Lucy was not quite certain what boskey meant, but didn't like the sound of it.

"No, I thank you sir, none for me. I'm persuaded I should not like it!"

"And I am persuaded, Miss, that you shall have it!" replied Sheldon, exasperated by her implacable demeanor.

Lucy put up a hand. "No, I thank you. I should not like it."

Before she realized his intention, his lordship had an arm round her, tilting her backwards, his other hand pouring the fiery liquid down her throat, saying a trifle breathlessly, as he did so, but in a voice resolved to be agreeable, "And I think Ma'am, that it will do you good!"

A LADY OF BREEDING

Delia Ellis

FAWCETT CREST • NEW YORK

A Fawcett Crest Book
Published by Ballantine Books
Copyright © 1987 by Delia Ellis

ISBN 0-449-22002-8

This edition published by arrangement with Malvern Publishing Co. Ltd.

Manufactured in the United States of America

First Ballantine Books Edition: September 1991

PROLOGUE

They sat in the orchard, two figures: the smaller neatly in one of two chairs placed side by side in an open, sunny patch: the other gangly, sprawled on cushions at her feet, her mass of red hair dangling into her aunt's lap as the girl read from the letter received that morning.

It was warm for so early in the year. Winter might yet make a further stand before relinquishing its fearsome hold on the land, yet today was too cheerful not to take advantage of such a generous respite, and even Mrs Chadwick had not protested too vehemently when Lucy had collected their shawls and dragged her off to sit amidst gnarled trees hung with young blossom, while they viewed her situation.

'Read that last part again, child,' said Mrs Chadwick, whilst adjusting the rim of her bonnet to keep the sun from her eyes. 'It sounds very abrupt to me.'

'I expect letters of business always are, Aunt,' said Lucy calmly, turning back to the letter. 'It only says that the Earl of Sheldon will be pleased to receive me on the twelfth of this month to see if I will suit his purposes. Does that seem so out of the ordinary?'

Mrs Chadwick absentmindedly twirled one of Lucy's curls around her finger. 'It sounds cool. I do not like to think of you being employed by such a man.'

'His secretary wrote the letter, Aunt. Not the Earl. *He* is probably perfectly amiable. It's my experience that most people are amiable if you treat them with respect.'

Her aunt looked down at her fondly, 'And you have such a deal of experience of people, my love, haven't you! Why you must have visited among at least a dozen or so families during your long life! And we number so many Earls among our acquaintances!'

'An Earl is only a person. I don't see that it makes so much difference what rank he holds. It need not make him the less amiable.'

'Amiable or not, your uncle and I would much rather you did not go. Your uncle won't argue with you, but he thinks your place is here with us, as Tom and I do.'

'But he isn't my uncle. That's just it. If he were, I might remain here without a qualm.'

'Lucy Tiversley! How it would hurt him to hear you say that.'

Lucy reached up to touch Mrs Chadwick's cheek. 'Does that seem hurtful, dearest Aunt Marianne? Forgive me. I never meant it to. My own parents could not have been more to me than you and he. But still, Uncle Chadwick has Tom to consider.'

'We are not wealthy, my dear,' said Mrs Chadwick, mildly pink, 'But we aren't penniless, you know. Providing for you will not prevent us from providing for our son. It is distressing that you should think so. Remember that we *are* your godparents, if nothing else. Even on that head your Mama would have expected us to ensure that you get a suitable dowry now that she is no longer here

2

to look after such matters. And your uncle's own sense of fitness makes him wish to do so!'

Lucy gazed anxiously up at her, wishing she could obey. It would be pleasant indeed to ignore the promptings of conscience and remain within the loving circle into which her mother had placed her so long ago.

'Uncle Chadwick has already done too much for me,' she said haltingly. 'If I were beautiful someone might be prepared to marry me without a dowry, but look at me, Aunt! Only think how much Uncle would have to provide to get me married respectably.'

'My dearest child! One would think you were a positive antidote! You have such a sweet nature that someone will be sure to wish to marry you.'

'I have yet to hear that men marry women for their sweet natures. In my experience, men marry either beauty or money, and, wherever possible, both! They don't marry beanpoles, with red hair and freckles!'

'So we are back to your experience again, are we? My dear girl, in *my* experience the reasons why men marry are totally beyond a woman's reasoning. You are forgetting how many accomplishments you have!'

'Indeed, Aunt, I am *not*. That's why I *know* that I can earn enough to keep myself. If you and Uncle hadn't given me so many opportunities to improve myself I should never have dared to apply to an Earl for a position. But now I am perfectly confident that I have all that is necessary to be governess to his niece.'

'No-one doubts your accomplishments for a second. When I remember how reluctant you were to apply yourself when you were small, I never cease to be amazed at you now. If you weren't such a romp you could be mistaken for a positive blue-stocking.'

'Which will make me the perfect governess.'

'I cannot help wishing that your father had paid more heed to things at Helmsworth instead of joining the army when your Mama died,' began Mrs Chadwick on a familiar theme. 'Knowing the estate was entailed away from you should have made him more prudent, not less. But there, he was always a shatterbrain. Only your Mama could keep him in order. With careful management the estate would have yielded you a more than adequate dowry. But he had to make it his personal mission to rid the world of that dreadful Bonaparte creature and get himself killed in the process. And now to see your cousin in *your* home and you with no dowry is what I have no patience with. Your Mama would turn in her grave!'

'It's not so bad, Aunt. I may yet enjoy teaching.'

'Only promise me, my dear girl, that if you are unhappy you won't be too proud to come home.'

Lucy sprang up, grabbed her hat from where she had carelessly thrown it down onto the grass, and put out a hand to pull her aunt out of her chair. 'No fear of that!' she said gaily.

CHAPTER

1

At the peremptory ringing, Jeremy, the porter, in his blue and white livery, jumped up from his chair and walked expectantly toward the imposing front door of his master's Grosvenor Square Mansion. He trusted that their visitor would be one of the Earl's more generous friends, anticipating the pleasure of adding say a golden guinea to his private little hoard of tips.

His fantasy dissolved in an instant when, on opening the door, he found himself confronting not a town swell, with money jingling in his pockets, but two young ladies. He eyed them narrowly, even his long experience being insufficient to place them socially with any certainty.

His instinct told him that the shorter was maidservant to the other, since she had modestly lowered eyes and clasped her hands before her in the proper manner. Her tall companion was more difficult. She seemed a mass of contradictions. Ladies who looked at him so squarely could, as a rule, be depended upon to be exquisitely turned out. They always wore dashing bonnets at just the right angle, above charming hairstyles and perfect complexions. They held elegant skirts carefully away from steps to preserve their neatness. If, like this lady, they were so unfortunate as to be cursed with red hair, it was at least arranged with propriety and not allowed to escape riotously in wisps from beneath an unhappy Villager straw hat. He couldn't actually recall any of his lordship's acquaintances having such an unfortunate case of freckles, but he was sure that anyone suffering from such an aberration would at least make some attempt to mitigate it by wearing a veil, when out in the sun, and carrying a parasol. This lady, he noted with displeasure did neither, indeed she seemed weighed down with what appeared to be a large portfolio.

He would have liked to tell her to use the servants' entrance, but her unwavering glance held him captive. Instead, with barely disguised insolence, he asked her her business.

'My business is with your master,' came Lucy's prompt reply, her chin jutting out alarmingly at his tone. 'You will find that he *is* expecting me.' And she held out to him a plain visiting card as she walked past him into the grand hall, to stand by an ormolu table, while she inspected a painting of a racehorse placed on the wall above it.

The card gave him few clues. 'Miss Tiversley?' he asked doubtfully. 'I—er—don't . . .'

'Miss Lucy Tiversley. Daughter to the late Viscount Tiversley,' she annunciated clearly, turning back to him.

His mouth dropped, and he was about to take up a more conciliatory stance when she ruined the effect by explaining, 'I am here in reply to the Earl's advertisement for a governess.'

'I see, Miss,' he replied, with heavy disdain born of enlightenment. 'I will enquire whether his lordship is at home.'

'There is no need for that,' came a cool voice from the upper reaches of the ornate stairway which led from the entrance vestibule to the other storeys of the house. 'Miss Tiversley is to come up at once.'

Lucy looked up, but could see no sign of the person from whom had come the command. But the voice was sufficient, for without more ado she was being ushered up the circular stairway and led through an impressive doorway to find herself in a book-lined room, her servant instructed to await her mistress on a straight chair stationed outside.

'Sit down, won't you, Miss Tiversley.'

The room being a large one she could not immediately perceive from whence had issued the instruction and looked about her with interest, finally locating the Earl in one of two armchairs placed on either side of a handsome marbled fireplace. He beckoned to her with his finger, his manner seeming so much to infer that she was too much beneath him to deserve more of his conversation than was absolutely necessary that she found herself fighting a wild desire to laugh. She struggled to control her features, apparently unsuccessfully, since he stared hard at her, and asked, 'You find something amusing?'

The sour glint he threw at her effectively squashed her humour and she hastened to reassure him before he turned back to a letter in his hand, which he now perused intently through his quizzing glass, leaving her to watch him from beneath her lashes.

Just for an instant she recollected her aunt's strictures on rank. It seemed odd to think that being an Earl could affect one's humour, but how strange that such a handsome man should make himself so fierce just by the simple trick of turning down the corner of his mouth.

The Earl interrupted her meandering thoughts, allowing his quizzing glass to fall. 'Well, Miss Tiversley, it would certainly *seem* from your guardian's letter that you have all the requisite qualifications.'

Lucy did not like his tone. 'I can assure you, my lord,' she pronounced clearly, looking him straight in the eye, 'that you need not doubt the veracity of Mr Chadwick's letter. When he writes that I speak

7

French and Italian, have a good knowledge of the globes, play the pianoforte, sew and embroider well, and draw moderately, it is no more than simple truth. I also sing a little, but my voice is not strong, so we did not include it in the letter. I say this to you, my lord, not because I wish to blow my own bugle, you understand, simply to reassure you that my uncle is the most truthful of men. Why, he would be incapable even of mild prevarication.' This last was said as a matter for congratulations.

Unable to believe her outburst, the Earl lifted his quizzing glass in her direction, thus allowing Lucy the hideous spectacle of one huge eye apparently suspended in mid-air, a sight which had, on occasion, unnerved more than one of his protagonists. Lucy was made of sterner stuff and did not allow her glance to waver for as much as a moment.

Not one to waste his time on lost causes, the Earl let the instrument of chastisement fall and tried another tack for her discomposure.

'You are very young, Miss Tiversley,' he said, looking at her intently. 'Perhaps you will explain how you come to be so gifted, for I am sure that none of the ladies of my acquaintance have such a list of accomplishments.'

'With respect, sir, none of those ladies was raised by my aunt,' replied Lucy with a smile, which drew an answering smile from him.

'You would not let your godfather provide you with a dowry, child, but tell me, did your father leave no estate?'

'It is entailed,' she explained matter-of-factly. 'My cousin takes the house and the title.'

'Could you not live with him? That would certainly be more suited to one of your birth and years than the governessing trade.'

His innocent remark brought forth strange results, for she at once rose up majestically in her chair, to cry out in ringing tones, 'Live with my cousin! I'd die rather! Why, he called Papa a . . . a ne'er do well, just because he went to fight for King and country instead of staying at home to look after me. And I don't see how he could presume, do you, for if I don't mind, how should Hector?'

He took this to be a rhetorical question and, with no more than a raised eyebrow, returned to the letter.

'Tell me, child,' he said gently, as she regained her chair. 'Did your father not provide for you at all?'

'He thought he had, you see,' she said regretfully, but with tolerable composure. 'It was always his intention that I would join him with the army abroad as soon as I was old enough. And in case the worst should happen, he left instructions that, meantime, some of the profits of the estate should be put aside for me each year as a dowry. Only there never were any profits, just debts.'

'So cousin Hector has in effect inherited a pig in a poke.'

'He is lucky to get Helmsworth at all,' she replied hotly, 'and to say, as he has done ever since, that it is only my father's ill-management that has left me in so poor a pass, is the greatest vileness. Papa could not help being cheated by his steward!'

From his chair on the other side of the fireplace the Earl stared at her thoughtfully, his eye wandering down from her mop of unruly red curls to her clear blue eyes set above the riot of pale freckles which chased across her nose: mouth and chin suggested purpose, but then he had already had occasion to see that! He began to wonder if she wouldn't do very well.

She was tall, of course. Too tall to be fashionable. But since she was wearing quite the most off-putting dun-coloured gown he had ever seen, she obviously had no ambition to take the town by

9

storm. No bad thing since the girl had to work to keep herself. Pity about the freckles, but Denmark Lotion was said to be very good . . .

Her cough broke through his thoughts.

'So, you want to be a governess, Miss Tiversley?'

'Well of course, sir. That's why I applied,' she said, with heavy patience.

The Earl damped down his own hasty temper with difficulty. 'I begin to think you might suit me very well, though we have, of course, to ensure that you have all the accomplishments your uncle claims for you before I make a final decision.'

Lucy had risen to her feet and was purposefully pulling off her gloves before he completed his sentence.

"I would be most obliged, sir, if you would show me to a pianoforte, should you have a music room here, for I can see that my uncle's word is not enough. I cannot be at my ease while you continue to think me an imposter.'

Since Sheldon House, the Earl's Grosvenor Square residence, boasted quite the most magnificent music room that Lucy had ever seen, she was able to satisfy him in a remarkably short while that she *had* all the musical talent claimed, and a few moments more convinced him of her linguistic superiority. He would have taken her word for the rest but that, on their return to his study, she insisted on treating him to a geography lesson: nor would she be satisfied until he had made his way through her portfolio of quite admirable drawings. He would not have put it past her to demand material and thread to prove her other claims, but he had long been satisfied as to her suitability and stopped her in her tracks by saying, with a lift of his brow, 'If it was your intention to prove that my niece is to have a governess without match, you need proceed with this no further. I admit it! Freely!'

She looked at him darkly. 'I was *not* showing off! It was only that you seemed not to believe me.'

'Then I am well served,' he laughed, holding out his hand to her.

She hesitated.

'Come,' he said, putting his hand nearer. 'It is necessary to shake hands on our bargain.'

Gratefully she slid her hand into his.

In the minutes which followed the Earl told Lucy all about her new pupil. Lucy's expressive features exhibited all her sympathy when she heard how the Earl had lost his younger brother, a soldier like her own father, in the French wars, and she fully understood too, how it was that not even her child's need for a mother had been enough to prevent the Earl's sister-in-law from subsequently giving up her hold on a life which no longer held any meaning for her.

'Mary has not been strong since her mother's death,' said the Earl, shaking himself with difficulty from his memories. 'Our doctor thinks London air not good for her, else my sister, Lady Oswaldeston, would have the child to live with her. As it is, she must stay at home in the country. Mary has already had one governess, but Miss Tring found the solitude at Arunfold not to her taste. It can be gloomy in the country at any time,' he warned, 'but especially when the surrounding families are in London for the Season, so think carefully before you take up the charge.'

'Oh, but I love the country of all things. I never *can* understand why people should flock to town when there is so much more to do in the country, can you?'

That such a view of things had never been one he shared became immediately apparent from his horrified look, but he was not obliged to answer since, oblivious to his confusion, she asked eagerly,

'And when shall I take up my duties, sir?'

'Tomorrow, if you agree. We shall travel by curricle. Your maid can travel ahead with the baggage.'

Since it was obvious that he expected no quarrel, it was just as well that Lucy agreed at once to his wishes, but the complete absence of mistrust she displayed disconcerted him and he wondered briefly whether he had made a wrong decision. He was further troubled when she informed him without a qualm, 'But I must tell you, sir, that Alice is not *my* maid. She's Aunt Marianne's, and goes home tomorrow. I never had a maid myself. It has always seemed to me nonsensical to suppose that an adult should not be able to dress himself, do you not agree?'

Since his lordship employed an exclusive and, incidentally extremely expensive valet, it was too much to expect him to agree and he found himself making a mental note, his notions being liberal, to provide Lucy with a maid as a matter of urgency, if only to make her less complaisant.

'It will suit me, Miss Tiversley,' he said then, 'if your baggage could be sent on today with mine. Have it ready by about three o'clock and my man will collect it. You will require to keep an overnight bag with you, for we shall interrupt our journey to stay the night at a friend's house at Reigate. It is my intention to stay with Lady D'Avergne for a while once I have settled you in your new home, so we may as well break our journey and call in on our way down. You would find it too fatiguing to complete the journey in a day, I think.'

Considerably impressed by his thought for her welfare, she promised to be waiting at her hotel for him at ten o'clock on the following morning, before being summarily dismissed from his illustrious presence.

CHAPTER

2

When Lucy had gone, Alexander Carne, Seventh Earl of Sheldon, continued to sit where she had left him, musing on the strange whim which had prompted him to employ such an obvious scamp of a young woman. His mind drifted to thinking of Mary, bereft of both parents, and then, on inevitably to his own great loss. As always when he allowed himself to think about his brother's death, the muscles around his mouth became taut and a feeling of such bleakness overcame him that he almost cried aloud in his anguish.

Folly! he thought, sheer folly to lose him that way! He need never have gone! After all, he was only two years younger than Alexander and war was a young man's game. Besides, he had Grace to think of, and there would surely have been more children, for certainly never could there have been more of a love-match. As he thought of his sister-in-law, a lady known to both brothers since childhood, the tautness became more pronounced. If only the son she had been carrying could have been safely born before the news had come of Frederick's death. It might have been the saving of his wife, and, if not, at least Frederick's son would have been heir to the Earldom of Sheldon. As it was now, it would pass to Samuel. True enough Sam was the best of good fellows, but it just would not be the same. Too late now for himself, of course, admitted Alexander ruefully, wondering at the idiocy which had allowed him to leave to his younger brother the task of begetting an heir for Arunfold. Idiocy indeed! But never, in all his thirty-five years of seeking, had he found a woman to suit both his fastidious eye and his whimsical taste. Having come into the title a full decade before, mothers of all Society's promising young girls of ten seasons had had every opportunity to try to entrap his handsome person, and his very considerable fortune—indeed, it was largely their machinations and those of their offspring which had been responsible for the habitual expression of haughty boredom which now disfigured his face—but he had defied them all. Yet nobody would have been more delighted than Alexander himself had there been one, just one woman who did not bore him. However, it was not to be. And he was too set in his ways to marry now.

Not that he had lived chastely. Any number of the fair frail ones had looked to him for protection and had not looked in vain. But love was a different matter: the nearest he had ever come to loving a woman had been with Grace, his brother's wife, and honesty compelled him to admit that her great attraction had lain more in the aura of happiness which had surrounded her when she was with his brother than in any personal attraction. With their passionate attachment before him as an example, it had seemed an absurdity to sully the word marriage with any lesser emotion. And so he had remained a bachelor. And so, Arunfold would pass to his cousin Samuel . . .

The thought gave him little joy, and his twisted mouth became more pronouncedly so—yet he would not marry only for an heir. After all, Samuel was one of the family, if not one of his immediate family, and they had always rubbed along well together. Indeed, he had a deep affection for him. At least he was no boot-lick. And it wasn't as if Samuel had ever traded on his expectancy as some heirs to large fortunes did. In fact, he was amazingly circumspect in his behaviour and had increased substantially the already respectable portion Alexander's uncle had been able to leave him. Never could it be said for a moment that Sam was eager to step into his shoes, and the Earl knew beyond a doubt that he would have been among the first to wish him joy had Alexander ever shown the slightest inclination to marry. No-one either could have felt more sincerely the death of a cousin than had Sam when Freddy had died, and that was the truth of it. No, there was no reason not to be fully satisfied with his heir on any count—except that he was not from his immediate family. Strange how that became more important as he got older.

He continued to sit and to reflect idly on what might have been until, suddenly, his eye was caught by a sheet of paper on the floor by the armchair just vacated. Examination proved it to be one of Miss Tiversley's excellent drawings—of Tom Chadwick, so she had said, and obviously fallen from her portfolio. Alexander found himself smiling inwardly as he remembered her indignation when he had cast doubts as to her father's business acumen, but he knew that anyone daring to spread even the slightest smear on any aspect of his brother's life would have met with a like response—the dead, after all, had only their loved ones to protect them. He liked her loyalty! Pity she was so tall, he found himself thinking—and those freckles! But he hoped that she would do the trick for Mary. Certainly he must find something for she had been sadly down since her mother's death. Perhaps it was foolish to send a girl to teach her, but he had a strange feeling that Miss Tiversley might be just what was needed . . . Why, just to think of her made one smile!

Thus it was that when Lady Oswaldeston whirled her way into his library some few moments later, she was greeted, not with his usual bored expression, but by a brother with a ghost of a smile still lingering in his eye.

'Dearest,' she cried as she flew into the room, the lilac-coloured feathers which adorned her adorable gypsy hat dancing frantically with her swift movements, 'How happy I am to have caught you still in, for I am in absolute fidgets to know what you have done about a governess! Did you see the creature Lady Sefton recommended to you, or have you decided to interview Lady Jersey's choice?'

'Yes, and it's delightful to see you too, Fanny my love,' interrupted his lordship, raising one black brow sardonically.

Fanny was all contrition. 'Oh, my love,' she squeaked, taking both his hands in hers and lifting her lips to plant a sisterly tribute on one cheek, 'Am I indeed impolite? How horrid of me, and I am truly happy to see you, you know I am. It is only that I feel so odiously shabby not to be able to have the child with me here in London that I can hardly wait to know that she has some company. In truth, my heart mislikes me when I think of poor little Mary alone in the country.'

If his lordship was quietly reflecting to himself that the prompting of her heart was not so strong as to make her spend much time down at Arunfold with her niece, he was too fond of Fanny to scold her for it, merely contenting himself with lifting an eyebrow at her. His sister knew him well enough to interpret his look and was honest enough not to try to prevaricate.

'How horrid you are to torment me so, Alex, as if I do not care at all about Mary, when I do!' she said crossly. 'I would give all I own to have Freddy's little girl with me, but you know that Dr Knighton said she must not live in town. And you *could* not be so cruel as to ask me to leave town in the middle of the Season?'

'I know, my love, I know,' comforted her brother, lifting one of her hands to his lips and then letting them both go. 'Poor Fanny. So awkward for you to be such a social butterfly and yet to have a conscience which plagues you.'

'Yes, indeed, it is,' replied his sister, gratefully, 'For I am ever ashamed at being so sad a romp, but yet, I am such a town bird that the country makes me out of temper cross! Was anything ever so vexatious?'

'Well, you may be quite easy my love and cease to be at odds with yourself, since the business is completed. I have just hired Mary's governess—for a six month period only, to see how she suits.'

'How clever you are to set a period. I should never have thought of that. And did you choose Miss Tenchwood or Miss Simcott?' she asked, seating herself comfortably in the chair so recently occupied by Lucy, and pulling off her grey Limeric gloves so that she could more easily smooth down the skirt of her fashionable silk pelisse.

'Neither, fidget, I have engaged a certain Miss Tiversley for the post.'

His sister looked at him blankly. 'I do not remember anyone mentioning a Miss Tiversley to me.'

'Not altogether surprising, my love, since I heard of her myself only when she replied to my advertisement in the *Gazette*.'

'You are roasting me,' she replied incredulously. 'Why you would never have advertised for a governess. Everyone says that the only way to ensure that one is not taken in is to choose one on recommendation.'

'Nonetheless, I did advertise, my dear, because I did not much like the sound of either Miss Tenchwood or Miss Simcott.'

'But they both came most highly recommended, Alex, and surely Lady Jersey and Lady Sefton have had more experience in the matter than we have?'

'True,' agreed her brother fairly, 'Yet it seems to me that my aims for Mary are a little different from theirs. Lady Sefton told me that Miss Tenchwood would teach Mary to be quiet and obedient, and Lady Jersey that Miss Simcott has managed, apparently in spite of perfectly dreadful odds, to bring complete harmony to the nursery of an Honourable Mr Purdey, whoever he might be. But when I think of Freddy's little girl I cannot think that discipline is her principle need, can you?'

'Well . . . no . . . I suppose not. And what is Miss . . . er . . . what's her name, what's she like, brother?'

'Miss Tiversley is nineteen. She is the daughter of a viscount, now deceased, and, if I am not out in my opinion, the veriest scamp!' replied Alexander, without hesitation. 'If I mistake not, she will draw Mary from her depression quicker than any Misses Tenchwood or Simcott ever could.'

'Nineteen?' shrieked his sister in amazement. 'Nineteen? You must be running mad, brother! However can a girl of nineteen know enough to be a governess?'

'Oh, but she speaks two languages fluently, plays the pianoforte, draws admirably, sews and embroiders well, is more conversant with the globes than the crustiest schoolmaster and even sings a little— though I have it on the best authority that her voice is not strong,' he added reminiscently.

'Is the girl a beauty? Is that what it is?'

18

'Good lord, no!' laughed his lordship. 'Why, she's a veritable maypole, has the untidiest mop of red hair you ever saw, blushes violently every other second and has freckles! What's more, she was dressed in the most unflattering gown I've ever seen! Good Lord! A beauty! That's a loud one.'

'Well then, why? Why her?' asked Fanny, considerably relieved. She herself was a tiny, winsome beauty of exquisite proportions and had no very high opinion of tall ladies. 'What makes you think her suitable?'

'Well, you mistrustful harpy,' he replied earnestly, and for once his haughty expression had deserted him, 'I cannot hit on a way to make Mary happy. I rather hope, for Frederick's sake and for poor Grace that Miss Tiversley may do so for me. She was orphaned herself by the war, but she has not let it destroy her spirit. Somehow she has come through; and I want to see if she can do the same for Mary.'

At the bleakness in his voice, Fanny's eyes misted. She too had been overwhelmed at losing Frederick, but it had been for her a temporary pain which had gradually faded. She knew that for Alexander it never did, and her heart suffered more for him in his grief than it ever had for a brother long past worldly troubles. Once again, her hand reached for his. 'Well my dear,' she murmured, 'if you think this girl is competent enough then I am content.'

'Good girl,' said the Earl gratefully. 'And we must hope that we are not both disappointed.'

Later that evening, Alexander was accorded an opportunity to inform another member of his family about his plans for his niece. Dining at Watier's in Piccadilly, he ran into his cousin Samuel.

'Ah, there you are Sheldon old fellow,' cried his cousin cordially, on catching sight of him in the vestibule. ''Pon my soul, it's good to see you.'

'Samuel!' replied Alexander, in his usual clipped manner, but in no way discourteously.

His cousin liked to fancy himself a Pink of the ton in matters of dress, but, giving Alexander's coat a long, lingering glance, remarked admiringly, 'Deuced fine coat, old man! Stultz?'

'Good God, no!' replied Alexander, horrified. 'Weston. Strange—always thought it hung rather well, too,' he continued to reflect, as if to himself.

His cousin began to stammer reassurances, then, glancing at Alexander's expression, grinned sheepishly, but without the slightest sign of rancour. 'Lord, Shel, if you are not the most complete hand,' he chortled, 'And I fall for it every time, like the veriest flat.'

'And that's just what you are not,' remarked the Earl comfortingly, linking his arm through Samuel's and leading him towards the dining room. 'Have dinner with me and let me make it up to you.'

Samuel Carne was thought by most to be a very well-looking young man indeed. Some years younger than his illustrious cousin, he yet looked older than his twenty-six years, for his face was prematurely lined around the eyes and mouth. They were lines, though, of laughter and not from any meaner cause and he was generally well-liked wherever he went for his good nature. He had friendly, rather bovine brown eyes which exuded amiability and which led even remote acquaintances to confide to him all their particular troubles.

Despite Alexander's haughty ways, he had an enduring admiration for his lofty cousin, which would brook no criticism and, though he was proud to be his heir, not the worst of his enemies, should he have such a thing, could suspect him of wishing Alexander into an early grave in order that he might the sooner take the title.

The cousins had made their way through one of Watier's splendid meals and were broaching their second bottle of port before Alexander thought to mention Lady Mary's new governess. Predictably, Samuel's response followed closely Lady Fanny's. Reassured on the point of her qualifications and as to her lack of countenance, however, he had no objections to offer and agreed wholeheartedly with the Earl's plan to drive down with her to Arunfold and introduce her to Mary himself. He gave his usual slow grin when Alexander casually mentioned his plan to break his journey at *Ormaie*, the home of his friend Lady D'Avergne, on the way down.

'And why, may I ask, are you grinning like a simpleton, Samuel Carne?'

'No reason, old man, not the least in the world,' Samuel hurried to reassure him, though his reassurances were spoilt by the tremor in his voice.

'You are thinking that I appear to have a discreditable inability to prevent my feet from making their way to the vicinity in which Lady D'Avergne resides, no doubt, and there you are entirely wrong,' the Earl told him tartly. 'It is only that I promised to attend her houseparty—though how anyone can be so foolish—or is it vanity?—to arrange a houseparty in the country in the middle of the Season . . . But since I am in the area, common civility compels my attendance!'

'My dear Sheldon, let me assure you I'm not carping. Only wish the lady wanted my presence. Can't tell you how quickly she should have it! Word of honour! Don't blame you at all for taking advantage of her . . . shall we say, er . . . plenteous charms!'

'Plenteous is just the word I'd have used myself,' replied his lordship agreeably. 'Quite a tidy armful, as you say, but lately, just a little too demanding, I think.'

'It's not like you to grudge your blunt in such a good cause.'

'Money's no problem, but her desires go a little further, if I'm not very much mistaken.'

Cousin Samuel looked up sharply at this, but only said mildly, 'How do you mean, further?'

'Fancies herself a Countess, I've a notion,' said the Earl calmly, continuing to sip comfortably at his port.

Samuel choked, then laughed out loud. 'Good lord, Shel, you aint serious?'

'I? Serious? Heavens, no! But I have an uncomfortable feeling that she is.'

There was a pause in the conversation as each gentleman looked deeply into the ruby liquid at the bottom of his glass, apparently lost in thought. Then Samuel murmured, 'What will you do if you find she is? Serious, I mean?'

'Do, dear boy? Why, I shall continue as I am. What else should I do? Should Valentine D'Avergne have the temerity to think that an Earl of Sheldon would stoop towards the gutter in looking for a wife, she would learn her mistake soon enough. Assure you, you need not concern yourself. In the meantime, I intend, of course, to continue to take advantage of her . . . what did you call them? . . . plenteous charms—for which I assure you, coz, I have already paid quite handsome enough!'

'Sometimes you are a cold fish you know, Shel?' muttered Samuel uneasily. 'Would it not be best to just drop her now?'

'Cold? Sometimes? But I have it on the authority of any number of ladies that I am always so, my friend!' replied his lordship icily, ignoring his cousin's well-meant advice as if it had not been spoken. 'Now let us have less of this curst addle-plotting, for you know that I always follow my own path. If people see such a grim look on *your* face they'll think you are boskey. I might pass it off, but never you. Come, m'boy, it's my last night in town for a week or so. Come and see me lose a few guineas at macao!'

CHAPTER

3

Arunfold, the Earl's country seat, was situated in the county of Sussex, close to Horsham. They were to travel the new Brighton Road, Sheldon's intention being to leave it at Gatton Tollgate where the old road branched off to Reigate, to reach *Ormaie* by late afternoon.

Miss Tiversley would not have dreamt of keeping his lordship waiting; she was a punctual girl at any time, but the impatient gleam which she had several times yesterday surprised in his eye, made her think that it would be unwise on this occasion to break her rule, so that, when the Earl arrived at Mivart's Hotel, precisely at ten o'clock, she had already been waiting with her one small portmanteau for several minutes, having earlier bidden farewell to Alice.

His lordship was accompanied in his curricle by a groom, perched up behind, and, as the Earl brought his horses to a graceful halt in the roadway before her, Lucy had time to observe that the vehicle he drove was a lightweight racer, painted a splendid dark green, wheels picked out in fashionable yellow, and the Carne crest prominently displayed on its door panels. Harnessed to the curricle were four high-stepping bays, handled by the Earl with the greatest ease.

Although it was late spring, the day was grey, and over his other clothing her new master had draped a many-caped white drab-coat, through the top buttonhole of which were carelessly stuffed some whip thongs; on his handsome head reclined a curley-brimmed beaver, at a rakish angle. Brusque though he was, Lucy could not but admire him.

His opinion of her was less enthusiastic, for, once again, she had ruthlessly crammed her hair under the unbecoming straw bonnet, though not quite as tidily as on the previous day, and he noted, with all the disapproval of the service of his fastidious nature, that some bad angel had put it into her head to wear a gown and a pelisse of a hideous shade of pea-green. Alexander's only thought on catching sight of her was converted instantly in his brain to a desire to quit town as speedily as possible before anyone saw him tooling the ribbons for so unprepossessing a female, for he was quite certain that even he could not survive such a blatant challenge to the ton. Thus, Miss Tiversley found that, before she had time for more than a shy word of greeting, the Earl's groom had dealt with her portmanteau and helped her into his lordship's curricle, which was then driven off at speed. More swiftly than Lucy could have thought possible, they were crossing Westminster Bridge, making for the Kennington turnpike and the Brighton Road.

Since the few remarks she ventured to make to his lordship were answered with only the curtest of replies, Lucy gave up any effort at camaraderie and contented herself instead with settling down to enjoy her journey.

From Kennington the travellers drove on towards Brixton village, by-passing the church as the horses pulled the carriage effortlessly up the hill. Then to Streatham Common, and, some miles later, Croydon and their first halt. As they drove into Croydon, Lucy's attention was attracted to a sign which straddled the High Street and betokened their arrival at the Greyhound, one of the two main posting houses boasted by that famous stopping place and the one always used by the Earl in preference to the King's Head in Market Street.

Peckham, his lordship's groom, blew his horn to announce their arrival and, by the time their curricle had turned under the archway and into the courtyard, shirtsleeved ostlers were running to the horses' heads. The Earl had had the forethought, as was his custom, to have his own horses posted at inns along his route and, as he helped Lucy from his vehicle, he instructed Peckham to ensure that his team of chestnuts had arrived and would be ready when he required them. The Earl himself undertook to escort Miss Tiversley to the private parlour booked for their comfort, where they could partake of luncheon together before moving on.

They were just making their way into the inn when the unmistakable sound of a vehicle, being driven at cracking pace into the courtyard caused Lucy and the Earl to turn swiftly. It proved to be a flashy, high-perch phaeton, driven by a very young gentleman dressed in the pink of fashion, if carelessly, a Belcher handkerchief knotted loosely round his neck to show that he fancied himself rather a Corinthian than a town smart. Around his shoulders, he wore a multi-caped drab-coat; he was hatless and windblown, his face bright red and sweating profusely from the effort of his drive. As he came under the archway, his team seemed wild-eyed and out of control and, as they saw the equipage enter the yard, grooms, ostlers and postboys all jumped out of its path in self-preservation. Peckham, walking across the yard at that precise moment, was not quick enough and, as the driver tried to steady his sweating beasts, the team's leader knocked the groom to the floor with a frightening thud. Sheldon reached him in a second and pulled him out from under the rearing horse as pandemonium broke loose all around them and ostlers ran to his assistance.

The phaeton's driver managed, after some considerable effort, to bring the team under control and, having handed his reins to a groom, alighted from the ungainly vehicle to make his apologies as best he could. He was in a race with some friends, he said, and had backed himself to reach Brighton before them. Cursing himself for a cow-handed fool, his shame was evident. As he stammered out his apologies, Lucy felt quite sorry for him, for to face Lord Sheldon's icy stare was not something she would relish. He was not made to suffer long, however, for with only a brief quiz through his dreaded glass, and without so much as a word, his lordship turned from him to speak to the landlady, who had appeared in the yard, wringing her hands at the commotion. On Sheldon's instructions, and throwing the poor young gentleman a last look of sympathy, Lucy was shown into a snug parlour with a splendid fire and some comfortable armchairs, where she waited while the Earl attended to his groom. Peckham, who had meantime been carried upstairs to a bedroom at the back of the inn, away from the noise of the yard, was embarrassed by such unaccustomed attention. Nevertheless, the Earl insisted that a surgeon be called, upon whose arrival examination was made and it was found that the groom had sustained no worse an injury than a broken leg. Not so terrible, but enough to overthrow his master's plans.

What to do next was a problem. Peckham should

not be moved, nor could the party remain at the inn for the night, since Miss Tiversley—the wretched chit—had no maid with her. It was vexing in the extreme to one used to having his arrangements run without a hitch and the Earl's face wore so saturnine a look as to quell helpful suggestions. Remembering, however, that another of his grooms had been sent ahead with his team of chestnuts to await his arrival at the Greyhound, he instructed one of the landlady's servants to find him. The groom, Sam by name, short and slight and with a sharp, knowing look, calmly received Lord Sheldon's instructions concerning the care of Peckham and the Earl's spent bays, and went off immediately to carry out his orders.

Having made the necessary arrangements his lordship joined Miss Tiversley in the private parlour, where he was in time to see her partaking of an apparently huge repast. The motherly landlady had obviously decided that Lucy needed fattening up and, following the enormous plate of ham and cold chicken she had already encouraged her to consume, was now pressing a second helping on her, and had in reserve, on a side-table, various pastries and pies to tempt her, as well as a mountain of fruit. Friendly soul that she was, Lucy was already on the most amicable of terms with her hostess and had informed her of all the details as to her destination and of her new situation. Had not the Earl lifted his quizzing glass at the good woman, in a manner too pressing to be denied, she would undoubtedly have remained in the parlour at his entry to learn more, but, having quelled her pretensions with his usual expertise, he was free to turn his attentions to luncheon.

His lordship ate sparingly but watched with fascinated eye as Lucy, having asked in a sincere fashion about Peckham, consumed not only her second helping of ham and chicken, but proceeded to help herself to a number of the delicacies the landlady had provided, as well as consuming a considerable quantity of ratafia. His lordship, slowly sipping a glass of madeira, watched her from under his lazy eyelids as she tucked in.

'Well, Miss Tiversley,' he remarked eventually. 'I trust you are feeling more the thing? I'd no idea that Mivart's failed so miserably with the breakfasts they supplied their guests.'

His irony was lost on her. She replied earnestly, 'Oh yes sir, thank you, sir,' hurrying to empty her mouth of the last few crumbs of a particularly tasty venison pasty before she spoke.

'I am much relieved, Ma'am. It would never do to see you starve, especially since we are in somewhat of a dilemma and must needs put our heads together to see what best to do.'

She raised surprised eyes to his. 'Dilemma, sir? Surely if the doctor is seeing to Peckham . . . ?'

'I see I must explain it to you,' he replied with heavy patience, making his way to stand before the fireplace. 'You have no abigail, so it is not possible that we remain here the night. We might have been able to pass you off as my niece had I been so fortunate as to be before you with the landlady, but I fear that your fast-developing friendship has led you to regale her with your life history. No doubt she is aware of the true state of things?'

Vexed at her foolishness, Lucy bit her lip before agreeing. 'What must we do then, sir?' she asked, instinctively certain he could arrange it all.

He thought for no more than a moment, absent-mindedly prodding the log on the fire with his booted foot, and sending a fountain of sparks up the chimney. 'I wonder, would you be prepared to go on with me alone? The day is not yet too advanced to reach *Ormaie* by dusk and it is most unlikely that we will see anyone who would recognise us. My friend, Lady Valentine, will be in no hurry to see you compromised for travelling with me alone and will provide you with all the chaperonage you could possibly need. How does the scheme strike, Ma'am?'

'By all means let us go on sir,' she replied, blissfully unperturbed for her reputation. 'Nothing is more dreary than to be hanging about.'

All was speedily arranged and, having checked once more that Peckham was comfortable, they climbed back into the curricle, now harnessed to four glossy chestnuts, and set off once more, this time without the comfort of a groom behind them.

The weather, when they left the Greyhound, had given them no cause for alarm, but, reaching the Foxley Hatch Tollgate in good time, his lordship began to look anxiously skyward. Storm clouds were gathering, and a strong breeze blowing up, dragging at the skirts of Lucy's pelisse and causing her to hang on tightly to the brim of her bonnet. When they had paid for the ticket which would open for them the remaining gates and pikes through which they must pass that day, his lordship, having whipped up his team again, confided his fears of bad weather to his passenger. Just as the words left his mouth, a flash of lightning illuminated the heavy skies. He managed to hold his shying horses, but when, a few moments later, a crash of thunder shook the ground, it became clear from their prancing that the team was already uneasy. At Godstone Corner large spots of rain began to fall, but the Earl could not stop to raise the curricle's hood as he could not risk his team running off when he got down to do so. By the time they had reached Smitham Bottom, it was sheeting down in earnest, lightning ripping through the sky every few minutes, each flash closely followed by a peal of thunder.

It was just after they had passed through the village of Merstham that disaster struck. His lordship, fighting his horses' fear, had yet managed to continue driving at a respectable pace and had just called out hearteningly above the mounting noise of the storm, that they had not too far to go before they could leave the turnpike for Reigate, when another flash lit the road ahead and he could see, lying across it, a massive fir tree, brought down in the storm and completely blocking their path. With only a girl to help him there was no chance of moving it, and, in his usual decisive way, the Earl said firmly that there was nothing else to do but to go back to Merstham, where he knew of an old trackway which he thought was a previously used route to Reigate. Lucy, having no alternative to suggest, agreed at once; the team was expertly turned and the half mile to Merstham retraced. At Merstham he steadied the pace until the old track was located and his horses turned onto it.

Lucy could see nothing through the worsening rain, except when occasional flashes of fork lightning momentarily lit the landscape, and even then, she could discern only that the narrow path they were travelling seemed to be running through a tract of well-wooded land which effectively cut out any means by which they might get their bearings, though, mercifully, the trees did keep off some of the rain.

With admirable skill Lord Sheldon negotiated the track through the woodland, though their ride became every moment less comfortable with the heavy rain, which filled old potholes and made it difficult to avoid them. After what seemed to Lucy an age, they cleared the wood and then followed the bumpy track as it continued across some open heathland. The shelter the trees had afforded was gone and the skies emptied onto the unhappy pair, until Lucy was soaked to the skin. Wordlessly, his lordship placed whip and reins into one hand, unbuttoned his heavy drab-coat, taking care first to remove the whip thongs from the top buttonhole, and handed it to his passenger.

'Oh no sir, really, I am quite comfortable, I assure you,' protested Lucy, making an heroic effort to stop her teeth from chattering as she felt a stream of water running down the brim of her bonnet to land in a pool in her lap. 'My pelisse is really quite warm. Quite warm! You must not on any account worry yourself about me.'

His lordship did not deign to turn his head. 'The coat, if you please, Miss Tiversley. I'd as soon not have your death laid at my door.'

There seemed no more to be said, and Lucy gratefully donned the huge coat, through which the rain had not yet penetrated, though beneath its cumbersome folds and capes, her thin dress clung soggily to her legs. She was just fastening the top button around her throat, when a flash of lightning which seemed much nearer than any so far, lit the sky in a terrifying manner, greatly magnified by the grandiose peal of thunder which followed it almost immediately. The Earl remained unconcerned. He gentled his horses once more and, to Lucy's relief, she heard him say in an almost matter-of-fact voice,

'There seems to be a building of some sort by that cluster of trees ahead, Miss Tiversley. If you've no objection, we'll stop there, for I've little liking for going on tonight in this. We seem to have small chance of regaining the turnpike anyway while the storm continues to rage for I'm hanged if I can be certain of the path. There don't seem to be any lights showing, but we can but try to see if we can't knock up the owner.'

Lucy, as may be imagined, had no objection at all, but when they came closer, disappointment awaited them, for the building turned out to be, not the respectable farmhouse they both hoped for, but a dilapidated, though largish, stone barn, and with rain streaming through the caved-in roof at one end. Lucy could have cried in vexation for she was now frozen to the bone not even his lordship's thick coat being able to prevent the icy clasp of her soaked clothes from making her body shake uncontrollably. One look at her dismayed face when she saw the barn was enough, and instead of whipping up his horses to continue, the Earl reined them in under some partial shelter afforded by the small cluster of trees near to the building, jumping quickly down from the box to get to their heads and calm them down.

'It isn't much, Miss Tiversley,' he cried out, his words carried away by the blustery wind, 'but I fear it will have to serve.'

CHAPTER

4

When they had an opportunity to look more closely, the barn proved to be not so neglected as they had at first feared, for despite its unfortunate state of repair, some bales of hay were stacked at the dry end. The Earl suspected that the owner used the barn to store his crops when he had filled his other storage places.

In a surprisingly short time the Earl made their quarters something like tolerable. Soon he had unharnessed his team, rubbed them down with some of the hay, and then tethered them in part of the dry end of the barn. Indeed, it looked to have once been used for that purpose since some stalls, though dilapidated, still remained.

Using some stones from a fallen wall and dragging forward an old piece of timber, Lord Sheldon fashioned a hearth and began to build a fire. He contrived a flame with the help of his tinder box and some of the straw, and then some old pieces of dry timber, which had once formed supports for an upper hay loft, long-since collapsed. It was all most interesting, thought Lucy with undisguised admiration, and she could not help reflecting on what a pity it was that so *managing* a person had wasted his time at home when he would have been such a useful addition to the forces at the Peninsula!

'Not a very good fire, Ma'am,' his lordship remarked as he watched her holding shivering hands as close as she safely could to the modest flames, which were still being wafted by the draught, 'But it'll perk up and you'll soon find yourself more comfortable.'

Without waiting for a reply, he disappeared outside into the storm again and returned shortly, dripping wet once more, carrying a small trunk of his own, and Lucy's portmanteau tucked under one arm. The trunk he placed on the floor near to the fire and to Lucy, who had removed her sodden bonnet and was now sitting bareheaded, her mop of bright red curls clinging in tendrils all around her forehead, he held out the portmanteau. 'It is very wet, Ma'am, but we must hope that some of your things have been spared. Try to see if you cannot find a change of clothing.'

'But there is nowhere I can change,' she said firmly. 'If I sit here by the fire awhile, you may be sure my clothes will dry.'

'Don't be more of a fool than you need be, girl,' replied the Earl curtly. 'I assure you you've no need to fear for your virtue. Find something dry and don't be tiresome.'

She blushed hotly at both his manner and his words, but did not dare to disobey, her shivering hands unfastening the case with difficulty. Thankfully she discovered that, although some of her things were damp, the dress that she had packed as a change of clothing for the journey was barely touched.

In the meantime, his lordship had opened his trunk and declared, in a satisfied voice, 'Good. As I thought. All is dry. You may not eat, Miss Tiversley, but at least you will not freeze,' and he drew from the bottom of the chest a highly patterned brocade dressing gown, padded and of immense proportions, the magnificence of which could not be disguised even in the uncertain light given off by the fire. 'Go and change into that dry frock,' (noting with distaste that it was the dun-coloured one of the day before) 'and then you may tuck yourself up into this for extra warmth. What about undergarmets? Are any in your luggage dry?' Seeing her cheeks redden, he went on testily, 'Oh heaven, spare me your blushes, I beg. This is not the time for them. Have you dry undergarments or not?'

A quick rummage and a blushing nod told him that she was supplied with those necessaries.

'Take off the coat then, girl, and I'll make you a screen behind which you can put on those dry things, for it's plain as a pikestaff that you're of the opinion that I've nothing better to do, being wet through, cold and miles from anywhere, than to watch you disrobing!'

Miss Tiversley blushed again, but handed him his coat gratefully. Her own clothes revealed were a pitiful sight, the pea-green dress and pelisse clinging miserably to her long limbs, the colour having run into the saturated pantalettes, which could just be glimpsed beneath her mud-soaked hem. Her jean half-boots were not only wet, but were covered in mud and squelched uncomfortably as she moved to where his lordship had contrived to hang his coat, with the help of two large stones to weight it, across the end of one of the old stalls. Ducking underneath, Lucy swiftly began to remove her wet things, his lordship occupied, poking the fire, and apparently unconcerned at her predicament. Lucy was far from being so unconcerned as she suddenly noticed that he had only to turn his head to one side to see where the newly invigorated fire threw up her silhouette massively onto the wall beside her.

Since Lucy had nothing with which to dry herself, it could not be said that she was immediately made comfortable, but, having peeled off the sodden garments (as quickly as she could and with nervous looks towards the fire to see that his lordship's head was still turned away) and replaced them, as rapidly as her shaking hands would allow, with dry pantalettes, chemise and stockings, the dun-coloured dress to cover them, she did at least stop feeling quite such a drenched rat. She had omitted to provide any change of shoes suitable for such unexpected circumstances, so was obliged to replace her half-boots with a pair of flat beige pumps which would have been more at home in a drawing room. Neither had she a change of pelisse, but she had packed a shawl, which she now pinned around her shoulders. Since it was an old angora one of Aunt Marianne's and a livid purple in colour, it could not be said to have added to the attractions of Lucy's costume, but at least it was warm.

Being uncertain what to do with the wet clothes, for she was unwilling to expose them to her employer's gaze, she left them, all excepting her pelisse and boots, in a neat pile in the corner of the old stall.

'Well?' asked the Earl, as she came out of the stall. 'Where are the rest?'

'I . . . I've left them over there.'

'But why, girl?' he said brusquely. 'Can't you think of anything for yourself. Must I do everything for you? Bring them over to the fire. How else do you expect to get them dry?'

She was forced to obey, and to her profound distress, he took them from her hands to lay them neatly all around the fire. He took her half-boots too, scraped the mud from them with some straw and lay them on their sides on two stones placed near to the fire. 'They'll never be the same again, but when they're dry they'll be more suitable than those slippers. Now, if you'll only tuck yourself into my dressing gown, I think you will soon be warm,' and he held the voluminous garment towards her, obviously intending to help her into it.

She thought of refusing, but commonsense told her that this was not the moment to be thinking propriety, so she let him drape it round her shoulders, murmuring her thanks. For such a fribble of a garment, it felt surprisingly warm as she wrapped it around herself and, as her companion had promised earlier, she really did begin to feel better, her natural resilience beginning to reassert itself.

'Well now, isn't this cosy?' she began, as she resumed her place on a stone by the fire, then looking up with compunction at the Earl, still wet through and dripping, she bit her lip, though not in time to prevent a giggle. Resolutely she closed her teeth over her bottom lip, and, for good measure, placed her hand over her mouth too, to ensure that it should not repeat the offense, looking up apologetically at his lordship in the most disarming fashion. Even he was not proof against such a look, and he smiled, if stoically, only remarking, 'Just so, Ma'am.'

He began again to poke at the fire, which sent the flames dancing, then he was off outside once more, soon to return with the rugs from the curricle for drying, remarking as he came in, 'If this storm doesn't abate soon, Ma'am, we will be very wet in the curricle tomorrow. I've pulled it as far under the trees as I can get it, though I fear it's little sheltered.'

'I wish you would not keep going outside, sir,' admonished Lucy in concern, 'For you will never get dry if you do not stay by the fire. Tell me instead what I may do, for you've made sure that I'm very comfortable.'

'Don't dwell on my discomforts, Miss Tiversley,'

he replied, amused and not a little touched by her solicitude. 'I think a wetting will not kill me.'

'Well of course it won't sir, how should it?' she agreed at once. 'Nor me. But that did not prevent you from wishing me to be as warm and dry as possible. And you are so much older than I that, to be sure, it is you who will catch a chill first!'

Lord Sheldon's movements were arrested. 'Just how old do you think I am, young lady? Methusala was not *so* much my junior, you know!'

Seeing she had bruised his feelings by her thoughtless words, and remembering Aunt Marianne's strictures on politeness to elders, she was quick to say, 'Oh I do not think you so very old, sir, but you must admit that it is best not to take chances as one becomes a . . . a . . . *senior* member of society,' and she settled back, happy that she had hit on just such an unexceptionable word as could not wound him.

She was wrong! His lordship was most sincerely wounded and it was a wound intensely aggravated by seeing her sitting there so self-satisfied! Well enough that he should tell himself that he was past a certain age, but it was mortifying to have it so ruthlessly confirmed by a chit of a girl. It was only with great self-will that he held his control. 'You are too kind, Miss Tiversley,' he replied, staring at her from under black brows. Then suddenly his face brightened in the firelight. 'And, since you are so good as to mind for my health, I shall take the liberty of using your dressing room and change into some dry things myself. No point in taking any chances, as you say, when one reaches my advanced years.'

Lucy blushed scarlet! This was not at all what she had expected.

The Earl busied himself about his chest of things as if unaware of her dismay. Then, in provocation, he began deliberately to hold up his clothing towards the fire, as if to examine them for damp. Lucy did not know where to put her eyes. Hers had been the suggestion that he should take care of himself: now she wished she had rather bitten off her tongue.

As for his lordship, he had not enjoyed himself so much for years and he entered into the proceedings with enthusiasm, examining the intimate garments minutely for her benefit, and piling them up before the fire, while Lucy, head down, turned resolutely away. Having collected all the items he required, which were apparently many and varied, he made his way to the stall and ducked behind the coat-screen he had made for Lucy.

His close-fitting morning coat being shrugged off, the Earl had just removed his cravat and was making a start on his shirt, when Lucy chanced to glance up before her, only to realise that she had inadvertently placed herself so that she was directly facing the wall onto which the fire threw silhouettes. Cheeks ablaze, she swiftly dipped her head again, before his lordship should notice, and began shuffling round the fire to find a place where she could keep her eyes both from the Earl and his shadow. Sheldon, being all the time aware of her movements, and of her thoughts, for her face had nothing in it of prevarication, was hugely entertained.

Strolling back to the fire presently, elegantly at his ease, and clothed more immaculately than would have seemed possible to Lucy under the circumstances, he was prepared to offer a truce. 'Well, Miss Tiversley, so we are both comfortable again,' he said smilingly, amused by her face, which showed only too clearly how grateful she was that her ordeal was over—or almost, for his lordship did not hesitate to arrange his own wet garments close to hers around the flames. Then he settled himself on a stone near to hers, remarking with relish, 'Well now, isn't this cosy?'

Spirited enough to blush at his provocation, she refused to be drawn and they each sat quiet for some few minutes, looking into the flames, lost in their own thoughts. His, apparently, were of a practical nature, since he was soon delving into the chest again.

'You must be hungry, Ma'am,' he asserted.

Lucy's spirits lifted. Could he really have things edible in there? Alas, no. Instead he drew out a small silver flask.

'What is it?' she asked suspiciously, as he poured a generous quantity of bright golden liquid from the flask into its sizeable stopper, which was fashioned as a cup. She had a good idea, and was absolutely resolved not to drink strong spirits. Why, at Aunt Marianne's she had never been offered anything stronger than ratafia and, very occasionally, a little wine and water, of which she was by no means fond.

'Great heavens, girl,' expostulated the Earl, 'It's brandy! What do you think it is? It's to take the edge from your hunger! And if you think I'm trying to make you boskey, you were never more out in your life!'

Lucy was not quite certain what boskey meant, but didn't like the sound of it!

'No, I thank you sir, none for me. I'm persuaded I should not like it!'

'And I am persuaded, Miss, that you shall have it!' replied Sheldon, exasperated by her implacable demeanour.

Lucy put up a hand. 'No, I thank you. I should not like it.'

Before she realised his intention, his lordship had removed himself from his place, and had an arm round her, tilting her backwards, his other hand pouring the fiery liquid down her throat, saying a trifle breathlessly, as he did so, but in a voice resolved to be agreeable, 'And I think Ma'am, that it will do you good!'

Lucy, choking furiously, was given no chance to spit out the brandy, for the Earl, all the time showing a determinedly pleasant countenance, threw down the empty cup and held her face tilted backwards roughly, between his fingers, until it was all gone, when he immediately resumed his original place, saying with maddening calm, 'There now, aren't you feeling much more the thing?'

It took Lucy, eyes now streaming, some little time to catch her breath, by which time she had recollected the impropriety of calling her new employer a 'vile snake', so she contented herself instead with throwing him darkling looks and replying in deceptively sweet tones, as she mopped her cheeks, 'Well sir, had I known that you were so certain I should benefit, I would not have thwarted you. No need, I assure you, to manhandle me!'

'Touché, Miss Tiversley,' he chuckled, admiring her spirit and just a little ashamed at his own impatience, 'But it really will do you good, you know!'

Lucy, on whom the brandy was already beginning to exercise a soporific effect, replied reflectively, as she put away her handkerchief, 'Yes, you may be right, for Papa never travelled into battle without some, I remember, or so he told Uncle William. Strange—for it tastes so horrid. As to your behaviour, sir, do not let it trouble you, for I expect that Earls are brought up to be autocratic and to wish always to have their own way, and Aunt Marianne always says that what is bred in the bone will come out in the roast.'

Once again his eyes sparkled appreciatively. 'A hit, Ma'am, you have scored a hit! I am wounded to the core.'

'Oh no, surely not,' she replied doubtfully, 'for Aunt Marianne says that the truth can never hurt.'

'I begin to think Aunt Marianne a force to be reckoned with,' answered the Earl, resolutely damping down his annoyance. 'A *grande dame* indeed.'

'Aunt Marianne?' she chuckled incredulously, her eyes little more than slits, 'How can you be so foolish? She's not at all like that. She's . . . well, she's funny and . . . kind and . . . and good, just like my own Mama must have been.'

His lordship, noticing a slight slurring in her speech, and recognising the first signs of maudlin, wondered if he had been rather too generous with the brandy.

'Perhaps, Miss Tiversley, you should try to get some sleep,' he said bracingly, noticing with some alarm the flushed cheeks and brilliant eyes. 'Let's see if we cannot make you a bed with some straw, shall we?'

That the brandy really had made good headway was apparent then, for Lucy's eyes glistened at him in her rosy face, and she pulled her knees up to her chin, encircling them with her arms, 'Oh no, let's not go to sleep yet, sir,' she coaxed, 'This is such fun now we are both warm and dry. I am sure that it must be just like this when one is a soldier campaigning. And I have not yet thanked you properly for all your kindnesses to me. I really must thank you so much for being so . . . er . . . so . . .'

'Yes, I know,' he interrupted hastily, for he had seen many a young man in a similar state of intoxication and recognised all the advancing warnings of drunken confidences about to be his, and for which he was in no mood. 'I'm like Aunt Marianne. Funny and kind. And so is everyone when one is oneself decidedly foxed! But you, my girl, must still get some rest,' and he began fashioning a rough bed for her from some of the dry straw, as much out of the draught as he could. In a matter of minutes it was done, but not quickly enough for, when he turned back to Lucy, she was already asleep, forehead resting heavily on her knees.

'That's it, m'girl,' he whispered, amused, tucking the large dressing gown closely round her and then lifting her effortlessly in his arms to carry her the few feet to the straw pallet, 'You just sleep it off. A nasty head you'll have tomorrow, if I'm not mistaken, but none the worse for it, I'll be bound,' and he laid her down gently, so as not to disturb her, folding his dressing gown tightly round her feet, still in the absurd slippers.

Then he walked across to look out from the barn, noting with satisfaction how the wind had dropped and that the rain had changed to a monotonous drizzle. Perhaps it would be fine enough tomorrow to resume their journey after all, but what was to be done about Miss Tiversley? Innocent that she was, she had not considered what must be her situation now that she had been forced to stay in this devilish place with him. If they'd been expected anywhere else but at Valentine's they might have got away with it, and indeed, it would not be Valentine who would make trouble. But with the high-flyers he suspected would be assembled with her for this deuced houseparty, there was no escape. The kind of people she attracted would be the first to scent gossip and would certainly make sure that it spread. What to do? What to do . . .

He walked back towards the fire and stood looking down at Lucy, now in a deep slumber, her glowing cheek cupped in one hand, brow cloudless as if adult cares had never yet touched her. Why, she was little more than a child, not much older than Mary. The dressing gown had fallen away at her shoulders, and he bent instinctively to tuck it around her again, then, after placing a large tim-

43

ber on the fire, he walked to the other side of it and lay down himself on the ground, a frown distorting his features as he looked into the flames trying to decide the future for them both.

As the fingers of dawn stretched themselves low above the fields behind the barn, bringing forth trees and straggling flocks of farm animals from the dimness of night, the Earl awoke to the pungent smell of damp horse hair and the muffled sounds of stamping hooves on straw-covered ground. For a few moments he could not recollect where he was; then he caught sight of Miss Tiversley across the dying embers of his fire and he remembered all, a cry of exasperation being wrung from him as he lifted his head from the ground. He remained where he was, half lying, half sitting, supporting himself on his elbow, chin resting on his knuckled hand, while he watched Lucy still asleep and apparently unmoving since last night, since she was still tightly tucked into his dressing gown.

Having come to a decision about Lucy before fatigue had finally claimed him last night, he debated with himself now whether he should inform her of her fate or leave it until a more auspicious time. Commonsense told him not to rush into anything. After all, who knew what might happen to make such a momentous step unnecessary. And if nothing occurred to alter the situation, it was still better to wait until they reached *Ormaie*, for then the girl would realise for herself that she had little choice in the matter.

'Poor little sweetling,' he whispered, 'I should have taken better care of Mary's clever governess, should I not? Now, how your life must change—and you have such a very low opinion of Earls.' A grimace curled his mouth, 'And especially very old ones.'

Reluctantly he got to his feet, stretching cautiously

to try to ease the stiffness in his neck and shoulders. He then moved towards the rough entry to the barn and, as he walked over to the curricle, was relieved to find that it had stopped raining and that the ascending sun had begun to paint a silver and peach landscape in the sky to announce a fine day.

Thanking Providence that his curricle was light-weight he began to pull it from beneath the trees to give it a chance to dry out, but it was yet not so light as to afford him no effort, especially in the mud, and he was still tussling with it, when Lucy peered out from the barn.

'Do wait a moment sir for me to put on my boots,' she called to him, 'then I shall be able to help you.'

'There is not the least occasion for you to do so, Ma'am. I can manage quite well, I thank you.'

'I am sure you can,' she replied amiably, 'but certainly it is absurd to do so when help is at hand.'

'It is not fit work for a lady.'

'Oh stuff!' she declared inelegantly, 'Treating women as if they were made of porcelain is just what I have no patience with,' and she disappeared inside once more, only to reappear moments later shod for action.

As she walked towards him in the morning sunlight, holding the hem of her dress out of the mud, the Earl was, for the first time, at liberty to encounter the full force of dun-coloured cotton, purple wool and bright red hair, and he winced perceptibly. Lucy did not appear to notice, saying brightly, 'Now, what must I do, sir? Where are we trying to move it?'

'Are you quite sure you feel up to it?' he asked doubtfully. 'Your head does not pain you?'

'My head? Of course not. I don't know how it should be, but I am never ill. Aunt Marianne says I have none of the airs delicately nurtured females should have,' she apologised, with disarming honesty.

'I rather thought you might feel a little under the weather this morning after your ... em ... experiences of last night.'

Either she chose to misunderstand or, and his lordship was inclined towards the latter, she really did not follow his drift, for she said airily, 'Pray do not worry about me, my lord. I have the constitution of a horse and a little wetting would not make me ready to stick my spoon in the wall. Now, sir, where are we to move your curricle?'

In a few minutes they had the vehicle in the open, Lucy heaving and straining to do her part.

'We will leave it to dry for an hour or so, Ma'am, if you agree, and then we must get on our way.'

'Whatever you will, my lord. I am sure you know what is best,' she replied, adding wistfully, 'But how I wish we might get some food. I am positively famished, are not you? Some eggs, perhaps, oh and some lovely sizzling slices of ham ...'

'Would you like some more brandy, Miss Tiversley? You do not like it, I know, but you will feel less sharp set if you take some.'

'No sir, I really could not,' she grimaced, 'and I beg you will not try to force me, for I should not take it at all kindly in you. I might even be sick.'

'I shan't force you, Ma'am,' he assured her hastily. 'You may not believe me, but it is not a practise of mine to foist brandy onto unwanting females. And anyway, it is my intention, as soon as the curricle dries sufficiently, to try to bespeak some breakfast at any farmhouse we may pass as we go. You will not mind a farmhouse, for I wish to avoid going to an inn where we might be recognised? We are already in deep enough water, without wading further in.'

'Frankly, sir, I do not care where we eat, so long as we do. Even the straw begins to look tempting!'

'I'd forgotten what a hearty appetite you have, but

I doubt that it will come to that. We are certain to find some good honest folk nearby willing to feed us.'

And so it proved. They had travelled no more than a half mile or so before coming to a prosperous looking farmhouse, whose mistress was only too glad to provide food in exchange for his lordship's guineas, and would probably have done so without them. Pretending that Lucy was his sister, they had encountered nothing but kindness from the honest woman, or indeed, from her mild-tempered husband, who not only told them the quickest way to Reigate, but who also insisted on guiding them part of the way back to the main track himself.

It was gone two by the time the travellers found themselves passing through a gateway and turning down the long drive bordered by some woodland dominated at its edges by the band of elms which gave Lady Valentine's home its name. The house, which they were fast approaching, was not a stately mansion in the grandiose manner, rather it was a large, modern, square hall of rose-coloured brick, situated in a pretty park, its immaculate, scythed lawns surrounded by woodland. Accustomed as she was to her Aunt Marianne's more modest home, it seemed to Lucy handsome.

Just in front of the house, on the gravelled forecourt, was gathered a group of horsemen and one or two ladies, obviously just preparing for a ride, their grooms and maids in attendance, and, as she caught sight of Sheldon in the distance, one of these ladies, a striking, dark-haired beauty on a fine chestnut mare, rode across the lawns towards them, two or three curious followers close behind.

She wore a mannish-looking riding habit of royal blue velvet, lavishly frogged on its bodice and sleeves, on her head a dashing black hat, styled like a shako, but with a feather tucked into its brim which exactly matched the blue of her habit and which fluttered in the breeze as she rode. On many a woman, such a masculine garb would have looked out of place; on Lady D'Avergne it was provocative.

'Ah, our gracious hostess, if I am not much mistaken,' murmured the Earl as she came nearer, and Lucy was shocked by his sneer. 'How delighted she will be to see you.'

'Alex, my dearest,' cried that lady, in a voice lightly accented, as the Earl halted the curricle, and she reined in her mare, 'at last you are come! But why so late, cheri? Your valet and grooms arrived yesterday and, certainly, your letter said that you would be here by last evening. I waited and waited, but still you did not come.'

The Earl smiled at the pout which had accompanied her complaints, reached to take her hand, and raised it to his lips. 'Valentine, ma chère, I am distraught! Accept a thousand apologies, but we were unavoidably detained on the road. An unfortunate accident.'

Lucy looked at him in surprise. His manner was not at all like the kindly companion in trouble he had been to her.

'But you are here now, mon ami, so all is well,' said Valentine smilingly, 'and we have wanted you so much.' Then, taking a hard look at Lucy, and noticing for the first time the absence of a groom, 'And won't you introduce me to your travelling companion?'

'Indeed I will, my precious,' replied the Earl sweetly. 'Lady D'Avergne, may I present to you Miss Tiversley. Miss Tiversley is the young lady who has today consented to be my wife.'

48

CHAPTER

5

An hour later, sitting in front of a dressing-table mirror in the bedchamber of unaccustomed splendour, Lucy was still trying to understand the strange turn of events.

At first, hearing Sheldon's words to Lady Valentine, she had imagined herself dreaming. When, to her dismay, she knew herself awake, she was indignant, but saved the necessity of any immediate remonstrances by the very eloquent ones presented by their hostess, rigid with anger as she pulled her hand furiously from the Earl's grasp.

'You are insulting!' she had said sharply, 'I think I have not deserved so much from you.'

'But I protest,' replied his lordship, who seemed to be enjoying himself. 'You asked me to introduce my betrothed and I have done so. Where is the insult in that?'

By that time, they had been joined by one or two of Lady Valentine's guests who had already heard enough to show each other amused faces, and their hostess, quick to realise that such public display could add nothing to her consequence, said only to the Earl,

'Come on to the house, won't you my lord, and we will discuss the matter there. The others shall ride without me today while I see you both comfortable,' and she had ridden back towards the rest of the party, her head high.

Then it was Lucy's turn to demand explanations.

'I do not understand any of this, my lord,' she had begun hesitantly. 'Why should you tell her such a dreadful lie?'

'Ah, but you see my child, it is not a lie. I regret that it must be so.'

'How can you say so, sir? Are you mad? Why must it be?'

'Do you not know? Can you really be such an innocent?' and with increasing incredulity. 'In taking you from the Inn at Croydon yesterday without a groom, I did you the greatest disservice—oh, believe me, the fault was not intentional, but that will not help us now. Had we reached here before nightfall as I intended, all would have been well. It is not so unusual to travel without a groom, and I thought I knew Lady D'Avergne well enough to know that she would ensure that any irregularities would be overlooked. As it was, we did *not* arrive here. You have spent the night with me alone and it is the one situation which cannot be overlooked. Don't you see why you must marry me? You will be compromised else.'

'But I don't care about such stuff! Better compromised than a loveless match. Why, I would rather die than marry you!'

A weird contortion around his mouth set his lordship's face fiersomely. 'Handsome of you to say so Ma'am! I had not realised I'd been such a bore.'

'Indeed you have not, sir,' said Lucy contritely. 'You have been all kindness to me, but that is no reason for us to marry. I never heard anything so gothic! And to tell her that I had consented to such a scheme was outside of enough.'

'Yes, it was very bad of me, wasn't it, but since

she must soon know that we have spent the night alone in the barn, it is much better for her to think also that it is an affair of the heart between us. She is just such a woman as will not forbear spreading such delicious gossip about. She will do her best to make us laughing stocks, you may be sure, and I for one would not relish that! If she thinks we were to marry anyway much of her story will have lost its bite.'

'It does not matter what story you tell her. I won't marry you.'

'Yet you must!' he said determinedly.

'I must not!' she said, equally determined.

'You know from experience, Miss Tiversley, that I do not take no for an answer, so put any such idea from your mind. If I have to put you across my horse and carry you to Gretna you will be my wife by the end of the week, though I see little need for such extravagances. My family knows the Bishop of London very well, and he will provide us with a special licence. I will not allow you, or anyone else, to sully my family's honour by refusing.'

Lucy had been almost speechless with indignation at his high-handed manner, but had managed to gasp out a final, 'I will die rather!', as the curricle halted before the house, to be met by the Earl's own grooms, watching for his arrival since the day before.

As he lifted her down from the curricle, Sheldon muttered curtly, 'That may be able to be arranged!' before taking her by one hand and dragging her after him into the entrance hall to where Lady Valentine awaited them.

Lucy was determined not to discuss so private a matter in front of Madame D'Avergne and sat in silence while her hostess berated the Earl in fine style. He would hear nothing she said, told her that the storm had made it necessary for them to spend the night alone in a barn, refused to believe Lucy uncompromised as Lady Valentine tried hopefully to suggest, and stood by his decision to marry her, declaring audaciously that, although Lucy was too modest to admit it, they had a strong and undying affection for each other. Lucy's lips pursed, but she would not demean herself in a public wrangle with him and, in spite of her obvious fury, Lady Valentine had little choice but to have Lucy shown to a guest room, where she was now at liberty to ponder the matter.

She had not been there more than half an hour when she heard a knock on her door. Having rung for a maid a few minutes earlier and asked for some hot water to be sent up, she was not surprised to hear the tapping and called for her to enter, but instead of a maidservant, in walked her hostess.

Embarrassed, Lucy rose from her chair and, still dishevelled from the exertions of a morning's travelling, began making some unsuccessful attempts to push her springy red curls into place.

'Well my dear?' purred Lady Valentine, as she stood watching her from the doorway.

Lucy felt herself blushing. She murmured nervously, 'How gracious it is for you to house me so royally, Ma'am.'

'Royally?' replied Valentine, her eyes narrow, 'You will have to get used to much finer apartments than this when you are a Countess.'

Her words rekindled the fire in Lucy's cheeks.

'You blush wonderfully, my dear, but you must know that it is true. It would not be to everyone's taste to live in such high style, but you seem to think that Arunfold will suit you. And I am sure that nobody will blame you for taking advantage of so excellent an opportunity. For the Earl, of course, it is not so good . . . but you must not worry what his friends will think of you. I am sure that they will be reconciled to it . . . at last.'

Lucy was tired after the rigours of her journey. She had been forced to travel dripping wet for miles, to sleep in a barn, to be hungry and miserable and now to be insulted. Suddenly it was all too much and, incensed, she said with vigour, 'My dear Madame, I think you must be under a serious misapprehension. I like the idea of my marriage to the Earl no more than anyone else will. In his usual high-handed way, *he* has decided that I am compromised and that *his* family honour is at stake. He *will* marry me whether I will or no. My wishes matter little, if at all. It is all on account of his being an Earl. Spoilt he has been and now I am to bear the consequences! And to have you speaking as if I had schemed it is mortifying.'

Recognising at once that she had been precipitate, Lady Valentine's demeanour towards her guest underwent some considerable change. She moved towards her, holding out her hands and taking one of Lucy's own between them. 'My poor child, what a brute you must think me indeed. I can see that I have entirely mistaken the matter. As a family friend it seemed my duty to try to prevent the Earl from being the victim of what seemed at first like an encroaching female. Now I see you are no such thing! Say you will forgive me.'

Lucy, only too happy to comply, was soon seated at Madame's side, not only regaling her with details of the previous day's events, but telling her all about her life as well, dwelling especially on the great kindness she had received at the hands of her Mama's greatest friend. Valentine was not slow to interrupt her.

'Ah petite, what a terrible thing it has been that you meet Monsieur the Earl, n'est ce pas, for now you have no choice but to marry him, and all your kind friends lost to you!'

'What do you mean, "lost", Madame?' asked Lucy in surprise.

'Well, the Earl he is, as you may say, very proud and would certainly not let you acknowledge such a connection once you were married.'

'Well, of all the . . . ! I can tell you, Ma'am, that they are worth a hundred Earls, so good as they have been to me, and nothing or nobody would prevent my acknowledging them.'

'It is not I who says this, petite,' Valentine placated. 'I only say what his lordship will surely demand of you.'

'You are quite out there, Madame,' said Lucy defiantly, 'for I had already decided that marriage was out of the question. Something will have to be contrived!'

'How wise, my dear. I have seen unequal matches before. They do not serve at all.'

Lucy nodded decisively. 'I shall certainly escape him.'

Valentine gave a trill of laughter. 'La child, you cannot know Monsieur if you think to defy him so easily. He is quite unscrupulous.'

'So I have learned to my cost. I think he would go to any lengths to obtain his way, for he is the most odiously overbearing man I have ever had the misfortunate to meet.'

She thought for a moment, and Lady Valentine, as much at a loss to know how to get rid of the girl as Lucy was to know how to go, also remained pensive.

It was some minutes before Lucy smiled enigmatically. 'I think I know how to go about it,' she said, with a certain amount of satisfaction.

'Mais non, petite, surely it is impossible.'

'Oh, I think not, Ma'am. Resolution is all that is

54

needed. His lordship has to get a special licence from his bishop friend before he can marry me, and I think he must also obtain the consent of my guardian, which gives us quite enough time for what I have in mind.'

'Just what do you have in mind? Surely it is impossible?'

'Flight seems to me to be my only chance, however much I ponder the matter, so I must leave *Ormaie* tonight!'

'He will never let you go.'

'How shall he stop me if he doesn't know about it?'

Madame was all interest now.

'What do you mean to attempt?' she asked, her air of languour deserting her completely.

'I shall leave the house when everyone is asleep and make my way back to Aunt Marianne before the Earl has a chance to persuade her to his mind.'

'It is impossible, my child. How do you expect to get there? You have no carriage and no abigail.'

'I did not say there were no problems, Ma'am. Only that we might overcome them with resolution!'

Madame D'Avergne listened intently as Lucy outlined her sketchy plan.

'First I will need to borrow some money,' began Lucy, amazed at her presumption.

'The money, it is nothing.'

'I must find a way home to Buckinghamshire and if I can only reach Gatton I shall then be able there to ascertain the most direct post-coach route. My problem is in getting to Gatton in the first place and I wondered if, Ma'am, if you don't think it is the greatest cheek, you might lend me a vehicle and coachman to take me?'

Now that she realised she had nothing to fear from Lucy, Valentine was in complete charity with her and said thoughtfully, 'Oh no, my dear, that would not do. If you are sure you are willing to chance his lordship's displeasure, I have a much better plan. I can send you all the way home to Buckinghamshire in my own carriage.'

'You really must not put yourself to such trouble . . .'

'It is no trouble at all,' interposed Madame, putting up a hand to silence protest, 'And I am persuaded you must take no more risks with your reputation, so I shall send one of my maids with you as chaperone. You will have to stay overnight on the road and will receive much better accommodation if they see you properly looked after. If only my brother were here I could have asked him to accompany you, but he does not return until tomorrow. My man Masters will have to do instead. He has been with me for ever and nobody knows better than he how to smooth the cares of travel. Just think how easily his lordship would trace you if you were forced to make enquiries as near as Gatton.'

'How kind you are, Ma'am,' said Lucy, controlling with difficulty her shudder at the thought.

'It is the least I can do,' replied Madame in perfect honesty, 'For it would never do for you to be obliged to marry Monsieur the Earl.'

'No indeed,' agreed Lucy, paling visibly, 'How do you think it best I should leave the house?'

'Leave all to me, petite. His lordship has gone to the stables to check his horses. When he returns I will tell him that you have no wish to join the company for dinner, if you are agreeable, for it is probably better that you do not see him again. He may bully you, you know?'

'Oh, I would much rather never set eyes on him again,' she replied firmly.

'How wise,' gushed Madame, congratulating herself on Lucy's gullibility. 'I shall have a meal sent up to you. See if you can get a little sleep, cherie, ready for the journey. I will get my guests early to bed. The two coaching inns at Croydon take in guests at all hours, and Masters will manage to get you there, never fear. We are in luck, for it is a good moon. Patty, my own maid, will accompany you, I think, for she is not one to chatter. You will send her back to me when you get home to Buckinghamshire. Tomorrow, you can be on your way in earnest and no-one the wiser. If the Earl wishes to see you in the morning I shall say you are still asleep and, if we are lucky, he will not discover your absence until luncheon. It will be too late to pick up your trail by then in time to prevent you reaching your Madame Chadwell. The rest then is up to you and to her. We must hope that she is strong enough to protect you from the Earl.'

Valentine thought for a moment, then, 'We do not want to bring into this any more people than necessary so I will myself knock on your door when I am sure my guests are asleep, and I will guide you to the back door leading to the stables, where Masters and Patty will await you.'

'How can I ever repay you, Madame?' asked Lucy fervently.

'To get you safely away, my dear, is all the thanks I need,' replied the lady candidly. 'But should our plans go awry and Monsieur the Earl catch us out in this, I beg you will back my story that I knew nothing of this plan. I shall try to persuade him that my servants helped you only because you were so frantic to escape from him.'

At the look of puzzlement in Lucy's eyes, she said hastily, 'I am not so brave as you, my dear, and I confess that my blood runs cold at the thought of his anger if he knew I was involved.'

This seemed so reasonable to Lucy that she agreed to it at once. 'Though I cannot see how he will find out,' she said decisively. 'Especially if you are able to delay him discovering I am gone. Once I reach Aunt Chadwell's he need never know who helped me get there.'

'We must certainly hope not,' whispered Madame devoutly, fingering her neck.

As she left the room, Madame was chuckling silently to herself. In that good humour she was indeed a fine-looking creature, tall and elegant, her heavy hair piled high, one or two ringlets falling to rest against handsome sloping shoulders and full bust. Her face was not just in the ordinary mould and had caused havoc in the hearts of more than a few gentlemen, with its dark inky eyes, set wide apart, and full, pouting lips seemingly made for love. But she had other moods, blacker moods of rage, when things did not go her way and at such times she lost all semblence of beauty, her face disfigured as she whipped herself into a frenzy. In such a mood she was capable of anything, none of the normal taboos being strong enough to hold her. Few people had seen her in such a rage; her brother, her late husband, one or two of the servants; but she was careful to keep a tight rein on herself to keep them hidden from the world. This afternoon when Alex had talked of marrying the Tiversley chit she had felt such a mood begin to take her. But it would never do to let him see her so! All her plans, all her schemes, would come to nothing if he did. Why, she thought, as she made her way back to the drawing room, well satisfied with her afternoon's work, she had been a nobody for long enough. Daughter of a poor emigrée, she had married Monsieur D'Avergne, her late husband, for money. Lascivious and elderly, he had been unable to withstand her youth and rounded charms. For her part, she had determined on marrying him as soon as she had learned of the considerable fortune he had amassed in En-

gland after being forced to flee France in the early
days of the Revolution. He had provided her with
her handsome fortune, dying providentially while
she was still young enough to enjoy it. But his
money had been made in the City and nobody could
take from him the smell of the Exchange. She might
call herself Lady D'Avergne, but those who mattered knew what she was. All that would change if
she managed to entrap Lord Sheldon. Give her
Sheldon's title and nothing would be beyond her
reach.

Shortly after Valentine had gone, a servant
brought Lucy a substantial repast on a tray, which
she ate with relish, though she drank hardly at all
from the decanter of wine which had been thoughtfully provided, wishing that she dared ask instead
for some tea.

She decided to take Madame's advice, and lay
down on the counterpane spread over the large fourposter dominating the room, but she removed only
her shoes, to be ready as soon as she heard Madame's knock.

After the exhaustions of the day, Lucy quickly
sank into a deep, dreamless slumber, and it was
many hours later, though she seemed to have been
sleeping only a moment or two, before she became
faintly aware of a quiet tapping somewhere in a
corner of her mind. At first her muddled senses
could not make out what it meant, for she imagined
she was still at home in the bright bedchamber she
had had at Aunt Marianne's. Then the haze cleared
and she remembered everything, starting up from
the bed in an instant. Thanking heaven that it was
a moonlit night, she swiftly donned her pelisse and
shoes, without needing to light a candle, and, tying
her bonnet, stopped only to pick up her portmanteau before making her way unerringly to the door.

When she opened it, there stood Madame, barefoot and dressed in a long white nightgown, a shawl draped carelessly around her shoulders and her thick black hair rippling down her back. In her hand she held a branched candelabra and she beckoned Lucy onwards while she lit the way. Lucy followed her down the corridor, feeling the skin at the back of her neck prickle as the flickering candles picked out ghostly-looking shapes, and lit the paintings of the mock-ancestors with whom Valentine had chosen to adorn her house and who stared down disapprovingly at all this untoward night time activity. She was relieved when, after descending two flights of stairs, she found herself at a little panelled door which Valentine pushed ajar to disclose the competent-looking face of Masters, behind which peeped Patty's scared one. Pausing only to whisper, 'Au revoir, petite, and may the Good Lord travel with you,' Valentine returned swiftly whence she had come.

Masters took her portmanteau, saying softly, 'This way, Miss, if you please. We must make our way to the stables where the carriage waits. Quick as you can, Miss, if you will; you too Patty, and for heaven's sake make no noise, for if his lordship should catch a sniff of this, we are all in the basket.'

Lucy needed no second warning and, holding her breath, followed Masters as speedily as she could to where the carriage stood in the moonlight, a young groom holding the horses' heads to steady them and try to stop them stamping too much and betraying their presence.

Taking her portmanteau back from Masters, Lucy climbed into the coach, dragging a petrified Patty in after her, leaving Masters free to jump onto the box and take the reins from the groom. They began to move, very slowly at first until they had reached the gates and were out on the road, and then, rapidly picking up speed as if Masters was as eager as herself to put as much distance between them and the Earl as possible. . . .

In a surprisingly short time, Lucy found herself back in Croydon and, determined to take no unnecessary risks, requested that they stay, not at the Greyhound as on her journey down, but at the King's Head. As his mistress had intimated, Masters was an efficient servant and arranged everything so easily that it was not long before Lucy was safely tucked up in bed in one of the best bedrooms the hostelry had to offer; Patty on a little trestle-bed near to her own. A good night's rest and a hearty breakfast in a private parlour and Lucy felt ready for anything.

She was just about to remove from the little breakfasting room when, to her extreme horror, in walked the Earl of Sheldon!

'Well now, isn't this cosy!' he laughed malevolently.

CHAPTER

6

Lucy stared at him, appalled, as he lounged nonchalently against the door, which he had shut fast behind him, his arms folded across his chest, on his face a wicked gleam.

'However did you find me? Who gave me away?'

'No-one had to give you away, you little goosecap!' he replied in much amusement. 'I may have known you for only two days, but that was quite long enough for me to know that you would try to run for it. I had only to instruct one of my grooms to keep watch for any unusual activity in the stables to prevent you, for I knew that Valentine would help you if she could.'

Remembering Lady Valentine's plea, Lucy protested, 'But you are quite wrong, sir. Lady Valentine had nothing to do with it. It is just that the servants realised that I was so very unhappy that they *would* help me!'

'Really?' replied his lordship pleasantly. 'How very clever of them to realise that you were so miserable when you spent your time confined to your room. And what winning ways you must have, to be sure, to persuade them all to put their employment in jeopardy, not to mention steal a carriage from their mistress, just to help a girl they had never before laid eyes upon.'

Even Lucy was forced to realise the thinness of her story, and admitted, 'Well sir, it is as you say. Lady Valentine did help me, but it was only at my most earnest request. She was most reluctant and cannot in any way be held to blame.'

'Loyal, handsomely loyal of you, my dear. But then I already know that of you. I only hope you will not find your confidence in the lady misplaced. But enough of her, now that I have you again. Really not a very clever plot. It was too simple for my servants to foil. Poor Miss Tiversley, having all this trouble when there was not the least chance that you could succeed. My groom had only to follow Valentine's carriage on horseback—at a discreet distance, of course—and then report back to me.'

'It makes not the slightest difference that you have found me, for I will never marry you. You still have to get a special licence and, meantime, I shall have time to think of a way to make good my escape.'

'It grieves me to have to inform you, Miss Tiversley, or should I say "my love" now that we are so soon to be related?' He saw her face! 'No? Well, perhaps not! As I was saying, Miss Tiversley, it grieves me to have to tell you that I have the licence already in my possession.'

'You could not possibly have it yet.'

'Ah but I have,' and he pulled a paper from the pocket of his topcoat. 'I sent one of my grooms to the bishop with a letter of explanation as soon as you went to your room yesterday.'

'But you must have my guardian's consent before the bishop may grant such a thing.'

'Poetic licence, my dear, if you will excuse the pun? He thinks I have it, you see. My groom returned not only with the licence but with a letter counselling haste considering, as he says, such untoward circumstances.'

'He may counsel as he pleases,' cried Lucy hotly. 'But you are the last man in the world I would think of marrying!'

'Come now, Ma'am,' he said calmly, advancing forward to lean against the table opposite her. 'No need to take it personally.'

'Personally! It is *me* you wish to marry.'

'Much as I hate to contradict a lady, I feel I should point out that I do not marry you out of any great personal wish of my own, but to save your honour! A small point, but relevant, do not you think?'

Lucy had the grace to blush. 'Yet I never desired such a sacrifice, sir, nor will I accept it.'

'Oh come now, we've sung this duet before. You are compromised, and, as another spirited lady was informed by her impatient suitor, or so we are told, "Will you, nill you, I will marry you".'

'How do you propose to make *me* marry *you* sir? You cannot think that I will make my vows willingly, and no man of the cloth will officiate where the bride is unwilling.'

'You are too sanguine, Miss Tiversley. I rather think I know more of men of the cloth than you. Why, my own man down at Arunfold would perform the ceremony in a trice! Aye, and convince himself easily that he was acting in your best interest. And should he not it would not greatly concern me. There is more than one way to skin a rabbit. I could, instead, simply take you to a little hunting box I own in Quorn country—quite remote and the area deserted at this time of year. It would be quite amusing, just the two of us. You might even come to beg me to marry you at last!'

'My Uncle Chadwell would have something to say to such a scheme!'

'He would know nothing of it until it was too late, if you follow my drift.'

Lucy was very much afraid she was beginning to. 'You would not dare!' she cried, her cheeks scarlet.

'My dear girl, when will you get it into your head that I will?' he replied quite seriously, his eyes boring into hers.

She was defeated. 'I see you leave me little choice, sir,' she admitted quietly, her eyes those of a frightened child. 'I must agree.'

'Aye, so you must—and today too, before you think up any more shatter-brained schemes.' Then, seeing her crestfallen expression, he added, 'Cheer up bantling. You've nothing to fear from me. I'm not hanging out for a family. I've an heir already, in m'cousin, so you need not think I'll make any demands on you! You and I will rub along well enough, since we'll see very little of each other. You will stay at Arunfold as Mary's very dear aunt. You will teach her, just as we planned, while I . . . well, I expect my life to go on much as before. Apart from being hostess for me when I bring down shooting parties or when the family comes to stay you will have few duties to perform. And comfort yourself with the thought that anything could happen! I might choke on a chicken bone tomorrow and then you would be free! Attend well to the duties I've asked of you, and I'll make sure you are well provided for in that event.'

His words made her realise more than ever how much she was in his power and she blushed a more fiery red than before. 'I'm obliged to you sir! You really are too kind,' she cried out with crushing sarcasm.

'How good of you to notice,' he agreed with maddening sweetness.

'One thing, sir. You have it all worked out, it

seems, but what if I should meet someone . . . someone I liked and wanted to marry in earnest?'

'We'll cross that bridge if and when we come to it!' he replied with a grimace. 'Come, let us find ourselves a preacher. I want to make Arunfold tonight.'

It was approaching five before they came off the Turnpike at Horsham and they then continued some way on a well-made road until they reached woodlands belonging to the Arunfold estate. They had been travelling almost continually since the ceremony that morning, which had made them one, and for most of that time had not spoken, each being sunk in his own thoughts. When they reached Arunfold woodland, however, his lordship politely pointed out the fact to his bride, who could not help but be interested.

Still they drove on until, eventually, they turned in through some impressive iron gates, passing a modern gatehouse, from the windows of which peeped the gatekeeper's offspring. Lucy waved, and the three heads bobbed out of sight. She smiled to herself, a smile which reached her face, and she found herself feeling suddenly more cheerful until she noticed the Earl looking at her thoughtfully. She returned her attention to her surroundings.

The Earl's carriage drove the lengthy track through the home park towards the house itself, a happy compilation of the building of three centuries, palatial and wonderfully sited, backed as it was by steeply rising, tree-covered hills. Extensive grounds before the house had been cleared to open up the aspect, and laid to grass when the house was undergoing some alterations early in the previous century. Herds of plump cattle now grazed these lands, chewing contentedly and noting their approach but without curiosity. Dotted here and there across the expanse of lawn, limes and majestic oaks softened the vista towards the old house and helped blend it into its setting. The estate had such a permanent and harmonious air as to make Lucy feel that it might be fine indeed to be mistress of such a place.

As Sheldon brought his curricle to a halt on the gravelled path before the Corinthian portico which fronted the house, an army of servants appeared, to relieve him of horses, curricle and luggage, while he handed Lucy down and led her inside. At the top of the flight of stone steps leading into the house, the dignified person of Frensham, the butler, awaited them and took from them their outdoor things, passing them in great style to attendant footmen, while offering his master greetings. The Earl replied in easy fashion, adding, as if he was speaking about something as trivial as the weather,

'Oh, and Frensham, I would like to make known to you Lady Sheldon, my new wife and your mistress. I expect you to show her the same courtesy you have always shown to the members of this family—but I know that I may rely on you implicitly.'

If, as was indeed the case, Frensham had been shocked rigid at this disclosure, he was not about to abandon his habitual dignity, replying impassively, 'Certainly sir. And may I offer, on behalf of the staff, heartiest felicitations.'

'We thank you for them, knowing that they are sincere. Now, will you inform Miss Mincham that we are arrived, and tell her, if you please that we wish to see Miss Mary. We will repair to the small drawing room. Perhaps you will have some tea sent in?' and without waiting for a reply, he led Lucy through the entrance hall and across a huge apartment to which he briefly referred as the Great Hall: then into the room known as the small drawing room, since it was used in place of the Great Hall in the absence of guests. This room was amongst those redesigned in the last years of the previous century. Lucy looked around her with pleasure at cream walls and jonquil curtains, noting incidentally that his lordship had a fondness for the Empire style. She was just reflecting that she would never have called such a house gloomy, when a knock sounded and in walked one of the most forbidding-looking women Lucy had ever seen. In a dress of stark black without trimming, her only ornaments were a belt to which were attached her housekeeping keys and, above a sallow face and hiding every trace of her hair, an uncompromising plain white cap. As she passed in through the doorway, hands clasped neatly and precisely before her, Lucy noted her sharp features and tiny, darting dark eyes and was chilled. It was as if she had walked from blazing sunshine into a shaded room.

'Ah, Mincham,' began the Earl briskly, 'so here you are. I sent for you so that I may introduce you to my new wife. I am sure you will wish to pay her your compliments. My dear,' he went on, turning to Lucy. 'Here is Mincham, who will save you a great deal of worry, I am sure.'

Lucy was almost certain that she heard her give a contemptuous snort as her mistress greeted her, but the housekeeper replied demurely enough, 'Indeed sir, I am sure that I *hope* Madam will be happy here.'

Was it Lucy's imagination, or did she stress the word "hope" in a strange way?

'And where is my niece, Ma'am? I wish to introduce her to her aunt.'

'She will be here directly, sir. I told her to run along to wash her hands and face before coming to you, for you know what children are with their dirt and grime.'

'I wish you had not bothered, Mincham. I must

confess that I have rather a weakness for grimy little children, especially if it means they have been enjoying themselves. Mary has had little enough pleasure of late, and I disremember seeing her mucky like other children, since her mother died. It would be quite a treat to see her so!'

That Miss Mincham did not share his lordship's prejudice was obvious from another snort, almost, but not quite inaudible, though since Mary arrived at that convenient moment, no reprimand was forthcoming.

As Mary stepped into the room, a tiny pale figure dressed pitifully in black, relieved only by the silver blonde of her curls, Lucy's heart went out to her: it seemed intolerable to add black crepe to the child's burden of grief. Lucy vowed that the first change she would make at Arunfold would be to get the child out of mourning and into something more suitable, for surely it was heathenish to force little children to rub up against death so closely.

As Mary saw her uncle, her face lit up joyously and she gave one or two running steps towards him, before Mincham called out sharply, 'Now, Miss Mary, remember how your poor dear Mama would have hated to see you act the hoyden.'

The child's face crumpled: she stopped in her tracks, clasped her hands demurely before her, head bent as if in submission, and walked quietly over to the Earl to hold her forehead up for his kiss.

Lord Sheldon directed one dark look at Mincham before bending to catch Mary up in his arms and sitting her on his lap, 'Well miss, and how is my favourite niece?' he asked, planting his kiss first on her forehead, then on her cheek. But her high spirits on seeing him were past; Mincham had worked the transformation.

'I am very well, Uncle Alex,' she said quietly, the

pulled look about her mouth showing how deeply she had taken Mincham's words.

'Ah, but you will be even better soon,' he promised, determined to get a smile from her. 'I have brought a new companion for you, my love, who will stay here with you and teach you your lessons.'

'And will she stay, sir, or will she soon have enough of me and leave, like Miss Tring?'

'Miss Tring did not leave because she did not like you, sweetheart,' replied the Earl, shaken by her bleak acceptance. 'It was Arunfold she did not like. It was too lonely for her.'

'Will my *new* teacher like it here do you think, sir?'

'Why don't you ask her. And, as a special secret, I must tell you that she is not only your teacher, but your new aunt, too, so is rather forced to consider Arunfold as home.'

'How can she be a new aunt, sir? I did not think you could get *new* aunts.'

'You can if your uncle marries, for then the lady he marries becomes your aunt. And as I have married Lucy, she becomes Aunt Lucy to you, do you see?'

Mary nodded, wonderingly.

The Earl turned then to Lucy, who had been watching in fascination this softer side to her husband. 'Well, Aunt Lucy, and do you think you will like Arunfold?'

'I think that I shall like both Mary and Arunfold very much.'

'Thank you, Aunt Lucy,' replied Mary politely, then, turning back to the Earl, she asked with far more eagerness, 'Does that mean you will stay too, Uncle Alex?'

The Earl shifted uncomfortably in his chair, 'I am sorry, my love, but it is not possible just now. Perhaps later on . . .'

The eagerness died almost before it was born; she was used to disappointment. 'And shall you leave soon?' she asked, careful to show nothing of her feelings.

'I must go tonight, darling. At once!'

'Then I shall not see you tomorrow,' and she carefully slid down from his knee, removing herself physically as well as mentally from further contact with him. He made to put his arms round her again, but she calmly stood back to avoid him, making him a deep curtsey, 'Goodnight then Uncle Alex, and, if you please send my compliments to Aunt Fanny. Goodnight, Aunt Lucy.'

She walked sedately from the room, Mincham following, obviously gratified by such a show of decorum.

For a moment Lucy was bereft of speech, a choking feeling at the back of her throat making it impossible for her to utter so much as a sound. His lordship was similarly afflicted but recovered sooner.

'Well, that is Mary,' he said unnecessarily. 'You see now what I meant when I said she is a trifle out of spirits.'

'A trifle! More than a trifle, I think! That dreadful woman, how came you to allow her charge of Mary?'

'Now don't start jumping to conclusions,' said the Earl testily. 'You do not know the facts. Mincham is not in charge of Mary at all. She is the housekeeper—and a deuced efficient one too, I can tell you.'

'That I can well believe!' flashed Lucy hotly, staring resentfully at him.

'Will you listen before you run on so, girl!' replied her new lord and master. 'When Miss Tring left, Mincham offered and it was most handsome of her, whatever you may say, to take Mary under her wing until a new governess could be found—and that is you! Mincham is severe, but she does everything for the best as she sees it.'

'So, I am sure, did medieval torturers,' cried Lucy wildly. 'And I suppose it is her idea to keep the child in mourning for ever! I was never more shocked in my life to see it.'

'I must confess that I'd no notion of it. The rest of us put off our black gloves aeons ago.'

'Aye, but you did not think to check that she had had the same privilege, did you? Poor child, she has been abominably used.'

'Well, isn't that just why you were hired in the first place, to see that she is made happy? Just because we are married, I see no reason why that should change. If anything it should make things easier for you. You will be able to do just as you think about her, I give you carte blanche—and that goes for the house, too. You are mistress here now, and I will ensure before I leave that the servants know they must obey your wishes. Whatever you think is best, for Mary and for yourself, you have my permission to initiate. Anything to see the child happy.'

'Not a moment too soon, sir, if you ask me, for she seems quite moped to death,' replied his wife, refusing to be placated. 'I really do not know how you have come to let that woman have such power. Don't you have a house steward? I would have thought she would have to be responsible to him?'

'We did have, but old Brackham was forced to retire through ill-health just about the time I took on Mincham. She stood in for him and was so deuced efficient that there seemed little rush to replace him. Mincham is responsible to my secretary, of course, but he is usually to be found with me, so she has assumed much of his authority.'

'Hasn't she, though,' said Lucy tartly. 'She's just

the style of woman who would!' She hesitated before going on to say haltingly, 'And are you really going away tonight? I declare the sight of Mary's little face when you said so brought a lump to my throat.'

'Do you think you are the only one with feelings? I too was upset by it. Yet I must leave tonight. I am going back to *Ormaie*. You know that I was invited for a prolonged stay.'

'Won't it look rather strange for you to leave me so soon after our wedding?'

'No stranger than for the servants to see you occupying one set of rooms and me another on our wedding night—and with your door fast bolted! After all, they know I'm no monk!' he replied grimly. 'I'm afraid we must face the fact that whatever we do our relationship is bound to cause comment. The servants know everything in such a house as *Arunfold* and will not be taken in for so much as a moment. No doubt we will become inured to their gossip in time, and, once our behaviour becomes established as normal, they will cease to think of it. It is always so.'

'I'm afraid I will have to take your word for that, sir,' said Lucy sweetly. 'In our family we have no experience of such strange marriages.'

'Until now, my dear Miss Tiversley, until now—ah, but I am forgetting, I mean Lady Sheldon, of course.'

'I prefer Miss Tiversley.'

'A pity, my love,' replied her spouse, smiling broadly at her flash of temper. 'But perhaps by the time I see you again, you will have become accustomed to your new name.'

'Are you really going back to *Ormaie* tonight?'

'Would you rather I stayed to share the bridal chamber with you for our wedding night?'

'Indeed I would not!' cried Lucy, her cheeks aflame. 'I'd rather share it with any man than you!'

'Dear me, how very indelicate of you,' scolded the Earl, his eyes alight. 'Then I must certainly not outstay my welcome longer. And I am sure that Lady Valentine will be more encouraging. So, until I see you again, my dear wife,' and he moved forward, took her firmly by the shoulders, and, before she realised what he was about, kissed her very deliberately on her lips. To her dismay, Lucy felt an answer within her, and she pulled herself away, raising her hand to slap his face. He caught her wrist in mid-air.

'Tut, tut, my lady! Such violence! You really must learn to accept my husbandly tributes more becomingly.'

Lucy deigned no reply, and turned from him, keeping her temper only with considerable difficulty.

He seemed to hesitate, then, in a few seconds she heard the door open and he was gone.

CHAPTER

7

Lucy woke next morning to find the sun streaming into her room. A maid was adjusting the blinds
she had just raised, while, on the small lacquered
cabinet beside Lucy's bed was placed a silver tray,
on which stood a pot of steaming chocolate, a rack
of thin slices of bread and toast, and to one side a
number of dishes of preserves.

Lucy had never breakfasted in bed and requested
that only chocolate should be brought in future. For
the rest, she would breakfast downstairs with her
new niece. It was a shock to discover just how much
influence the Earl's words of the previous evening
had had, for the girl went puce in her attempts to
reassure Lucy that all would be as she wished.

She had been given the rooms always occupied
by previous Countesses, pleasant airy rooms, furnished with the elegant Chippendale furniture chosen by a predecessor. Pink flowered wallpaper,
curtains of a deeper rose and a luxurious carpet
made the rooms friendly and welcoming, but Lucy
had been afraid and miserable on entering them
the previous night. Her sensations had been a curious mixture of relief and regret that Lord Sheldon
had left her, for at least she knew he could be kind.
Now she was alone in a strange house. And why

had he said that Lady Valentine would be encouraging when he returned to *Ormaie*? What was he suggesting? Did that in some way explain the lady's extraordinary desire to help Lucy escape from him? Trying to understand what was happening to her, she had lain awake for hour after hour, wracked with indecision and fear, until eventually her exhausted frame could resist sleep no longer.

Now, as always, in the morning sunshine things appeared less appalling. She was soon dressed and making her way downstairs. The house was a maze, but she eventually found her way to the small drawing room. To her surprise, when she opened the door Mincham was there, sitting at a writing desk in a corner of the room, a mass of papers in front of her. She rose when she saw Lucy, her darting eyes working furiously, but only said depreciatingly, 'You will not mind my being here, Ma'am. It has become my custom, the house being so often empty.'

To Mincham's surprise, Lucy said firmly, 'The house is empty no longer, Mincham, and such tasks will need to be carried out in your own rooms now.' Lucy was not used to such a *large* establishment, but she knew an encroaching servant when she saw one.

Mincham's eyes narrowed, but, without so much as a word, she gathered up her papers and went to leave the room. Before she reached the door, Lucy called her back. 'Oh Mincham, have you seen my niece this morning?'

'Your niece, Madam?' she questioned impertinently, as if puzzled to know whom she meant. Then her brow cleared. 'Oh, you mean Miss Mary, of course.'

Lucy flushed. 'Who else should I mean, pray? Well? Have you seen her?'

'I've not exactly seen her, Ma'am,' she admitted,

not wishing to be helpful, but unwilling to pass up an opportunity to lay a familiar complaint, 'but I know where she'll be, and if I've told her once that it's unbecoming, I've told her a dozen times! In the kitchens is where you'll find her, with Perry! And what kind of influence she'll be on a growing child, I'll leave you to judge for yourself, tempting her with all sorts of sweet things until she minds nobody.'

'That will do, Mincham,' cut in Lucy icily. 'You may go.'

Left alone, Lucy found herself curious as to what Mary could find to interest her in the kitchens and decided to investigate. When she reached the kitchens the scene which met her eyes came as something of a shock, for there, amidst numerous contrivances for roasting, baking and steaming, were a dozen or so maids and scullions all engaged in a frenzy of activity. Calmly directing proceedings from a big armchair by the open fire, was a large, white-haired lady of uncertain years. On her lap, her face tear-stained, sat Mary, clutching her doll in one hand and a sugar plum in the other and resting her head on her friend's matronly bosom. Seeing Lucy, the lady rose slowly to her feet so as not to jolt Mary off too quickly, and bobbed a curtsey, calmly straightening her cap and voluminous apron as she did so.

'Good morning, Madam,' she said, her voice, with its soft burr, surprisingly sweet and showing no sign of embarrassment at being found so. 'I am Anne Perry, your ladyship. Your head cook.'

Lucy noticed that, though Mary was now on her feet, she still clutched Mrs Perry's apron.

'Good morning, Perry,' said Lucy in reply, determinedly cheerful. 'I came down to find Miss Mary. Mincham said she would be here.'

'She's often here with old Perry, Ma'am, the poor

77

little lamb. Nothing much else for her to do. She finds the kitchen a comfort after the spiteful words of *some* people.'

'You will not stop me from coming to see Perry, Aunt, will you?' begged Mary, finding her tongue. 'Mincham says you will.'

'What a strange notion,' said Lucy, annoyed at Mincham's presumption. 'When I was small I liked nothing better than the kitchens at home. I'll join you if I may.'

Mary's eyes opened widely.

'There you are, my duck,' said Mrs Perry, putting her arms round the child and holding her close to her, the little girl's head buried in her apron. 'I told you that your Aunt would not say so,' and her kindly eyes met Lucy's over the child's head in a nod of approval. 'But shouldn't you fetch a chair for her ladyship?'

Mary rushed off willingly and struggled back with a small Windsor armchair, running off again to fetch a cushion.

While she was gone, Mrs Perry outlined graphically for Lucy how Mincham had tried to keep Mary in the other part of the house, 'almost as if she was in some way jealous, Ma'am, if you know what I mean, and Miss Mary only wanting love where she could find it. I've known women like her before—sour creatures who enjoy taking their ill-humour out on little ones. It's "Miss Mary this" and "Miss Mary that" all day long. "Don't you know that young ladies do not run about wildly, Miss Mary" and "Only think how your poor Mama would turn in her grave to see you so grubby, Miss Mary", until I'm past all patience. It's happy I am to see you here, for she certainly needs someone young around. The kitchen's no place for her to be sure. That's the only thing I'm in agreement with Mincham on, but

I've not the heart to send her away to face that Friday-faced creature alone.'

In the middle of all her talk, Mrs Perry continued, seemingly without effort, the work of directing men and maidservants all around her, her calm, bright blue eyes missing nothing, and Lucy watched fascinated as she told one to "stop rubbing that pastry as if you were trying to make a bread pudding, girl, can't you. It'll be so heavy it'll weigh more than that pan over there", and she pointed to the largest of the great number of highly polished copper stewing pans hanging on pegs on the wall. "Move over and I'll show you again."

While she was so doing, Lucy had plenty of time to take stock of her and the little world she ruled over. She liked what she saw. Gruff she was, almost to the point of rudeness, to the girl she was teaching, her ruddy face sharp with concentration, but when the girl got it right at last, she was rewarded with a smile which broke through as if a window had been opened to let in the light.

Lucy could not help noticing how clean she kept all around her. 'How unusual, in such a large house, for a woman to be in charge of the kitchens' she observed, as Mrs Perry resumed her place by the fire, having first wrapped Mary in one of her aprons and given her some pastry cuttings to play with.

'You'll find a lot of things different at Arunfold,' she agreed pleasantly. 'It's how the old Earl wanted them, God rest his soul, and the new one never seems to want them changed either. Good plain cooking is what he always likes when he is in the country; English food. Time enough when he is in town for him to faddle his insides with foreign messes and French chefs, and so I tell him!'

'You . . . tell him?' asked Lucy, surprised, thinking of the haughty Earl she had faced in London.

'Bless you, Ma'am. Miss Mary's not the first child

to find her way into Perry's kitchen. I well remember when he and poor Master Frederick—little scamps they were . . .'

She broke off in confusion, realising the impropriety of gossiping to the mistress of the house.

'Please go on, Mrs Perry. I would so much like to know about Arunfold now that I am to be living here.'

Perry obliged, much relieved.

'Of course, a Carne's been Earl of Sheldon for centuries,' she explained. 'And Master Alex brought up as the heir, you might say. Him and Master Frederick were always into mischief, and Miss Grace too, she would come over to join them whenever she could. Merry as grigs from morning till night, all three of 'em; Miss Fanny being much younger of course. And then Miss Grace, she married Master Frederick, and never was there such joy. The Earl's Mama being dead, Miss Grace came to the house as mistress, Master Alex, him never seeing a girl to please him until now. It was a grand time, and no mistaking. Only then Master Frederick was taken from us,' she went on, her voice thickening, 'and things were never the same again. Master Alex taking it so hard and blaming himself for letting him go—though how he could have stopped him, I'm sure I don't know! And then Miss Grace—such a gentle, sweet lady as she was, with never a sour word for anyone—well, she just seemed to fade, and losing the poor little babe an' all. That's when Mincham came. And to give him his due, Master Alex only brought her here to save Miss Grace worry—her being so weak.' Her voice hardened. 'But it was a bad day for Arunfold. Place has never been the same since. She does her work well enough, but she hates to see folk happy. And our chick here hounded by her day in and day out. It was Mincham drove Miss Tring away. Right fond of the little 'un she was, but poor girl couldn't stand the atmosphere. *We* do our best to keep Miss Mary out of Mincham's way—for I've been here too long for her to try to trespass on my territory—but she has her at her books all day if she can, much more than is right for a little girl. And it's Mincham who keeps her in black too!'

'She'll be in black no longer if I have anything to say about it,' declared Lucy resolutely, turning to Mary. 'How would you like a pretty new dress, my love? Are not you made dull by that one?'

To her surprise, Mary replied, 'If you please, Aunt, I would rather keep my own dress. Miss Mincham says that my Mama would think I did not care to remember her if I did not wear black.'

Lucy smothered her indignation with difficulty. 'Well I never heard anything so silly. My Mama and Papa are dead too, but I know they loved me too much to want to see me in the glooms. Do not you remember the pretty dresses you wore before your Mama went to heaven? Did your Mama have you dressed in black then?'

Mary stared at her doubtingly. 'No,' she replied slowly, clearly considering the matter for the first time.

'What makes you think she would like you to wear it now, then? Depend on it, she would like to see you looking pretty, for that is how she thinks of you while she waits for you in heaven.'

'Do you really think she would be pleased?' asked Mary, with rising hope.

'I do,' declared Lucy firmly.

CHAPTER

8

Having left his wife at Arunfold, Sheldon rode back to *Ormaie*, reaching it just after Lady Valentine's last guests had sought their bed-chambers. Their hostess was still giving last minute instructions to her servants before seeking her own apartments. After the scene she had had with Sheldon when he had berated her in round terms for contriving Lucy's flight, Valentine half expected to see him no more, so it was with gratification that she met him in her hallway, muddied and fatigued from his ride.

'So, you've come back to me,' she purred softly in the echoing vestibule, her face alight as she held out her hand. 'You decided not to marry after all. How wise of you.'

The Earl took the hand and bent low over it, just brushing it with his lips, enjoyment on every feature. 'Au contraire ma belle, we were married this morning by special licence, and I have now deposited my bride at her new home as promised.'

Incredulously, she snatched her hand from his light grasp, her features distorted. 'You dare! You dare to tell me this?'

'But, you asked me! Would you have me tell you less than the truth?'

'Truth? You speak of truth? It is the truth when I remind you that you swore you wanted me! It is the truth when I tell you that you say you care for *me*!'

'So I do,' replied the Earl pleasantly, 'So I do. None more. Assure you!'

At his tone her self-control drained and, as if with a will of its own, her hand moved, fingers curled viciously towards his face. Before it found its target, however, she was faintly aware of movement behind her, felt her wrist clasped tightly in a firm, cool grasp, and heard a voice saying smoothly,

'Alex, mon ami! How glad we are to have you with us, are we not, Valentine? We missed you tonight. Nobody to play cards with—at least not to any sense. Really, my friend, it is impossible to enjoy playing for sixpences. And these fellows think themselves all the go!'

By the time Valentine realised that it was her brother who had stayed her hand, she had also recollected the impropriety of scratching her guest's face and said with a hard laugh, 'Hardly sixpences Léo, though, to be sure, Alex would have been more amusing for you.'

The nasty moment had passed. Quick to make amends Valentine excused herself and went to order refreshments, while her brother led the way into one of the carefully restful salons which led off from the hall.

'So, you are a married man now, mon ami. How very amusing,' he began, nonchalantly leaning an elbow on the mantelshelf as Alex settled himself comfortably into an armchair by the fireplace in which a log still glowed brilliantly.

'Not as amusing as it might be, old fellow,' replied Alex drolly, 'since I am here and my bride at Arunfold.'

Both men laughed in the insinuating way men

have on such occasions and the Earl went on, 'But you know my reasons, so I shan't bore you with them.'

'Indeed no, you need tell me nothing. And I quite see that you had no choice in the matter. A man's honour . . .' He shrugged his shoulders in a peculiarly Gallic gesture, and left the sentence uncompleted.

'Your sister seems not to share your complaisance, my friend.'

'Valentine? She is like all women; a victim of her emotions. But she will come round, my friend. I am sorry that I wasn't here when you brought your Lucy to the house for I could have explained matters to Valentine. But she's an intelligent woman and will come to see that you have acted only as you must.'

It seemed he knew his sister well, for on her return all trace of ill-humour had gone. 'Well gentlemen,' she said calmly, not so much as a line to spoil the smoothness of her exquisite brow, 'I have asked that some supper be sent to you, Alex dear. I hope you excuse me, for I have been wanting my bed any time this last hour.'

Alexander rose at her words and took her hand between both his own. 'Am I forgiven, cherie?' he asked coaxingly, lifting each hand in turn to his lips in the familiar gesture.

'Silly boy,' she replied playfully, patting his cheek with the hand he had just released. 'How should I not?'

'I think Alex will not wish to be long from his own bed tonight, petite,' commented Léo. 'For he must be worn to the bone after his ride and all the events of the day.'

'I *am* tired,' agreed the Earl co-operatively. 'A little supper only, and then bed I think.'

'Sleep well, mon ami,' replied Valentine mildly,

and swept gracefully from the room, the silk of her dress rustling as she moved; her face a picture of indifference. It began to change as she mounted the stairs to her apartments and by the time she had reached the privacy of her bedchamber, the familiar dark expression disfigured her features. As she entered the room, tearing viciously to unfasten the fine emerald bracelet on her wrist, the two women who waited on her recognised her mood and each moved nervously around the room, dealing with her allotted tasks as quietly as possible as if unwilling, by any awkward noise or movement, to draw attention to herself. It was with a sigh of relief, breathed in unison, that they found themselves outside their mistress's door some half-hour later, without having brought down her wrath on themselves.

When they had been dismissed, Valentine, now in her long white nightgown, moved slowly and thoughtfully, towards the bed from her place at the dressing table, where she had been examining herself critically in the glass. Her expression was not pleasant as she restlessly moved across the carpeted floor and threw herself down on the silk coverlet on her bed, a frivolous, tented concoction. Her fury released itself as despair, and when her brother walked unceremoniously in on her some few minutes later, she was lying with bunched masses of the pink silk clutched in her fisted hands, while her tears produced spreading patches beneath her face.

Valentine's brother Léo, Monsieur Marechal, was not consciously an ill-disposed man; that is, he would never deliberately hurt someone only for the pleasure of it. But he was cold-hearted and selfish so that his schemes often resulted much as they might had he done so. Being entirely aware of the paucity of social respectability in his background, it seemed only commonsense to climb to the apex of society by whatever means necessary. If he could do so by fair means, well and good. If not, he was not one to baulk at the foul. He liked to be popular, but it was not entirely necessary to his sense of well being.

Now, as he came into the room, his sister looked up at him, her face blotched and patchy.

'What is this, Tina my precious? Tears?' He shook his head slowly, as if she was a child who had disappointed him. 'Surely not for Sheldon. I am surprised at you.'

'Surprised?' she cried fiercely, lifting her head from the bedcover, her accent becoming more pronounced as always when she was agitated. 'How can you say so? It is not I who fawn all over the Earl for marrying this stupid little halfling. I don't say, "Oui, m'lord and Non, m'lord," like a serving wench! You know I want him and that he has shown himself familiar with me, yet you do nothing! It is not kind in you!'

He did not reply at once, and continued to stand by the door looking not at her, but down at the carpet, as if in concentration. Then, 'You never were very wise, my dear, were you? Always such an impression of wit, but in reality. . . ?' Again the shrug and again the unfinished sentence.

She was instantly curious. 'If you have something to say, Léo, just say it. Don't strike poses!'

'So gracious, petite soeur, but yes, I do have something to say,' and he came over and sat beside her, his ugly face peering intently into hers.

'Now listen, stupid one! You rage at me, because I welcome the English lord to our house and stop you from acting like a fury. But ask yourself how it would serve either of us to drive him away? Would it suit you not to have entry to *his* house any more? Think of it; no more house parties or pleasant al fresco afternoons. What would it serve?

Will you be happy to have him cut you when you meet? And not only him, but all his friends.'

He had her attention entirely.

'Try to think clearly for once. You want his lordship; his title, his fortune; and yes, I believe you are not averse to his person. Well, and you have my blessing even in that, if you do not let it cloud your judgement. As for his fortune, well, we have money enough—yet not so much that his could not be useful. But his title we *must* have, and you should never allow yourself, even in your passions, to forget it! Think what doors it could open to us. You have done well for yourself, I admit, but so you should have with such natural advantages.' He lifted a handful of ringlets to expose her white shoulder and, like a man inspecting a familiar horse or hunting dog, he allowed his eyes to rove over her body. 'Yes indeed, my dear, such lush promise! How many men could resist? It is that body which has made it possible for us to call you Lady Valentine without being directly challenged, but it is not enough. Your husband juggled with the best of them in 'Change Alley, but he couldn't juggle you into the ton. Too many people know he came from the City for us to be comfortable. Quite enough to ensure that you will never grace St James's. You can get any number of men down here, but how many ladies? Even when you are Sheldon's guest at Arunfold he is, shall we say selective, as to which ladies he invites with you. Yet it is with the modest fair ones and not the little *barques of frailty* that your future must lie. Marry Sheldon and you will have entry everywhere. Nobody would dare to refuse his wife. And that will be of the greatest value to me!'

'You seem to forget one small matter,' said his sister curtly, nettled alike at his tone and peremptory manner. 'There is a Countess of Sheldon already.'

'I forget nothing! I ask you only to think! How long do you imagine this marriage will last? Six months? A year? Such a disparity in age, in fortune, in ton! Have patience and you will see it crumble. Think, if you can, how she must come to grief as his hostess! Do you really imagine he will suffer the embarrassment for long, when he marries only to keep face? Why, he is not even attracted to her. When he finds it not *convenable* he will find a way to dispose of her. Divorce is not impossible these days. And if he is to be believed, only annulment will be called for. It will not prevent him from returning to society with a new wife—and, if you are clever, that will be you. You are beautiful, a brilliant hostess and you are his own age. Everything this Miss Tiversley is not. Why should he not turn again to you?'

Valentine was smiling as he went on.

'Of course, if it does not go as I think it will, it may be necessary for us to take some action of our own, but there are a hundred and one ways to speed things on a little. You will not mind what we have to do to free him, I know.'

Some time later his lordship heard a scratching at his door.

Alexander was surprised; he had not been misled by Valentine's change of humour and knew her to be still in a fury, which caused him not a moment's unease and several of malicious enjoyment. Now as she walked in on him without waiting for his permission to enter, he was reclining in an upholstered armchair by the fire, dressed in a long, silk dressing gown and enjoying a glass of brandy before bed, his valet having already bidden him a punctilious goodnight. Seeing Valentine, still in her nightgown, walk in on him unannounced, he was surprised and a fraction off-guard. He sprang up, spilling some of the contents of his glass on the arm of his chair: on his face a twisted smile: in his eyes suspicious hardness.

'What a delightful surprise,' he said caressingly, as she came to him, reaching to place her arms around his neck and lifting her mouth to his. Before their lips could meet, she felt her hands unclasped unceremoniously from behind his neck, and pulled downwards to be brought to rest on his chest, his own hands gripping them cruelly. 'Naughty little Valentine,' he murmured provokingly, 'trying to play at housekeeping with a married man. I find that I'm shocked.'

'As well you might, my dear,' she replied unruffled, 'if that was my intention. But you mistake, my love. Your charm is enticing, I admit, but not quite that enticing.'

He cocked an eyebrow at her, his interest aroused by her dismissal as it could never have been by flattery.

'Not housekeeping, then?' he said, reflectively. 'Then why the kiss, my sweet?'

'A kiss? It means nothing to such old friends as we, Alex. But I am here to talk, my dear—and even you must see we need to talk, so strangely as we are placed?'

He knew she had a point and drew her over to the fireplace, where he poured her a glass of brandy and offered her his chair, as if she, and not he, was a guest in that house.

'No, my dear, you sit down, for I know how fatigued you are,' she said smoothly, pushing him down again into the seat he had just vacated. 'I will sit here,' and with her usual guile, she placed a cushion at his feet, seating herself on it and leaning her head heavily against his knees, while allowing her luxuriant curls to cascade over them. Without thinking, the Earl reached out a hand to stroke her hair familiarly, as he might with a favoured pet, and they sipped their brandy in companionable silence, each of them looking into the flames.

He was the first to break their silence. 'Well, now, cherie, so we have agreed that we are not to play at housekeeping. So why all this? I would be the last person to cavil at such comforts, but I confess myself puzzled.'

'How strange you are, Alex,' she replied, turning round towards him to rest her arms on his lap, her beautiful face glowing in the firelight, hair spilling onto creamy shoulders. 'Surely you can understand why I should come to you. Can you have forgotten how close we have been?'

'I doubt it would be in any man's capability to forget you,' he replied with honesty, coming unwillingly under her spell, a reminiscent smile playing about his mouth.

She joined her smile to his: their memories were the same.

'Thank you for that, at least,' she said graciously, bending her head in a dignified gesture, scarcely bothering to disguise her satisfaction. He saw her smile and was once more on his guard.

'So, petite, we are agreed that we are here only to talk. What shall we talk about. I cannot think that we have anything to say to each other.'

She hid her anger with difficulty. 'I find, my lord, that you must explain matters to me, you see?' she said, wrinkling her brow in concentration. 'It is that I do not comprehend.'

'And you are usually so perspicacious, my love! What must I explain to you?'

She almost refused to continue with this charade, but her brother's words still sounded, so she said plaintively, 'But you must have known that it was thought that you and I would make a match of it?'

'You and I? A match, my love? But no! Are you sure? But how could I guess? Why, I could only imagine that such a pretension would have been seen as an act of piracy by any number of my friends. Only think with how many other admirers I have been forced to share you and you will see my problem.'

She turned her face away and bit her lip and, rising from her cushion, moved towards the fireplace to stand with her hand on the high mantelshelf. She knew she had to be careful now, for she had always thought him unaware that he shared her favours. 'Yet I would have been faithful to you had you made me your wife, Alex. Men are so cruel. Free to take a mistress, they do not understand that women can be just as lonely, need someone just as much as they! Had you stayed with me I should never have looked elsewhere.'

The Earl watched unmoved. 'My dearest Valentine, I am appalled! I'd no idea you had such strength of character. I'm distraught! Assure you. Ma'am, it must ever be so!'

It says much for her brother's influence that Valentine did not fly at him, but she was angry enough to say unwisely, 'Perhaps you *will* be distraught when all your friends are laughing about this marriage. You will not feel so clever when the story is spread that you were forced to marry a penniless child, just out of the schoolroom, and who means nothing to you!'

'But such a rumour won't spread, my dear, will it?' he said unpleasantly, rising to his feet and bringing his fearsomely set face close to hers.

His expression frightened her and she pulled her face away. 'See now what you have me saying, Alex.

But you are safe from me. I'd never hurt you, however much you have trampled my feelings!'

She touched his hand placatingly, but his response startled her, for he pushed her hand away and grabbed her shoulder, his fingers pinching at her flesh.

'Enough of this play-acting. Let us have an end to this threatening and let us both understand why! You will spread no rumours about me because I know enough about you to ruin you. I could make certain that you never enter another London salon, as well you know, and I'll listen to no more threats from you. You and I have had a pleasant little friendship—that is all. It was never more than that. I have given you some expensive trifles and you have given me . . . well, let us just say that we have enjoyed each other! And now it is over.' His last words were spoken slowly and deliberately, with all the coldness with which he had so often been charged. Now was not the time to change his mind. There would be other times for that if she was clever, so she only said, 'As I say, mon ami, you know how to hurt; but it is as you will. I am not one to make myself offensive to those who do not wish my company.'

The Earl was deceived by her gentleness.

'Come on Valentine,' he coaxed, 'you will always be welcome where I am.'

As soon as she spoke he knew he had been foolish to let down his guard, even for a second, for she said persuasively, 'Then you will not turn me from your door, Alex, should I come to visit you and your bride at Arunfold?'

They both knew that, given his own inclination, he would never introduce her to the ladies in his family. Now, however, he could not find it in himself to refuse her, so, with a laugh of acceptance, he said,

'Go on with you, girl. Of course you and Léo may visit me. Lucy will make any friend of mine welcome.'

'Thank you Alex. How happy I am that you and I may still be friends. This country is so civilized. And do stay at *Ormaie*, my dear, as long as you wish.'

'As to that, I must leave you in a week or two at most. My heir must be told of my marriage and my affairs put in order. My sister, too, must be told, though what she will say . . . So, it must be London for me.'

'We shall miss you, my dear, but perhaps all is for the best,' she acceded graciously. 'And now, since'—and here she made a provocative face—'we are not to play house, I must leave you.'

Her expression changed once she had left his room. Her cheeks burned and she vowed that no matter how long or what it cost her she would repay him for his insults. The Earl and his wife!

CHAPTER

9

It says much for Madame D'Avergne's powers of persuasion that it was three weeks before the Earl returned to London, driving into Grosvenor Square just before midday, in scorching sunshine, and staying only long enough to divest himself of his travelling garb before going off in search of his heir. Having tried all his usual haunts in vain, he eventually tracked him down at Manton's shooting gallery, where Samuel, an excellent shot, was wont to spend the odd half-hour perfecting his eye.

As Alexander walked into the gallery, he was in time to see Samuel perfectly culping six wafers in a row, and, amidst general congratulations from his cousin's cronies, he came up behind him and clasped him on the shoulder to add his own.

'Well done, my lad, well done indeed!' were his first words, uttered with a warmth which might have surprised those who considered the Earl to be top-lofty.

'Sheldon, what you here?' cried Samuel with similar cordiality. 'Well, by all that's famous. I never expected you to tear yourself from your cosy berth down in Sussex so soon.'

'Reasons, old fellow,' replied Alexander enigmatically, touching the side of his nose to suggest that now was not the place to go into them. 'And it was worth it just to see you do that little trick,' with a little flick of his head towards the other end of the gallery, where Samuel's friends were inspecting the clipped wafers. 'As neat a bit of shooting as I've seen anywhere.'

'That's nothing,' said his cousin modestly, replacing his coat. 'Just a knack. It's when the target's moving that the skill comes in.'

'I remember you down at Arunfold last year, old fellow, so if you are trying to bam me into thinking you can't manage that too, best forget it. M'keeper's still trying to restock the West Wood.'

They laughed together with the ease of old companions and made their way from the gallery arm in arm.

'Where are you taking me, old man?' asked Samuel, amused, suddenly realizing that he was being borne off without so much as a by-your-leave. 'Don't like to be inquisitive, but it'd be nice to know.'

'Don't be awkward, Samuel,' replied his cousin pleasantly. 'Want a word. Got some news for you. Thought we'd go back to Grosvenor Square if you've no objection. I've only just got back to Town and I'm famished. Laid on luncheon and a bottle or two. Thought you might share it with me.'

Samuel had no objection at all and they were well into luncheon before Alexander broached the reason for his return.

Samuel was too surprised at Alexander's news to utter more than startled exclamations at first, but when he was over his initial shock he became calmer.

'I don't understand any of this, Shel,' he said wonderingly. 'A few weeks ago you told me that marriage was the last thing on your mind. Also said, if I remember, that the chit was a dowd. And now you're married to her. What possessed you?'

'No point in wrapping it up in clean linen, old fellow. I was dogged by ill luck—we both were,' and he told Samuel all that had happened to him on the fateful day, and the night which followed.

At the end of his cousin's recital, Samuel looked at him thoughtfully. 'What a frightful mess! But what made you marry the girl?'

'You're not thinking clearly, Sam. She comes from a respectable family; she's not some village girl I could buy off for a few pounds. Her father was at Waterloo! A viscount! The girl would have been ruined, and none of it her fault. There was nothing else for it. Believe me, she's just as sorry as me.'

'I'll wager she is! It must be dreadful to become a countess overnight! I should rather imagine she must think it the best night's work she's ever done!'

'Well there you are quite out,' said his lordship tersely. 'Though it's what everybody will believe. As a matter of fact, she ran away from me rather than marry me.'

This caught Samuel's attention. 'Ran away! You don't mean it?' Amused in spite of himself.

'It's true! And I would prefer no laughing, if you can contain yourself!'

Samuel did his best to obey as his cousin went on, 'So you are not to be imagining this is a love-match—on either side. It is to be a marriage in name only—I am quite content with my heir, so your inheritance is secure. And, in any case, my wife has impressed on me that, not only am I the very last person she would have chosen to marry, but that I am too old as well. She tells me that I am—ah, let me get her precise words—a senior member of society.'

'She sounds like a romp to me!' cried Samuel, slightly shocked.

'I've always said that your mild exterior hid a needle-sharp brain, my boy! She is precisely as you say—a romp. But we will go on well enough: no worse than many another couple. She agrees to stay with Mary at Arunfold: teach and generally look after her, that style of thing. We shan't have to see much of each other.'

'You say it's to be a marriage in name only. Does that mean that she will have her own suite of rooms?'

'Lord, boy, don't you turn mealy-mouthed on me!' returned Alexander impatiently. 'It means that I do *not* share her bed, if that's what you want to know. In fact I haven't seen her since our wedding day. As I said, I am perfectly happy with my heir. And any comforts I want in the petticoat line I can get elsewhere! I've told you, your inheritance is still your own.'

'Good God, Shel, as though that matters a jot! If you had found someone to make you happy, you must know that I would be content to stand down. I never heard anyone yet say that I am hanging out for a fortune.'

'I didn't say you were, but it's as well to know where you stand.'

'But what about her? What about the Countess? You say that you can go to the muslin company when you wish, but it's not so easy for a woman.'

'I admit I had some qualms, but since she was going to be a governess anyway, it must have occurred to her that marriage would be unlikely. It seemed to me that being Countess of Sheldon, even if only in name, would be better than being a nobody in a schoolroom. Her future is assured, at least, and it will be a mighty comfortable one. I'll make suitable provision for her in my will should I predecease her, but it won't take much from the estate and money's not a problem with us. She's taken to Mary and if she looks after her we'll owe her that much. Lady Sheldon's a deal too young to have fixed her affections yet, and I think she would always be too honest to try to foist someone else's brat on to me. I'll give her a season or two in London later on, for my part of the bargain. Plenty of pin money. It'll be alright. And if she *should* fall for someone later, well, as I told her, we'll cross that hurdle when we come to it.'

'You seem to have thought it all out, but surely it can't be so simple? Suppose she should have a liaison, and a child be born. Arunfold would pass out of the family.'

'She can hardly expect to pass off someone else's child as mine if we don't share a bed!' replied the Earl, with a deliberate coarseness unusual to him. And with that Samuel had to be content.

Less easy to quiet was his sister, Lady Fanny. He met her that evening at the opera, dressed all in celestial blue, a besotted admirer on each arm, hanging onto her every word; a few steps behind, and looking on with huge enjoyment, her husband, Lord Oswaldeston.

There were many among the ton who had accused Lady Fanny of marrying Piers Oswaldeston for his fortune, which was prodigious. And indeed, it is difficult to know how that lady, whose name was a by-word for extravagance, could have managed with anyone of less means. Those who imagined however, that that had been his only fascination were out in their reckoning, for, although he was some years her senior, she had a deep and abiding affection for him. Indeed, for her, he represented the solid foundation on which her happiness rested. Bowled over as he had been by her charms, having failed to succumb to those of the many who had set out to tempt him in earlier years, he had been too wise and too experienced to allow her to perceive just how much she had affected him, showing himself always pleased to be in her company, but never languishing for a sight of her as his younger rivals were wont to do. He was happy to partner her at any ball, but if, to tease him, she bestowed her hand on someone else in the dance, he had shown no sign of ill-humour, continuing to partner other ladies with apparent pleasure, and never flattering her by watching her every movement down the set. If she failed to wear his flowers and studiedly pointed out that those she wore came instead from one of the moon-faced youngsters who surrounded her, no look of dismay crossed his features (whatever his private thoughts) and she heard him say instead, and quite infuriatingly, how much they suited her. Never for her edification did he enact Cheltenham tragedies as he knew some of her followers did, but he could always procure for her a glass of ratafia when she was hot and thirsty, be the crowd by the refreshments table ever so thick, nor was she forced to stand when her feet hurt because he could not obtain for her a comfortable chair. He showed his affection in a hundred different ways by his care of her, but never once in his pursuit did he allow her to think it in her power to take that affection for granted. Used as she was to adulation, his controlled quest at first piqued and finally won her.

No more than of middle height, and well into his forties, there were still few ladies who could resist him when he set out to charm, for he had the kind of face which would still be handsome when he was old—high cheek-boned, and furrow-cheeked. He did not make the mistake of trying to copy younger members of the ton with his costume: his dress was enough in the mode to be called fashionable, but there was nothing about it to inspire the young to follow him, nor, indeed, to allow his contemporaries to say that he tried to keep pace with his wife by making himself ridiculous.

There was a great affection between the brothers-in-law, and when Lord Oswaldeston caught sight of Alexander's head just appearing above those of the people around him, he immediately made his way to him through the crowd of people thronging the gallery which led to their box, his eyes meeting those of his lordship warmly before he was close enough to speak to him.

'Ossie, old fellow, just the person!' said Alexander, taking his hand in a hearty handshake as they finally reached each other. 'My spoilt sister with you, old chap?'

'Sheldon! Good to see you looking so fit. Thought you were down in Sussex. Fanny's here somewhere—with two of her *admirers*!'

Again their eyes met, this time in shared amusement. Alexander knew, as well as Lord Oswaldeston, how little his sister's husband had to fear rivals.

'If I were you, old fellow, I'd have her penned up. Girl needs a good whipping!'

'Good God, Shel, it'd take more of a man than me to attempt it,' he laughed. 'But if you want to try . . . ?'

Again they grinned, as Piers led the way to his wife, now sitting demurely on a velvet chair in their box, playing one of her admirers off against the other while waiting for the performance to recommence. Should that particular young man have been feeling encouraged by her warmth it was quickly dispelled when, on catching sight of her brother coming through the curtained-off doorway, she interrupted him without compunction by jumping up in the middle of a particularly complicated flight of poetic fancy, to squeak,

'Alex, my love! How wonderful to see you. We have been so dull without you, haven't we, Piers?'

'Devastated.'

'Pay no heed to him, Alex,' remonstrated Fanny, pouting. 'I declare that it has been *trés fatigué* without you, dearest.'

'Would that I could flatter myself that the rest of the ton shared your admirable taste, Fanny. And are you enjoying the opera, or is that, too, *fatigué*?

'Oh, it's only "L'Agnese", you know and a bore. Ambrogetti is in perfectly horrid voice. And there's no-one here of the slightest interest to talk to.'

'Poor Fanny,' replied her brother, wickedly entertained by the crestfallen expressions on the faces of the two young men the Lady Fanny had been enchanting a few moments before. 'And how gracious of you to say so.'

Fanny did not pretend to misunderstand. 'Oh Mr Badgcombe and Viscount Munro never mind me—do you my loves?' she said audaciously.

Both young men blushed fiery red and murmured incoherent, but reassuring sounds in the back of their throats, by which the Earl was led to believe that they were as much under her spell as ever.

'But I'm afraid they will mind me,' he said, regretfully, 'for I must drag you away from them.'

'Darling Alex, how delightful: where are you taking me?' replied his incorrigible sister, unaware of the despair she was creating.

'Nowhere exciting,' he apologised. 'Just off to supper. I need to speak to you—you too Ossie, if you've nothing else on. Family affairs.'

'Oh no, Alex,' wailed Fanny. 'You cannot be so mean as to drag me off now, just for a chat. The next act is ready to start!'

'What about Vauxhall for supper, love? Will that make up for missing La Camporese? If we set off now we shall have ample time to get there,' coaxed Alexander, putting a hand under her chin and raising her eyes to his. She was about to protest again when she noticed an underlying urgency which intrigued her and said instead, 'Vauxhall! That is more like!' and turning to her unfortunate cicisbei, she dismissed them without another thought.

In their supper box in the grounds of Vauxhall Gardens, some little while later, partaking of some excellent shaved ham, she found that she had not been mistaken, and when Alexander had finished telling her his news, she was so shocked that her husband was moved to say in congratulatory manner, 'Well done, Sheldon old man. That's the first time I've ever known your sister silenced.'

Even *his* words failed to rally her and she continued to stare at her brother for several moments longer, her mouth slightly open. Eventually she found her tongue.

'I'm dreaming, Alex! Tell me I'm dreaming.'

'Not, I'm afraid, Fanny,' he replied gently.

'But why? Why marry her? Surely with that type of female you could have paid her off?'

'That's just the point. She isn't *that* type of female!'

She ignored him. 'But you said yourself that she was a . . . a maypole, and . . . and that she had freckles! How could you, Alex?'

'Well you know, Fanny,' he replied, as if seriously weighing the matter, 'if I'd guessed beforehand that I was going to have to marry Mary's governess, I'd have been far more careful to choose a smaller one without freckles.'

'But I shall be expected to give her precedence,' wailed Fanny, suddenly struck by this monstrous realisation. 'A nobody.'

'Not quite that, love,' admonished her husband, knowing how improper her words might later appear. 'Daughter of a Viscount can't be called a nobody!'

'You always knew that you might have to give place to my wife one day, Fanny,' said her brother, adding his words as extra weight. 'In the nature of things the possibility must have occurred to you before.'

'That was different. You cannot think me so odious as to imagine that I would have minded in the least had you chosen someone from our set. Why, I've had any number of girls in mind for you, for ever!'

'Yes, I rather thought you had, love,' he said pleasantly.

'Oh, it's all very well you giving me that look, Alex, but I've always known it to be a hum when you've gone around telling everyone you were past an age to marry! Why, only look at Piers! I just knew that if I did not get you properly settled you'd fall for the intrigues of some harpy or other, and that's just what has happened. It isn't fair! Just as I was beginning to think that you had a particular affection for Beatrice Hollander. She'd have been quite unexceptionable.'

'Heaven forbid! Girl's a dead bore!'

'She is not!'

'She is, you know, Fanny,' interpolated her husband with unco-operative promptitude. 'Though she hasn't got freckles, of course.'

'Oh do be quiet, Piers,' replied his wife, ruffled. 'It didn't *have* to be Beatrice. Why, he might have had that latest chit Lady Melbourne is for ever bringing forward, or the Falkenders' niece. Both nice girls in their way, and excellent ton!'

The two men looked at each other in horror, but seeing Fanny's petulant look descend, thought better of teasing her, and settled themselves instead to trying to reconcile her to the match.

They seemed to be making some headway when a chance remark of Alexander's explained the exact nature of the marriage. Even Piers was surprised: Fanny shocked rigid!

'A marriage in name only?' She stared at him in disbelief. 'Now I know you are mad, Alex. You could never hold yourself to it—unless the girl is a positive antidote.'

'No, she isn't that,' admitted her brother, reflectively, beginning to feel uncomfortable at her probing.

'Then why should you agree to such a thing?'

'She wouldn't have me else,' he explained ruefully.

'Not have you? Not have you? A little nobody of nineteen not have the Earl of Sheldon? You are jesting!'

'You cannot think how reassuring I find it to hear you say so,' he replied with a smile, 'But you may be certain that I don't find it something to jest about. It's the most damnable situation possible—and made worse by the fact that she has taken me into dislike. I had to threaten to take her off to Gretna by force before she would agree to the wedding, but I doubt that any threats of mine would have made her go through with it had I not promised to keep my distance from her person.'

Knowing how many women of her acquaintance would have given all they possessed to prevent his lordship from keeping his distance, Fanny was at first amazed and then intrigued. Later that night, in her husband's arms in the privacy of their bedchamber, she continued to speculate.

'Mark my words, Piers,' she murmured, as her lord began gently to kiss her hair. 'The girl's playing a deep game. It's my belief she set out to catch him from the first. I've half a mind to go down to Sussex to look her over! Not this week, of course,' she amended hastily. 'For there's the Melbourne House Ball, which is a nuisance. But when that's over and done with I could well spare a few days. I wish Alex hadn't got himself into such a scrape.'

'At this particular moment, my precious,' replied her husband, kissing the lobe of her ear persuasively, 'I wish so too—you cannot know how much.'

She giggled, turning sparkling eyes towards his own, now dark with meaning. 'Don't be cross with me, Piers,' she coaxed, 'Say instead that you will go down to Arunfold with me.'

'You are a designing baggage, my love,' replied Lord Oswaldeston, a reflection which seemed to afford him considerable satisfaction, since he enfolded her, none too gently, into his arms. 'Of course I will go with you. You are not the only one curious to see this minx that Sheldon has saddled himself with.'

CHAPTER

10

At about the same time that the Earl had arrived back in London, his house at Arunfold received an unexpected visitor. Having had terse conversation with the housekeeper, the new arrival asked permission to stable his horse, and went in search of the mistress of the house, who, as he was informed by a transparently disapproving housekeeper, was to be found with her niece somewhere in the woodland behind the house, perhaps near to the stream which skirted the East Wing, for Madam had taken (and it was said with a haughty sniff) a quantity of fishing equipment with her, though what young ladies had to do with such things, she could not say!

The stream was quickly reached from the stables, once the way was pointed out and, not seeing Lucy on its banks, he followed the stream upwards, following the cutting worn by its relentless passage through the wooded landscape which backed the house.

It was very hot, now that the unsettled weather of the past few weeks was calmed, but the woodland was so thick that the sun was only occasionally able to break through, its rays straight and misty in the distance. After the heat of his ride he was content to be in the blissful coolness and, as he climbed, he occasionally bent to scoop up a handful of the clear, cold water to drink. Nothing stirred nearby, not a rabbit or squirrel to suggest habitation. Once or twice he heard the schip-schip-schip of the marsh tit, as from a great distance and, a little afterwards, it's mate's answering cry, but nothing closer disturbed the forest.

His path rose steeply in places and in spite of the shade, he began to feel warm again, pausing to remove his coat, which he swung nonchalently over his shoulder. Coat over shoulder, he made to move on again, when his ear was assailed by the sounds of giggling ahead. He recognised one of the voices immediately and moved forward with greater certainty. As he came through the trees into a small clearing an extraordinary sight met his eyes, for there before him stood Lucy, barefoot, her shoes and stockings lying discarded in an untidy heap with some fishing gear by the stream, the hem of her dress muddy from the forest floor, so often of late deluged with rain. Balancing precariously on her shoulders and peering into a bird's nest in the upper branches of a small laurel, was Mary, the pitch of her laughter climbing ever higher. On hearing him crackling his way through the undergrowth, Lucy turned round, with more speed than caution, threatening every moment to upset her burden, but managing somehow to keep her safe. As she saw who it was, her eyes widened in pleasure and she cried out, 'Tom, how wonderful! What on earth are you doing here. Only see, Mary, it is Tom!'

'What am I doing here? Well, I like that,' replied her friend, rushing forward to lift Mary from Lucy's shoulders, and noticing as he did so that she was barefoot and muddy like Lucy. 'What did you expect when we got your letter. "Dearest Aunt Marianne, you will be surprised to hear that I have become the Countess of Sheldon." Not a word since the letter you sent home with Alice and then that!

Surprised! Mama was frantic! Papa wanted to come to you straight off, but he's been laid up with the gout since you left for London, and I persuaded Mama to remain with him.

'Poor Uncle William, but I knew he would suffer when he *would* eat all the splendid things Aunt Marianne put out for my farewell supper. Turbot never agrees with him, and my Aunt warned him that he was taking too much wine!'

'Never mind all that,' said Tom crushingly, cutting her off in mid-flow. 'What's going on? And don't give me all that stuff about Countesses. Mama couldn't be easy until one of us came, but I told her it'd all be a hum, for I know what *you* are!'

'A hum is it?' she replied grimly, stung by his injustice. 'Well that shows all you know!'

'You mean you really *are* married, and to Sheldon?' He looked astounded. 'Whatever made you do it? And why the hell didn't you write to tell us sooner? Three weeks and not so much as a word!'

'There wasn't much I *could* do about it, gapeseed. I didn't become Lord Sheldon's wife because I wanted to! And when I came to trying to write, I didn't quite know what to say!'

Tom's cheeks turned a fiery shade of red, a nasty suspicion forming which caused him to clench his fits instinctively. 'Perhaps you had better tell me, what made you marry him!'

At these tell-tale signs of brotherly rancour, Lucy promptly said, 'Don't get on your high ropes, Tom, I beg. It is not at all what you imagine.'

He did not noticeably relax, and repeated grimly, 'Tell me why you married him,' his voice so testy that Mary instinctively reached for Lucy's hand.

Lucy's tale was tangled and not a little confused, but Tom had not lived in the same house with her all those years without result and had no difficulty at all in following it. As she progressed further into her story, he showed distinct signs of feeling easier, and, by the time it was completed, his brow had cleared entirely.

It wrinkled again when she explained that hers was to be a marriage in name only. Lucy thought it would put his mind at rest, but it had precisely the opposite effect.

'But that's preposterous, Lucy. You of all people will want children some day. Whatever made you agree to such a thing?'

'What choice did I have, addle-brain? I tried to run away, but he's devilish clever. And when he found me, he said he would run off with me to Gretna if I did not marry him. Said it was a matter of his family's honour. And only think how Aunt Marianne would have liked hearing that I had been married across the anvil! As for children, well, I doubt I'd have received any offers while I was a governess, so I most probably wouldn't have had children anyway.'

Tom shook his head. 'What a damnable situation, Luce. But I must say that the Earl is doing the gentlemanly thing. If it'd have got round that you'd spent the night in that barn together and he hadn't married you, you'd have been ruined.'

'Well, I'm sure the niceties of my situation are very clear to you, but I'm only a humble female, and it seems to me that if he'd made a bit of a push to do so, he could have stopped it coming out.'

'Don't be so green, Luce. Servants sent on ahead. Guests at the house expecting you. Everyone at the inn knowing when you both left. Stands to reason it would have come out. He's the Earl of Sheldon. No way of stopping it. Nothing like a servant for having a big bonebox! No ... he did just as he ought, all right. Just a pity that you've taken each other in dislike. Like to see you have children, the way the little things take to you. And as for that governessing business, you can't think that Mama and Papa ever intended to allow you to go on long with that type of slavery! They only let you have your head because you insisted. We had a wager among ourselves, 'matter of fact, about how long it would be before you were ready to do as m'father wished and allowed him to settle some money on you. Mind, there's no denying that this is better. It's a splendid match—if a little irregular. From all I've heard, he's top-of-the-trees. Regular "Go" among the "Goers". And nobody could have expected you to contract a brilliant alliance. There's no denying you've done well for yourself. Can't get much better than a Carne.'

Lucy chose to pass over his imputations as to her staying power as a governess and latched on to his last words.

'Well, if that isn't just what I'd expect you to say, Tom Chadwick, for a more cork-brained fool I've never known,' she cried. 'For your information I'd rather stay a governess all my life than be married to that . . . that . . . monster, top-of-the-trees or no!'

'That just shows that you are far more cork-brained than me,' said Tom, quite willing to spar with her on this one. Seeing that Mary was unsettled by their customary verbal warfare, however, Lucy thought it prudent to say no more on the subject and asked instead, and quite pleasantly, 'How did you know how to find us, Tom? What made you come up here?'

'Well, I wasn't going to stay in the house with that Friday-faced creature, was I? Frightened me to death. Told her I'd come to look for you. Whatever made you choose that hatchet-face for housekeeper? If it isn't just like you to make a mull even of such a simple thing as that.'

Lucy was quick to take umbrage, seeing her olive branch rejected out of hand. 'Well, that's all you know. She was here before I came. I had nothing whatever to do with choosing her, Mr High and Mighty.'

'What in the world has that to say to anything? I wouldn't have thought it beyond you to get rid of her! Can't imagine m'mother suffering her for so much as a day! Regular horse-face! Enough to make anyone think twice before staying the night! Remember, if I'm not mistaken, that you mentioned in your letter that the Earl don't get many visitors. Suppose you never so much as thought to wonder why!'

Lucy laughed in delight. 'Tom, you may be the greatest simpleton in England, but you certainly lift the spirits. I'll be bound that Mincham won't put you off, for I never knew of anyone who could stare you out of countenance.' And she looped her arm through that of her late protagonist in the friendliest way, telling him that she counted on him to make a prolonged stay.

'And what will his lordship have to say to that, m'girl? Some of these Tulips of fashion are stiff-rumped about the company they find themselves in. He may not wish you to keep up the connection.'

'Oh, stuff!' cried Lucy elegantly. 'I'd like to see him try to stop me from seeing you. And anyway,' she added with simple truth. 'He's not here to try it. His man of business writes me that he's gone to London.'

'His man of business? Don't he write to you himself? Well if that don't beat all. And what's he doing leaving you so soon after the nuptials? It seems a curst rum business to me.'

By the time she had completed her explanation, Tom was as indignant over the Earl's behaviour as had been Lucy.

'I'll tell you what, m'girl,' he thundered. 'It's lucky I came! What with that gorgon of a hausfrau and a husband who thinks he can use you as he pleases, you need some help!'

Like Lucy, Tom was easily able to withstand Mincham's disapproval, which was just as well, since on being told to prepare one of the best guest rooms for him, it was manifested in every way.

If she expected Tom to feel overwhelmed by the grandeur of Lucy's new estate, Mincham was doomed to disappointment. His own was modest in comparison, but the Chadwicks had never had to do without the niceties of life and he was, in any case, the type of English gentleman who would feel at home wherever he found himself. The fact that he could settle himself in snugly when he visited the meanest of his father's tenants, did not prevent him from appreciating the beauties of a house like Arunfold, and any of the social gradations in between would have found him equally content.

He soon became as much a favourite with Mary as Lucy for, like her, he was always ready for fun. Each fine afternoon, when Mary's lessons were over, the carefree trio went off in search of enjoyment; if they were not fishing, or bird nesting, they were out with a net collecting butterflies, or lying on a grassy hummock watching interesting insects scurrying along.

Mary had begun not to be troubled when, on her return home, she passed Mincham on the stairs and heard her loud snort at seeing Mary with her hair hanging in tendrils round a less than spotless face, her fingernails grimy, and her muddy shoes held in her hand. Every day seemed like a holiday, for Lucy had the knack for making even lessons pleasurable, and when, at noon, they took a picnic lunch off somewhere and Tom taught her how to tickle fish, or Lucy helped her with her sketching, she knew that she had never been happier in her life.

CHAPTER

11

It must not be supposed that, before Tom's arrival Lucy had been entirely confined to Mary's society. Unceremoniously as she had been deposited on her wedding night, it would be too much to expect surrounding society not to be curious as to the lady who had led its most important landowner into matrimony after so many had failed before, and indeed, her unceremonious deposition made her more of a celebrity than otherwise.

Since Lucy had not thought to refurbish her wardrobe on becoming a Countess it is not surprising that she made no very great impression among the more elegant members of that rural community, many of whom came only to reassure themselves that the new arrival was less smart or less pretty than they were. The human creature being what it is, instead of being relieved to find in Lucy no rival, they were, for the most part, ready only to ridicule, many a modish daughter being moved to wonder that the Earl should have married so dowdy a maypole of a creature and one fine gentleman going so far as to say that, having done so, it was small mystery that he had then run for his life!

But rural society has its variety and there were one or two families to whom the pressing matters of wardrobe were not paramount and with whom Lucy, with her sunny disposition, quickly made friends. By far the most agreeable of all her neighbours was a family called Thorne, which had at its head a certain Viscount Thorne, a widowed gentleman, whose lands marched close to those of the Earl. He paid an early courtesy visit to Lucy with his son the Hon. Charles and daughter the Hon. Gwendolyn; the Thornes professed themselves pleased with Lucy, and, since it was a simple matter to take a carriage the few miles which separated Arunfold from their mellow-bricked Elizabethan mansion, morning visits had become quite customary by the time Tom's worried Mama took it into her head to send her son post-haste to investigate matters.

Lucy lost no time in introducing Tom and he was quite as pleased with them as was Lucy, though his pleasure in their company seemed to owe more to an inclination to spend time with the divine Gwendolyn than with the others.

Miss Thorne was indeed a creature to charm all hearts, from her dusky, naturally curling ringlets to the tip of her shapely slippered foot. Having too, a handsome portion to be given to the fortunate man who won her, it is not surprising that most professed her to be as delightful a creature as ever lived.

As soon as he saw her, Tom joined with the majority, for never had he been privileged to behold a girl half as lovely. Lucy was his chum, but Gwendolyn—a goddess!

Lucy had expected Tom to be smitten: what was more surprising was that Gwendolyn appeared to be similarly taken with Tom, for indeed Lucy could think of no other way to account for her friend's countenance on being introduced to him. To Lucy's wonderment, when Tom took Gwendolyn's hand she had blushed entrancingly and lowered her eyes in confusion as Lucy had never before seen her do, be she ever so much flirted with. Nor did she seem able to raise them to his for more than a second without the colour flooding her cheeks again. Lucy watched fascinated, for here, clearly, was a case of love at first sight, a phenomenon which, within the marbled covers of the books in her aunt's library, had engrossed her for many an hour, but which she had hardly expected to encounter in any dealings with Tom! The idea that anyone should fall in love with him she found so droll that she was hard put not to laugh, but Tom would probably not have noticed, for his eyes never left Gwendolyn's face and, as one in a daze, he asked her father's permission to take her off into the quiet embrasure of a window to look at a collection of her watercolours.

Mary ran off to find the gardener, with a promise that she might help herself to a new crop of fine strawberries just ripening, leaving Lucy sitting comfortably with the head of the household.

Viscount Thorne had once been what is commonly termed a very personable man. Tall and elegant in his youth, with a fine shock of fair hair, his middle years had been dogged by an arthritic complaint which no amount of doctoring had been able to arrest. Though he still insisted on being helped from his bedchamber to sit each day either in the drawing room, or the gardens, he was unable to move from his chair without assistance. In latter years, his hands had begun to display the twisted characteristics of his illness. He never complained, but the lines of suffering on his face and his prematurely white hair had their own tale to tell. Yet he was rarely out of humour, and seemingly never out of spirits. He counted himself blessed to have so affectionate a son and daughter and good servants pledged to his comfort and, when he was too ill to visit neighbours and none came to call, he managed to fill his days with a variety of interests. Not the least of these was an abiding one in the history of his own family, which, as he had informed Lucy proudly on more than one occasion, could be traced back to before the Conquest. He took an extraordinary delight in adding to his already considerable demesne, small parcels of land as they came up for sale, to consolidate and enrich his family's holdings. It was this interest, indeed, which presented the only source of conflict between the two families, for, as he lost no time in informing Lucy at their first meeting, some pernicious, sixteenth century ancestor of Sheldon's had wrested from the Thornes—"by fair means or foul, and I leave you to guess which, my dear!"—a particular piece of land which had once formed part of their borders.

Today, as soon as Mary was out of sight, the Viscount unrolled a map to prove his point, and showed Lucy how, for miles, his borders ran smooth against those of Arunfold, except where this little bite of land had been stolen.

'Do you see there, m'girl?' he said pettishly. 'The Carnes have no right to it! Breaks the whole line. Offered to buy it from that husband of yours a dozen times and at a fine price, but he won't take it. Carne pride! He knows I'll not rest easy in m'grave if I can't see that little piece fitted in before I go, but there's no changing his mind. If his cousin Sam was Earl he'd sell. Nothing top-lofty about him. But he'll not get a chance now you've wed his lordship. And your sons will be brought up just the same, you'll see. Carne pride—no end to it, dammit!'

Lucy, who had every reason to dislike Carne pride as much as the Viscount, found herself making excuses for her husband, which surprised her. Since the old gentleman, of whom she had become very

116

fond in recent days, showed every indication of becoming disturbed, she greeted with relief the sound of a soft footfall behind her, and a male voice saying soothingly, 'Now now, Father. Don't get yourself in a pucker! Lady Sheldon will think you as crusty as an old bear if you nag at her like that.'

The gentle voice was deceptive, for it might have led its hearer to prepare for a personage of quite a different stamp to its owner. But Lucy was familiar with the appearance of the Viscount's son Charles, and turned her head to gaze up at a perfect giant of a man! Six foot four in his stocking feet, and with a breadth of shoulder any pugilist would envy, he was the only man who had ever made Lucy feel petite. Now, as he came round from behind the back of her chair and stood before her, she could not resist the temptation to stand up to greet him, since it was so very agreeable to have to raise her eyes to look into a gentleman's face after so many years of having either to look down, or, at the very best, to measure herself eye to eye with them.

'There you are y'young scapegrace!' said the Viscount, looking up at his son with affectionate approval. 'I'm *not* in a pucker, as you so elegantly phrase it. And Lady Sheldon understands me. She won't take offence at an old man.'

Lucy, who had found herself becoming embarrassingly enmeshed in the difficulty of trying to justify her husband's intractability was relieved at her unexpected reprieve and assented willingly to the Viscount's suggestion that she join young Mr Thorne in a ramble down towards the shrubbery to see the rose garden the Viscount had had planted in the late Viscountess's memory. Mr Thorne needed no second command and with an alacrity surprising in one so large, had placed Lucy's hand on his arm and was guiding her through the French windows and across rolling lawns almost before the suggestion had left his father's lips.

Tom was not *so* involved with Miss Thorne that he missed the exchange between Lucy and Mr Thorne and now it was his turn to be surprised. In the years he had known Lucy, he had seen her by turns naughty, penitant, affectionate, kindhearted and downright mischievous: never had he seen Lucy blush so winningly as when Mr Thorne placed her hand, as if it were an object of the greatest value, on his arm. Certainly he had come to Arunfold not a moment too soon if Lucy was to be kept out of a scrape.

Meanwhile, Lucy and her large companion were making their way into the shrubbery, a mathematically formal garden, quite a distance from the house and surrounded by a high hedge, pierced only by a tall wrought iron gateway. The day was fine and, although Lucy had for once remembered her parasol to protect her face, the sun felt pleasantly warm through the thin material of her frock.

When they reached the centre of the formal gardens, they found the rosebeds that the Viscount had mentioned, to one side of which was a pretty arbour covered by rambling roses, under which had been placed a stone bench embellished with cupid faces. Mr Thorne suggested that this was a good vantage point from which to view the rest of the rose garden, but it was soon plain, once Lucy had seated herself at his side, that he had something other than horticulture on his mind since, almost immediately he sprang up again, placing himself in what he felt to be an heroic posture, and cried out in ringing tones, quite unlike his own and which made Lucy want to smile, 'And have you still not heard from that scoundrel who calls himself your husband, ma'am?'

With difficulty Lucy controlled her quivering lips.

'Why, no sir, not yet. I am afraid he is not a very good correspondent.'

Mr Thorne was shocked by her levity. But of course it was all a ruse. She was hiding her feelings with a sweet courage he must applaud!

Never a great man for the ladies, he had passed lazily through his thirty years almost oblivious to the romantic snares set for him. His notions of womanhood had been gleaned from heroic poetry, of which he was extraordinarily fond! To Charles Thorne, all ladies were delicate; precious creatures, to be cherished and guarded. Convinced that it was every man's duty to fight off hordes for the lady of his choice, it was only a pity that in rural Sussex so few opportunities existed to put him to the test.

Vaguely, yet pushed firmly to the back of a mind absorbed by the pressures and pleasantries of a life he enjoyed, he had recognised that at some time he must get himself an heir, but one morning spent in company with Lucy had convinced him that his neighbour and friend had been before him in taking to wife the only woman he had been thus far privileged to meet who would have suited him. The more he knew of her the more certain he was that here was a woman who needed his protection. Now that they had become friends, he was fully conversant with all the facts of her strange nuptials and his sympathy had increased tenfold to see how she had set to slot herself into an alien world. And overriding all, was a disgust that Sheldon, a man whom he had always considered a friend, could treat his wife in such a cavalier fashion. Impressed by Lucy's ability to run her own life, he was appalled that the Earl could allow it!

'It's damnable. Why should you be placed so ill and by no design of your own?' he exclaimed now, much to Lucy's surprise, for she had grown so used to her absurd marriage that unless it was brought forcibly to her attention, she hardly ever gave it a thought. She had long agreed with her husband as to the relative merits of living at Arunfold as its mistress rather than a lesser dependent, and as a result now only replied to Mr Thorne's outburst laughingly.

'You refine too much on the disadvantages of my situation, Mr Thorne. Only think how much greater they might have been had I come here as Mary's governess. Think how Mincham would have ruled over me.'

'That creature!' he replied grimly, but a reluctant grin forced itself across his features, as he realised she was joking. 'Walked all over you—eyewash!'

'But, Mr Thorne,' sighed Lucy affectedly. 'I declare myself ready to faint each time she utters a harsh word. Were it not for my hartshorn bottle, which is never far from my side, as you may imagine, I should not know how to support my spirits!'

She glanced up at him winningly from under her eyelashes, a dimple at the corner of her mouth.

'It's all very well trying to pretend that all is right and tight, but you know that the Earl had no right to leave you to fend for yourself, or to give rise to the rumours as to his destination when he left you here alone.'

Lucy was no longer amused. 'If you mean his visit to Lady D'Avergne, I wish you would say so and not be mealy-mouthed about it. But Mr Chadwick assures me that his lordship has done his duty by me and that, I suppose, is all I may expect!'

'Much as I like your Mr Chadwick, he can go to the devil,' choked Mr Thorne, with heat. 'Sheldon certainly does not do his duty by you. Of course he was right to insist on your marriage—you know my thoughts on that—but no man with the slightest sensitivity would have left you in such a way having done so. He must have known what people would say.'

'Ah, but there you have it, Mr Thorne. Nothing I have so far seen of his lordship has convinced me that he has the slightest degree of sensitivity—nothing at all!' said Lucy with vigour.

'Indeed no,' he agreed gravely, calming himself with effort as he saw her agitation. Then, looking at the gravel on the path, he made a swirling pattern in it with the sole of his boot, saying hesitantly as he did so, 'My dear Lady Sheldon . . . I know I should not, but yet I cannot help but tell you how nearly your situation touches me.'

Lucy looked up startled towards his averted face and the tell-tale flush in his cheek, which made her fear that he was struggling with a declaration. Her heart beat agitatedly, her one thought to prevent him from saying anything which could preclude the propriety of their meeting again. Much as she liked him, with his flights of heroic fancy he fell far short of her idea of a lover. She enjoyed having an admirer, but the oddness of her marriage made it no less binding to her.

'You forget yourself, Mr Thorne,' she said firmly, her own face now as hot as his. 'However much I may deplore it, we should *both* remember that I am married to the Earl!'

'Do you really think I am in danger of forgetting such a monstrous fact?' he asked, with a tortured expression, taking one of her gloved hands between his, in the approved way. 'You do me an injustice if you think I would embarrass you by improper attentions, however careless a guardian Alex may be.'

She was at once contrite. She should have realised that his feelings would be of the high poetical! 'Of course you would not. I know you too well to really fear it, but yet, in the heat of the moment . . .'

'Not even in the heat of the moment. I honour you too much to insult you—and if your husband honoured you as much, this conversation would not be taking place! Warm as is my regard for you—and I make no pretence to the contrary—my only wish is to serve you. I cannot pretend that, should you ever find yourself free, I would not try to make you my own, but while you are married I can never be more than your affectionate friend'—His code, you see, was strict!—'and, as such, willing to smooth your path as *you* see fit. Ah, I can see that I *have* embarrassed you, which is just what I promised not to do. I must, and shall, say no more.'

'No indeed,' declared Lucy briskly, removing her hand from his and determined to change the atmosphere. 'Tell me instead what you think of Mr Chadwick. Your sister and he seem remarkably taken with each other. Should I warn him off? He will not be wealthy. Would your father disapprove? I know how he values adding to the estate.'

'He values our happiness more, my dear, so if m'sister likes Chadwick, Father won't stand in the way. There's only one piece of land he wants.'

'You were a deuced long time in the grounds with Thorne, Luce,' said Tom truculently as, after a pleasant luncheon, they made their way home in the grand chaise which was one of a number of smart vehicles which Lord Sheldon kept for his convenience. 'What can you have been doing to take so long?'

'I'm surprised you noticed how long I was gone, Tom dear,' replied his friend sweetly, popping a large strawberry from a basketful provided by the Thorne's gardener, into Mary's mouth. 'I rather thought your mind was on other things.'

'By gad, yes, Luce. Sweetest thing in the world,

aint she? Angel! Man'd have to be crazy not to be
entranced by her!'

He lapsed into reverie and Lucy thought that she
had succeeded rather well in giving his thoughts a
less dangerous direction. She was wrong.

'That's neither here nor there, Luce!' he said in
a little while. 'Haven't told me what you were doing in the shrubbery. Nice fellow, Thorne, but not
the thing for you to be walking off alone with him
for so long. Married lady now, y'know!'

Lucy nearly choked.

'Not the thing! Since when have I needed you to
tell me what is the thing?' she cried, her quick temper roused in a moment. 'What exactly do you think
we were *doing* in the shrubbery?'

'Ssh, Luce! Not in front of Mary, if you please,'
he replied, very properly, with an anxious look toward the child, sitting regarding them both with a
sparrow-like expression of expectancy.

'Well then,' said Lucy, exasperated, 'Get James
to put us down here and he can take Mary on to
the house. We can walk the rest of the way and
have this out in peace.'

Tom made no objection and the two made their
way by foot up towards the house, arguing hotly as
they went. They had reached no result even by the
time they reached the French windows of the drawing room, which were ajar, the weather being so
warm. Lucy was just about to cross the threshhold
to continue the argument indoors when her sharp
ear caught the sound of Mincham's voice from inside the room. Instinctively Lucy halted, and looking back to quieten Tom with an urgent gesture,
listened from outside. What she heard was enough
almost to drive her to an apoplexy, for Mincham
was conversing with Jenkins, the chambermaid,
perhaps the only person in the house with whom
she was on any terms of intimacy, though even that

was an uneasy intimacy and their conversation took its usual form of a monologue, punctuated by Jenkins' occasional agreement. Mincham had obviously been expounding at some length on the animadversions of her new mistress and Lucy arrived in time to hear her saying maliciously, 'As to her having the bare-faced gall to bring her so-called *friend* here, I've never heard of such goings-on in a decent house. That young lady, it seems, is not content with having tricked the Earl into marrying her. No sooner does he leave her in possession than she brings in her cicisbeo. Brought up as brother and sister? If you believe that you'll believe anything, else why should she have me make up the Green Suite for him, so near her own? And then there's his lordship, no better than he should be! Off with that French woman that he had the nerve to bring here and expect *me*! a good, honest, God-fearing Christian to prepare rooms for. And I leave you to recall how close they were to his own!'

Just as she reached this point she happened to turn her head towards the windows, only to see her mistress silhouetted in the afternoon sunshine.

Tom had been too far behind Lucy to hear all that the unfortunate woman had said, but he had caught most of it and, knowing Lucy's temper, even felt sorry for her. Enough a man to wish to avoid an unpleasant scene, he muttered faintly, 'Think I'll go to m'room, Luce old girl. Like to try to see if I can't tie that knot Thorne had on his cravat this morning. Liked it! Not too elaborate,' and with an eye on Lucy's face, by now contorted with pure rage, went from the room.

What followed was swift, sharp retribution, and ended with Mincham being ordered to pack up every one of her belongings and leave the house that very day, on the assurance that no application need be made to Lucy for references.

By four o'clock her things were being placed in a gig brought round from the stables, and Mincham was climbing into it, declaring her intention to revenge herself on them all, 'Quite like a Malvolio really,' giggled Lucy, flushed with triumph, when she described the scene to Tom, who had continued to cower in his room until the unpleasantness had passed. 'I half expected to see her lift her skirts to show me her stockings, cross-gartered!'

'Lucy, behave!' he protested with dignity, shocked that she should speak of such intimate garments to him now she was a Countess. 'You are as much a romp as ever, but I'm glad to see the back of that onion-face. Now we may be comfortable. Be careful when you choose the next one though.'

'As to that,' she replied, with characteristic unconcern, 'I've spoken to Perry and she thinks, as I do, that a house is best run by its mistress, so I mean to make a stab at it. Aunt Marianne gave me excellent notions of economy. And anyway,' she continued, lifting her arms in a luxuriant gesture, 'it is so *wonderful* not to have Mincham under my feet that I would be a perfect gooby to risk having another like her.'

One warm afternoon, little more than a week later, found Lucy, her sketchbook on her lap, sitting on a fallen tree trunk near to the roadway on the undulating section of land leading up towards the house. Tom had taken Mary off for a riding lesson, and Lucy was trying to capture a view of the house which had fascinated her since her arrival. She had already been sitting there for some considerable time, her hat thrown carelessly to one side, curls escaping riotously from the almost orderly bun in which she had earlier constrained them. On the skirts of the old dimity dress on which she conferred the rather grand title of her "sketching out-

125

fit" a messy array of chalk marks blended unbecomingly into a gypsy print, which she occasionally attempted to rub off with chalky hands.

At the sound of wheels approaching, she chanced to look up from her work. One glance was enough to satisfy her that the only person she knew who drove in such fine style was her husband, so she was not surprised when the curricle got closer to see the Earl, attired in his usual precise fashion, looking curiously towards her.

'Well met, madam wife,' he called over to her as he brought his horses to a halt at the side of the roadway.

Lucy blushed to hear herself so addressed and, putting down her drawing things, rose to her feet and walked over to his curricle to shake hands with him, having first made another futile attempt at brushing her skirts.

'Tell me, do you never dress in anything becoming, Ma'am?' he asked, as he took her hand.

She stared up at him, laughing to herself at his appalling rudeness.

'I trust that I always dress suitably, my lord,' she replied demurely, her eyes dancing.

'Well then, let me tell you that you are sadly out!' he replied, letting go her hand and driving on without a backward glance.

CHAPTER

12

By the time Lucy returned to the house, about half an hour later, his lordship had been apprised of the fact that he no longer had a housekeeper, but when she walked through the open French windows into the drawing-room, he only remarked mildly, 'I see you have been making changes, Ma'am,' which led Lucy to think that he was by no means dismayed.

'And we have a visitor,' he went on, thoroughly at ease in a comfortable chair near to the fireplace, a tea tray before him set on a small table. 'I shall be interested to see how well you captured his likeness.'

'Are you still trying to suggest that I cannot draw, my lord?' asked Lucy, furiously. 'I should have thought that you would be happy to see my accomplishments as claimed, since you have taken me for wife!'

'Still as hot to hand as ever, I see my love,' he replied, maddeningly calm, swinging his quizzing glass slowly from its black riband.

'I am not hot to hand, sir, any more than I am your love,' she replied indignantly, throwing her hat and drawing things carelessly onto a nearby sofa, 'it is just that you always insinuate that I tried to get a place by underhand means.'

'I certainly seem to have an unhappy knack for offending you, but on this occasion you are unfair,' he replied pleasantly. 'To my untrained eye, your drawings of your friend Tom seemed admirable, so naturally I am curious to see the original.'

His gracious speech effectively silenced any retort she might have made, and she, determined to be equally gracious, offered to pour his tea and join him in a dish. She was beginning to think that his visit need not mean the end of her comfort, and was not even very offended when he said, with a certainty he must have been far from feeling, 'You will be glad to know that I have had my man engage a lady's maid for you, a Miss Havering, for a Countess cannot go without one, even if she despises them as you do. She comes in a day or two, for, as you may guess, after our own mishaps, I no longer drive females any distance.'

Reluctant to admit his right to engage a servant on her behalf, a few seconds reflection were sufficient to make her realise that he must know the exigencies of her rank more than she, so she inclined her head in agreement. If he was determined to be pleasant, he should not have a chance to hold her manners against her.

But it was impossible that such geniality should long exist, when he said, without any attempt at tact, 'I have engaged, too, for Mrs Gardiner to visit us tomorrow morning, with a view to seeing if she cannot make something of you. It behoves me at least to try to prevent my wife from looking like a scarecrow if at all possible and away from Town, Mrs Gardiner is considered a modiste out of the ordinary. We shall see if we cannot try to find something to make you look halfway to a Countess,

128

though little can be accomplished until I get you to Bond Street and choose some things for you there.'

'I prefer to choose my own clothes, my lord,' she answered coolly, rising from her chair.

'I was not aware that your preferences had been called into question,' he replied, with an astonishing bluntness which effectively silenced his wife, who only gave an infuriated mew of wrath, turned on her heel, and stalked from the room.

His lordship was undismayed, for, when she left, he rose languidly from his chair and walked towards the French windows as if to take some air. He was just in time to see his niece running across the lawn, hotly pursued by a young gentleman whose face he recognised. Seeing her uncle, the little girl squealed loudly and ran towards him, arms outstretched in a warm, grubby welcome. Behind her, now more restrained, came her faithful follower, no longer running and trying to appear nonchalent.

'Ah, Mr Chadwick, I believe,' drawled the Earl pleasantly, as Tom reached the house, putting out the arm he was not using to hold Mary to offer his hand in a friendly handshake. At the signs of good-humour in his face, Tom began to wonder just what maggot Lucy had got into her head to make all the fuss about. Why, anyone could see at a glance that he was a great gun!

Lucy did not see her husband again until dinner, and had spent the intervening period making the best of herself. She had decided to wear her only evening gown, a white confection which she thought made her look rather attractive, and was certain he could not help but admire. When she met him at the top of the stairs, and he winced palpably, she knew herself mistaken, though it was not so much the dress which offended, even if, to be sure, he guessed it to be at least two years out of date, but the way she had so carelessly scraped her hair back in the semblance of a style and had provided herself with a rainbow-coloured shawl every other colour of which clashed horribly with her curls. He omitted to comment, however, only muttering, if rather audibly, 'Thank Heavens Miss Havering comes tomorrow!' before offering her his arm to lean on while going down to the drawing room. As they walked down the wide, elegant stairway, he remarked, 'I have you to thank, Ma'am, for the remarkable transformation in my niece.'

Secretly pleased by his terse praise, she was in no mood to appear complaisant towards him and only bent her neck to acknowledge it.

But Lucy's changes were not confined to his niece, for when Frensham announced dinner and the Earl took Lucy's arm ready to lead her through to the dining room, she turned calmly, saying, 'Ah, sir, you are behindhand. We no longer eat in that draughty place. You must tell me what you think of your new dining room,' and she led him instead to the small salon which now served for the family. The Earl was suspicious of change, but when he saw how snugly she had had things arranged, said in a gratified tone, 'Now why hasn't anyone done this before? How clever of you, my dear, to realise what was needed. You cannot know how I have always disliked eating in that mausoleum when only the family was present. This ... well, this is just the thing.'

The evening passed off better than Lucy could ever have anticipated, and when Mary had been sent reluctantly to bed, the two men played a rather casual hand or two of piquet, while Lucy played for them at the pianoforte. Neither the Earl nor Tom was much interested in their game and soon gave it up, preferring to listen to Lucy's music, an odd little smile transforming the Earl's face, so that Tom was privileged to see him in a light denied to most of his acquaintances. At the end of a beautiful sonata, Tom cried out, 'Come on, Luce, let's have my old favourite!'

'Oh no, Tom, not "Bethgelert"!' she wailed, with a gurgle of laughter.

'Go on Lucy,' he insisted. 'You know how I like it. It always makes me remember when we were children and Mama used to sing it to us before we went to bed.' Then he looked winningly at the Earl, saying deferentially, 'You've no objection, sir, I trust?'

' "Bethgelert"!' laughed his lordship reminiscingly, 'I can never hear it without recalling a time when I was down at Panshanger for a houseparty. A group of us were playing cards and concentrating, as one does, when about three rooms away Emily Cowper suddenly started up with "Bethgelert". Princess Lieven gave a great start and cried out, "Oh my dear, there's that dreadful song. Just think that it is about a dog which goes on dying during thirteen verses, and I've heard it twice and that makes twenty-six"!'

They all laughed, but Tom was tenacious, giving the Earl an opportunity to hear his wife's singing voice for the first time. It had, as she had admitted, no very great strength, but was of such clarity and sweetness that he received no mean pleasure from hearing it.

'Your Uncle Chadwick and I are agreed that you should have included your voice on your list of accomplishments, my dear,' he said with sincerity. 'Truly a delight, and I can well understand why "Bethgelert" should be Tom's favourite when he has been used to hearing it sung so well. It will be one of my own from now on.'

Her cheeks turned a furious pink. 'Well, I'd no

idea that the ton could be so easily pleased,' she said briskly.

It was not until after Lucy had poured the tea and they were taking their leave of each other for the night that her husband thought to mention to her that, in a few days, his sister and her husband would be joining them at Arunfold and that his heir, Samuel, might accompany them. He was surprised at how calmly she took the news of her forthcoming inspection and gratified that she was not to be put out by any attempt of his to intimidate her. He was also surprised to realise with how much pleasure he had passed his first evening in the country, though the company was such a small one, and he would have said of just such a nature as to be insipid.

When he handed Lucy her candle at the bottom of the stairs, he felt much in charity with her, a feeling which she was near to reciprocating until he was moved to remind her not to dawdle, since she must be up early next morning to receive the dressmaker!

His lordship need not have spoken, for Lucy was up betimes next morning, and ready for Mrs Gardiner when she came, though she had lain awake for some little while the previous night, wondering if the Earl might try to visit her apartments, and listening for him to go along the corridor. She had been in bed not more than half an hour when she heard what she thought were his footsteps, strolling unhurriedly along the gallery outside, and, though she was not quite sure whether she had imagined it or not, thought they hesitated just outside. Next morning when she remembered, she still could not decide whether to be more relieved or more cross that they had gone past, but surely it argued a strange disposition when a man was willing to be banished quite to the other end of the gallery without making the least push to ingratiate himself in his bride's good graces?

The thought that he might feel his banishment to be no unpleasant thing gave her little joy, for much as she disliked him, she had the usual woman's wish not to be despised for her person, and Mrs Gardiner found her rather more receptive than she had been led to expect. Though she shuddered to see her new client, she comforted herself with the thought that the Earl, having met her in the hall on her way up, had assured her that a fashionable London dresser had been employed by him and would soon do something with his wife's dreadful hair, and that it was her job only to persuade Madam into garments more befitting her rank. It should not be too difficult.

An hour later, she felt rather less sanguine as to the outcome of her first encounter with such a formidable failure in the art of costume. One glance at Lucy had been sufficient to give her a fair idea of the patterns and colours which would be suitable for her: convincing her esteemed client seemed to be taking rather longer. Each time she suggested a dove grey or delicate cream, Lucy would turn in her pattern book to a deep red, or multicoloured stripe which, even with so small a sample, clashed abominably with her hair and seemed to make her freckles more pronounced.

Lucy had no firm idea as to style and was willing to be led by Mrs Gardiner as to the changes which had occurred in the fashionable world of late, so that the hard-pressed lady had some hopes, at least, of producing dresses for her which minimized the unfortunate impression of height, but, as to colour, she could make no headway at all, and was beginning to despair when, to her relief, in walked the Earl, entirely unannounced, and obviously not embarrassed, though Lucy was in her undergarments and had to dash behind a screen.

'Ah, Mrs Gardiner,' he said amicably, not so much as glancing in his wife's direction, 'how do we go on? What have we chosen so far?'

Mrs Gardiner hardly liked to meet his eye as she showed him what Lucy had ordered, though she hastened to assure him that she was not precisely of the same opinion as Her Ladyship as to colour and hoped that, anyway, the Earl would like her designs.

Recognising at once a woman in a dilemma, the Earl had no hesitation in saying kindly to her, 'I am sure I shall, Ma'am, but won't you show me what colours you would have chosen instead for my wife? Sometimes a third person's opinion can be so useful where disagreement exists.'

In a strangled voice, Lucy called over to him, 'I have made my choice, sir.'

He lifted his quizzing glass towards her, his eye twinkling hideously at her rage. 'And admirable choices I am sure they are too, my dear, but this is England, you know, and the majority always take the day! Now, let me see, Mrs Gardiner—oh yes,' and he calmly cancelled all of Lucy's orders and replaced them with his own.

Mrs Gardiner, a startled frown on her face, following one glance at her livid client, did just manage to say, 'But madam does not seem to like . . . ?'

His lordship settled the matter at once. 'Ah but she only has to wear them. I have to look at 'em.'

He would not chance leaving Mrs Gardiner to Lucy's tender mercies and helped her collect her things together and showed her to the door, having ascertained that at least two dresses would be ready before breakfast on the morrow.

If the rest of the day passed uneventfully, it was miserable, for Lucy in a rage was no very edifying sight and her fury failed to abate at hearing Tom tell her sagely, 'Best take Alex's advice, Lucy,' (for the two men were already on first name terms). 'Never did have much eye for colour. I disremember ever hearing Mama agree with your choice and his lordship has such excellent taste.' This piece of wisdom was so little designed to calm her down that they were all pleased when the day ended.

Nobody was less surprised than Lucy when her husband again chose not to visit her rooms, though she wished more than anything that he would, for she had taken a sharp-cornered book from the shelf in her room and had stationed it on the little table by her bed, ready to use as a missile should he be foolhardy enough to show his head there.

Waking next morning to find one of the despised dresses from Mrs Gardiner—a charming cream-coloured morning dress of jaconet muslin trimmed with bows of narrow mushroom coloured ribbon—hanging ready for her beside her bed, was the last straw, and instead of putting it on, she studiedly went to her wardrobe and took out her pea-green. Not only that, but she draped Aunt Marianne's old shawl round her shoulders, and arranged her hair even more negligently than was her custom, before making her way with carefully assumed nonchalence, downstairs.

It was no great shock to her to see her husband waiting for her, arms crossed, at the bottom of the stairs, though she was a little alarmed by the martial gleam which mounted in his eye as he took in her resplendence. He waited for her to reach the bottom stair before so much as moving an inch from his place, then, very deliberately, stood before her, arms now outstretched, to allow her no opportunity to go further.

'I believe, ma'am, that a dress has been chosen

135

for you to wear,' was all he said, his voice as infuriatingly calm as ever.

'But *I* did not choose it!' cried Lucy, wishing she could control herself as well.

'Of course not, my love, I did. We are agreed, are we not, that such matters are best left to those who understand them?' he replied sweetly.

'Which, I suppose, means you!'

'Which, as you so very correctly surmise, means me!'

'Perhaps I do not like your taste!'

'I thought we had decided, too, that that was very little to the point.'

She ground her teeth loudly.

'Suppose I tell you that I refuse to wear what you have had put out for me and prefer to keep my own things on?'

'I cannot think you are so foolish, my dear, for they are abominable. And anyway, should you refuse to comply with my wishes, I will carry you upstairs myself, and take those dreadful things off your back with my own hands! Do I make myself clear?'

Her eyes narrowed dangerously in consideration.

'Don't doubt it!' were the only words he said, but the gleam which accompanied them made certain that she did not disobey and she flounced furiously back upstairs to do his bidding.

She had barely finished changing when, as once before, he walked in on her unannounced.

'How dare you come into my room without knocking,' she cried, her rage by no means blown.

'But I am your husband, my love,' he replied urbanely, not remotely upset at her spurt of temper, and then lifting his glass to look at her said, 'Ah yes, that is better. I thought it would be. Now we only have to await Miss Havering, for she will, I am sure be able to control your hair. Perhaps then you will be something like.'

'Not everyone wants to be as foppish as you, sir,' she said witheringly.

'And not everyone has the knack to be so, my dear,' he replied pleasantly. 'Now, I will just call in your maid,' (for the poor girl had retreated into the dressing room as soon as their altercation had begun) 'and she may get started on taking out your old clothes to be burned.'

'Burned! Now you are being provoking!'

'Oh come now, Lucy, do not be foolish. Of what possible use can they be if you may not wear them? They will only take up closet space that you will need. Ah, there you are my girl,' he said as the maid came cautiously into the room. 'Just take all her ladyship's old clothes and throw them out, there's a good girl,' and he strolled unhurriedly from the room.

Recognising the impropriety of arguing in front of a servant, she followed him downstairs, and into the little breakfasting parlour. Nobody else was yet down, so she was able to have her say in peace. It made not one jot of difference, for, far from going back on his word, he added to his sins by telling her, in a voice which suggested that he expected congratulations, that he had ordered an entire new wardrobe of undergarments for her, as well as night things and that she must expect the shoemaker later in the day, oh and also the milliner!

'You must realise, Ma'am, that you have a position to keep up. Your own commonsense must tell you how much easier it will be if you look the part. It might be comfortable prancing around like a hoyden, but it is not the thing for a Countess. Only think how depressed you would be to have to meet my sister today in one of those old frocks.'

Even Lucy was forced to admit that a modicum

of truth lay behind his words and was prevailed upon, when Miss Havering eventually arrived, to go upstairs with her and allow her to cut her hair into a new and dashing style. Lucy sat in amazement as her springing curls were coaxed just as she would have them go, and even admitted that the improvement was striking.

Miss Havering shook her head when she saw the freckles, standing out livid from the results of Lucy's careless meanderings in the sun without hat or parasol, but she immediately applied some Denmark Lotion to them and began to look up receipts for other well-known remedies, refusing to be daunted by such a challenge.

Lucy did not go down again until she heard her new sister-in-law arrive, but one quick peep at her from her window was enough to make her glad that the Earl had had his way, since Fanny looked as adorable as ever in a handsome carriage dress of pale blue cambric, worn under a matching short pelisse: on her head the sauciest poke bonnet trimmed with roses. Lucy could only be dismayed when she saw how tiny and ethereal she was.

CHAPTER

13

Surprising even herself, Fanny did not immediately take against Lucy. Perhaps it was Lucy's straightforward friendliness that made it impossible for Fanny to administer the carefully rehearsed rebuff she had planned on her journey down, though it might as easily be accounted for by the fact that against Lucy she knew she must look more fairylike than ever. And anyway, Lucy was not half so impossible as her brother had said. Her taste in clothes was by no means as bad as she had prepared for, though not quite up to her own exacting standards, of course, and even her hair (though red must ever be a sad trial!) was quite elegantly styled for someone fixed in the country. Charitably, she put her brother's prejudices down to a natural disinclination to be wed to one not of his choice, though she quite saw how the dreadful freckles might offend him and good-naturedly made up her mind to look up an old receipt of her Mama's for Roman Balsam which, if she could persuade Lucy to wear it overnight, would take away their worst effects.

For her part, Lucy was fascinated by this sprite of a creature who seemed in only a few minutes to have turned the house upside down, having brought with her numerous presents for them all, which she insisted must be inspected at once, and which included for Mary the prettiest little long-haired tabby kitten whom Mary, on seeing his velvety blob of a nose, had no hesitation in naming Smudge.

The day being fine, Lucy told Frensham to arrange for luncheon to be served outside, and garden furniture was carried forth and arranged picturesquely in the shade of a spreading chestnut tree situated near the house.

"What a splendid idea Lucy, and how comfortable a family party is. One can have too much of company,' said Fanny languidly, peeping from under the wide-brimmed hat which protected her delicate complexion from the sunshine, while she watched Mary teasing the kitten with a skein of wool. 'Such a waste not to make the best of this lovely weather. And there can be little harm in it so long as one wears a hat. Not that I should like to chance it either without a long sleeve and glove, but then my complexion is so easily scorched.'

'My wife is full of surprises, aren't you, my love?' said Lucy's husband teasingly, watching in unholy amusement as his wife hid her ungloved, weather-roughened hands among her skirts. 'Only wait until we dine this evening and you will see another of them.'

'If they are all as good as getting rid of Mincham,' declared Fanny, who had heard with the greatest satisfaction how Lucy had routed her, 'she has *my* blessing.'

'Rather!' said Samuel, with feeling. 'Woman always was the very devil. Don't know how you dared, though. Must have been a deuced delicate matter.'

'Delicate?' asked Lucy, as if the word was unknown to her. 'No, why should it? My Aunt Marianne has always brought me up to consider the feelings of any servant, for she has the very highest principles, but she would not expect me to keep a servant who held me in aversion.'

'Lucy's Aunt Marianne is, I understand, even more of a Tartar than Lucy,' said the Earl grimly.

Piers and Samuel both laughed at his tone, but were caught by the tolerant affection they saw in his face as he looked at Lucy.

They had not long finished luncheon when Frensham, at his usual stately pace, came across the lawn, a silver salver in one hand, in the centre of which lay a neat visiting card sent in by Viscount Thorne.

Charles Thorne had always been a favourite with Fanny, though she had often been piqued by her inability to bring him round her thumb as she had countless others. Nevertheless, he was a most personable gentleman and, as such, fair game, so she whiled away the few minutes before he appeared in making imaginary adjustments to her already perfect coiffure and straightening a neckline which had never been allowed to become crooked, while her husband watched her preparations comfortably diverted.

The Earl was less comfortable when he noticed similar preparations from his wife, who had assumed the easy flush to her cheeks on hearing their guests announced. Now what was going on with the girl, he wondered?

There was little time for speculation, however, for, on looking toward the house he saw the old Viscount being helped by his son toward the gardens: on his face the usual stoical expression he wore when he was in pain and did not mean to allow the others to feel sorry for him.

The Earl moved at once to meet him before he took so much as a step outside.

'My dear Viscount,' he said amicably, shaking his hand. 'How good to see you, sir, and you too Miss Thorne: Charles. Tell me at once if you would prefer to stay inside for we can easily move. We are being perfectly indolent as you observe.'

'Good God, boy,' he replied tetchily. 'I'm not ready to stick my spoon into the wall yet, y'know.'

'I'm very glad to hear it, sir,' replied the Earl without rancour, showing his old friend to the seat he had just vacated, as a footman hurried to bring out more chairs.

'Heard you were here, my boy,' said the Viscount, ashamed at his temper. 'Thought we would make it our business to do the pretty. Didn't expect to see you *all*, though. Most gratifying.'

Alexander's eyes twinkled to see how speedily Tom rose to offer Miss Thorne his seat, and even more so when he realised that Tom's admiration for the pretty creature was returned. Alexander had always thought Gwendolyn insipid. A little in awe of him, she was never at her best in his company. But he knew her to be much admired, and today, with the bloom of summer on her, he could not find it in himself to blame Tom for his prejudice. He could not help glancing at the Viscount to see if he objected, but seeing only complaisance, the Earl was disposed to like the budding romance.

He was less happy to see confirmed his mild suspicion that his wife, too, had an admirer, though Mr Thorne knew his duty too well to make his way to Lucy's side before paying his respects first to Lady Fanny and then to the rest of the company. Seeing the intimate glance which passed between them when Mr Thorne finally shook hands with Lucy, the Earl knew a distinct pang of alarm.

The visit, like many another, passed amiably and lazily in the sunshine, with pleasant exchanges of gossip and news. Like others too, it was marred when, on leaving, the old Viscount was unable to resist bartering again for his precious plot. It was an old game between them, and Alex had not changed his mind, refusing even to consider the Viscount's offer. This time, however, Samuel surprisingly intervened.

'Why not sell it, Shel? I will, when I am the Earl. Surely it isn't worth having that little piece of land, so far from the house?'

The Earl stared quizzically at his heir for a moment, saying nothing, but Viscount Thorne went so far as to forget his manners and say, 'Aye, m'boy. *You* see sense! That's because your head's not filled with proud nonsense.'

'I can only hope,' interpolated the Earl mildly, 'that you may reconsider, Samuel, when—or should I say *if* you become the Earl. As things are, perhaps I must hope—if only for the sake of the estate—that I may outlive you. Stranger things have happened after all.'

Samuel had the grace to look ashamed and apologised handsomely for his presumption.

'Small difference now,' said Viscount Thorne undaunted. 'Always hoped you'd come into the inheritance one day, Sam m'boy, and then we might have settled the matter. Won't come off now that he's taken to wiving. Your cousin'll have a parcel of brats around the place before we can look about.'

Embarrassment hushed the company, a silence which seemed not to touch the Earl, though Lucy could feel her face burning. It lasted only a moment, however, and ended as such embarrassing moments will, with a welter of nothings all spoken at once.

Charles was mortified at his father's clumsiness and found a moment in the general goodbyes to apologise to Lucy.

'Don't mind father, Ma'am. You are the last person in the world he would wish to embarrass,' he said, earnestly. 'He wouldn't have said anything had he known as I do what your marriage really is.'

He could say no more, for Fanny was with them pressing her demands for his attention.

The Earl, meanwhile, had seen the affecting little exchange and, on turning back to the house, his

143

face wore a thoughtful expression totally devoid of its usual indifference.

When Lucy went up to change for dinner, her maid had laid out another of Mrs Gardiner's creations for her, this time a ravishing, white evening gown of figured silk, its neckline low and square-cut about a tight-fitting, high-waisted bodice. She was surprised to see, lying on her dressing table, two long rows of fine pearls, and asking Miss Havering where they had come from, she was told only that the Master had given them into her hands not half an hour before. Lucy could not decide whether to be annoyed or delighted. Surely, if the Earl wanted to give his wife a present, should he not place it in her hands and not pass it to her via her dresser? She was half a mind not to wear the pearls! And yet . . . they were lovely . . .

An hour later saw her dressed in all her new finery, hair neatly curled, pearls hanging from neck and with a shawl of the palest peach draped becomingly over her arms. She felt that she looked rather well and her husband's nod of approval as she entered the drawing room lifted her spirits.

Fanny, agreeably surprised at Lucy's smartness, was inclined to be quite envious of her pearls, and said, in a tone not quite free from pique, 'Wherever did you get such delightful pearls, my dear? I had not thought you had anything so fine.'

Her brother, seeing Lucy's confusion, was quick to intervene.

'Naturally, they were my wedding present to Lady Sheldon, weren't they, my dear?' and he stared at Lucy, daring her to deny him.

She did not dare, nor would she support him, prevaricating instead by saying, 'Indeed yes, they are charming aren't they,' before leading her guests into dinner, herself taking Lord Oswaldeston's arm while her husband escorted his sister.

Fanny thought Lucy's rearrangements inspired, and could not forbear remarking every half hour how she wished she had thought of it herself.

Fanny had come to Arunfold to criticise, but instead found her sister-in-law, if not quite the dasher she herself might have chosen for Alexander, no less acceptable. She was as much impressed by Lucy's housekeeping skills as by her decided accomplishments, declaring that it had been years since Arunfold had been so comfortable to visit. Listening that night to Lucy playing, she found herself wondering if Lucy might not work out very well after all, especially when she glimpsed the tolerance with which her brother seemed to regard her. Whatever he might say, Fanny could see little reason for him not to like his wife, and she was inclined to think that their silly bargaining for a match in name only must surely come to nothing.

All they required was a little encouragement and Fanny became determined to do all in her power to promote the match. Never subtle, she began her campaign at once. Lucy was the most accomplished creature in the world, she told her brother. Her playing was simply heaven!

'Wait until you hear her sing if you are so eager to find something to praise,' was all her maddening brother had to say in reply. But nothing else was needed. Almost before he knew what she was about, Fanny demanded, in a loud voice not to be denied, that Alexander and Lucy join together in a duet.

'My brother, you know, is a fine baritone,' she told Lucy, 'and he tells me that your voice is delightful.'

Lucy disclaimed at once, saying that she would much prefer to listen to the Earl singing with Fanny, but she would not allow her plans to be thwarted and, to her dismay, Lucy found herself expected to sing with her husband. Guessing Lucy's disinclination gave the Earl the required determination that she *would* sing with him and she soon found herself embarking with him on a spirited rendering of "Nor Robin Lend to Me Thy Bow". The others listened admiringly, for their voices were far more in harmony than the pair had ever been, and gave the company so much pleasure that they were not allowed to cease until they agreed to sing again. Lucy pithily suggested "The Berkshire Tragedy", but the Earl would not agree.

Lucy blushed when Lord Oswaldeston, having watched his wife's scheming in his usual quietly amused way and prepared to add his mite, asked for "Greensleeves", but since the Earl chose to think his brother-in-law's choice unexceptionable, "Greensleeves" it was. She felt hot with embarrassment as she forced her way through the intimate words, keeping her eyes on her hands as they played, never allowing so much as a glance to fall her husband's way throughout, though had she done so, she would have been as surprised as were the others to see there, not the cynical glint he so often showed to the world, but a kindlier gleam with which not even his sister could be dissatisfied.

Determined not to have to sing with the Earl again, Lucy ordered the tea tray early, pleading a fatigue which Fanny declared she shared and which led to them both taking their candles up to bed.

The gentlemen left to their own devices, Tom challenged Samuel to a game of billiards, and the two younger men took a bottle to the billiard room, leaving the others to sit until bedtime, a decanter and some glasses on a table between them. Having spoken in a desultory way about trivialities, Lord Oswaldeston could not eventually resist saying, 'I like your wife, you know, Sheldon.'

'Oh, Lucy,' he replied, concentrating hard on his brandy.

'Yes, Lucy,' persevered his brother-in-law, smilingly. 'And she is not at all what you led us to expect, though I admit to the freckles! And very sweet they look, too. She's quite charming.'

Since there was still no response from Alexander, Lord Oswaldeston tried again a few moments later.

'She's tall, of course, but it suits her. And as to her clothes and hair, I cannot see what offends you. I think she dresses charmingly.'

'Of course she dresses charmingly,' replied Alex, nettled, 'I dress her! She thinks she can wear puce and mauve with that hair! Though don't for heaven's sake tell Fanny, for that would certainly be enough to damn her for ever.'

'Good grief, man, you don't mean that *you* had to choose her clothes, do you?' he asked, horrified. 'Why, I shouldn't have had the vaguest idea.'

'Yes, well, don't suppose I would really,' replied Alexander slightly mollified, 'only I chanced to remember that Grace always swore by Mrs Gardiner, so I told the poor woman to call. Thought she would fix everything right and tight. Didn't reckon with Lucy, though,' and he went on to give Lord Oswaldeston all the details of their encounter. By the time he had finished, Lord Oswaldeston's shoulders shook, and even the Earl, forced to see the funny side for the first time, was able to join in.

'If you ask me, Sheldon,' said his brother-in-law, feelingly, 'this business of a marriage of convenience can't last! You're both of you too headstrong for it to be possible. And anyway, Lady Sheldon's far too attractive for me to suppose you would want it to.'

'Perhaps you should talk to her rather than me,' declared Alexander brusquely. 'She seems to dislike me more since we married. Thinks me some kind of monster, and says it would have been better to have been a governess all her days than my wife. I am the last person she wants to live with.'

'Don't try to bamboozle me into thinking you could not make her love you if you wanted to, my friend. Coming it too smokey by half! And what I want to know is, why don't you do it!'

'Perhaps it is more fun this way,' replied Alexander, and for the first time that evening his lip curled downward.

Lord Oswaldeston looked thoughtfully into his glass.

'I don't mean to interfere, Sheldon, but perhaps it would be wise to make the girl fall for you before she realises there are alternatives.'

'Ah, so you saw him too, did you Piers?' replied the Earl, the curling lip more pronounced. 'Not much escapes you, does it? But you see, I find myself curious to see how far she will go.'

'Isn't that rather a dangerous game, my friend?'

'Dangerous, perhaps, but amusing, you will agree.'

'It might be anything but amusing, Sheldon. She's little more than a child, you know?'

'While I'm a senior member of society. You see, I have not forgotten. It's true that I am experienced enough to turn her head, should I decide to do it (though it makes me sound a coxcomb to admit it), but I have the strangest desire—you will think me mad—to see her come to me of her own free will and not because I've dazzled her into it with compliments and the like.'

'God, man! Does it matter how you do it? She's your wife! Only make her love you before someone else does.'

'If you mean before the blockish Thorne does, why don't you say it?' he said harshly, finishing the words abruptly as he saw that Samuel, followed by Tom, had walked back into the drawing room.

CHAPTER

14

It had become Lucy's habit to breakfast at nine in the parlour which led from the gardens and which adjoined the small drawing room. It was a comfortable room filled with an odd concoction of elegant satinwood furniture and family clutter, and Lucy enjoyed lingering over breakfast there, especially when, as this morning, the sun had already visited it with the promise of another fine day.

Neither Tom nor Mary were matutinal and the Earl rarely bothered with breakfast at all. Now, with the arrival of Lord and Lady Oswaldeston, no change in Lucy's solitary state occurred, the men going off early to seek what little sport was to be had in the woods, while Fanny could not be expected down until at least noon. Fanny, not an early riser, had then the added worry of always appearing at her best, a demand which sometimes exercised her powers of contrivance for as much as two hours at a time.

Lucy was happy to be left in peace: she would not readily have relinquished her tranquility to the demands of courtesy. Today, however, she was not entirely alone, since Smudge had decided to keep her company and was busy exploring the skirts of yet another of Mrs Gardiner's creations, this time of palest buttermilk muslin, high waisted, long sleeved and flounced at the hem in a style which Lucy privately thought became her very well.

Mary had, the night before, begged that Smudge share her room, but the Earl, who could not approve cats upstairs, had forbidden it and the little creature had, as a result, to wait eagerly for a friendly face in the breakfasting room, though he was already a fair way to having all his wishes conferred to in the kitchens, whence he had been sent at Mary's bedtime. He had an instinctive notion, however, that the company there was of an inferior kind, and had managed to sneak out through a small opening left by a maid when she carried the breakfast things along to her mistress. Lucy had not the heart to send him back and settled him on her lap while eating her toast and drinking her usual cup of coffee.

Smudge was at first quite content to subject himself to such gratifying attentions, purring softly, arching his back and stretching his claws in his ecstasy, but surely he could do even better! He put a tentative paw toward the table and, seeing that Lucy did not prevent him, was soon exploring among the china on the breakfast table. Lucy's eyes crinkled as she saw him making his way unerringly round the coffee pot and the Worcester coffee cups towards the cream jug, and she picked him up and carried him carpetward in one hand, while placing a saucer on the floor beside him with the other. This looked highly promising to Smudge and he was not mistaken, for a second later he viewed with delight a creamy waterfall falling into the saucer from a silver jug obviously meant for him. This was something like! He set to finish every drop, then, after a thorough grooming of paws and whiskers, curled himself into a ball, just where the sun fell on the centre of a rug, and began his nap, his bulging tummy pleasantly overfull.

Mary had still to make an appearance, which made Lucy wonder if she might not steal a half hour or so for a project of her own. While walking in the woodland close by the house a day or two before, she had seen a formation of fungus growing at the base of an old beech, which she had a fancy to capture in chalks. Now would be her chance, and collecting her sketching things from the drawer in which they were kept, she put on a spencer and neat, plain straw morning bonnet, and made her way through the French windows at the side of the house, across the lawns towards the part of the wood where the beech tree grew.

At that time of day, the wood was chill once she had advanced beyond the edge, the heat of day not yet having pervaded the thickness of the foliage.

Dew still lay heavily on leaves and hummocky grasses, where it hung like strings of transparent pearls caught in the dim light which found its way down from gaps above. Wetness from the long grass reached over her pattens and dampened her jean half-boots and skirt hem. Here and there where the sun tried to break through far ahead, eerie straight rays fell to the forest floor and, all around, the air steamed. There was no sound anywhere. Not as much as an insect clicked or whirred in the brooding silence and Lucy felt the loneliness of the place. It seemed for the first time sinister. Somewhere in her mind apprehension held her spirit: a feeling that she was being watched refused to be quieted and she was conscious of a tingling at the top of her spine, the fine hairs on her skin all standing away!

But yet, she was still Lucy and declined to be intimidated, so forced herself on to find her beech tree, glad that it was not in the thick of the forest but at the edge of a small, sunlit clearing a few yards across, though still uneasily aware, all the time she was sketching, of the certainty that she was not alone.

Her sketch was poor, for her hand was unsteady and her usual powers of observation had temporarily deserted her. Only stubbornness made her continue with it. She *would* not leave the place without her drawing, though as soon as she had filled her page sufficiently, she began, over-eagerly, to collect her things together, aware that her face and palms perspired.

She had almost collected the last of her chalks from where she had carelessly placed them when, lifting her head slightly at an apparent movement beyond her vision, she saw, just out of the sunlight on the other side of the clearing, in the faint haze of shadow, a woman's figure, dressed from head to toe in black. There for no more than a moment and then gone, yet Lucy had not seen her move. And surely she knew her? Surely it was Miss Mincham in the shadow . . .

On the strength of her observations, Lady Oswaldeston delayed her return to London. She had seen enough not to despair of a happy outcome and was determined to leave no stone unturned to reconcile her brother to his wife.

For several days it seemed she had been right to hope. Thrown together in the midst of a family party, their intercourse unmarred by any unfortunate appearance from Mr Thorne (who had not enjoyed seeing Lucy with her husband), it seemed as if all might be well. If, at first, Fanny's brother had shown a lamentable tendency to tease Lucy rather as an uncle might, and if Lucy, for her part, seemed sometimes determined to find her husband autocratic, yet, as the days passed by amidst such obvious family goodwill, their bickerings became

harder to sustain and Fanny became quite sanguine as to the future.

On hearing that Lucy did not number among her
many talents the ability to tool a carriage, the Earl
even went so far as to offer to teach her himself and
their neighbours were either gratified or not, ac-
cording to their dispositions, to see almost every
afternoon, the Earl and his young wife bowling
along nearby lanes in fine style and seemingly on
excellent terms.

On her seventh day at Arunfold, Lady Oswaldeston, coming through to the drawing room for luncheon and seeing the Earl and Lucy together at the
pianoforte was able to reflect contentedly on the fe-
licity of having a brother well married, convinced
that this nonsense of a marriage in name only must
very soon be a thing of the past.

Luncheon was another prolonged, leisurely affair, this time indoors, for Fanny was certain that
she had been too careless and that the sun had
roughened her face, even under her hat.

While they were eating, Mary played her piece
on the pianoforte. As his eyes rested on the child,
Lucy saw again how fond her husband was of his
niece, his obvious pleasure sufficient reward to Lucy
for all her hard work. Without warning, Alexander's eyes shifted to Lucy's and held them for a moment, then moved on so quickly that she wondered
afterwards if he had really looked at her so ten-
derly.

They were still in the drawing room when Frensham placed a calling card at his master's elbow.
Alexander took it from the salver, stared hard at it
for a moment and appeared uncomfortable when he
read the sentence or two, written in flowing hand,
on its back. He seemed to consider denying himself,
gave a shrug and declared to Lucy, in tones abnor-
mally loud,

'You will be pleased to hear, my dear, that some friends of ours have this moment arrived.'

'Friends? Of *ours*, my lord?' asked Lucy pleasantly, still influenced by his late gentleness.

'Lady D'Avergne and her brother, finding themselves "almost on our doorstep", I am quoting, you see!, wonder if we would think it an impertinence should they ask to avail themselves of our hospitality for a few days. Do we think it so, my dear?'

Whatever Lucy thought, Fanny seemed inclined toward strong hysterics!

'Valentine D'Avergne! Stay here? She must be mad, brother. Does not she know that you are now married? For sure, but what a foolish question. She cannot, for even she would never think to foist herself on your wife. You will refuse her, of course.'

'Dearest, dearest Fanny,' replied the Earl, lifting his sister's fingers to his lips in a butterfly soft tribute. 'Nobody understands these little social niceties so well as you, but you have forgot, have you not, that Lucy and I stayed with Lady D'Avergne on our way here? She knew about my marriage even before you did and knows too,' and this was said in his mildest voice, 'that any friend of mine must always be received by my wife.'

Lucy bit her lip, but met her husband's gaze squarely, her face a mask of indifference, 'Naturally your friends are welcome, sir,' she replied evenly. 'Was not that our agreement? I am to be left in peace to enjoy Arunfold: your wife in name only? In return I am to receive your guests and teach Mary, as well as receiving my most generous allowance. What possible cause could I have to complain? Our arrangement is perfectly agreeable to me, I assure you. Won't you go out and bring them inside?'

'Bring them in? Are you mad Lucy?' cried Fanny, her voice faint with amazement. 'Bring in that

154

creature with ladies in the house? Do you know what she is? She is just the kind of ingratiating personage as if given the slightest encouragement would haunt one should she once get a foot in the door. She has been trying for an age to become accepted at Almack's, but we have kept her out. Bring her here and she will plague us for ever. You cannot, indeed you cannot! This comes from your determination to avoid girls of your own class, Alex! But Lady Sheldon will know better.'

'Don't be a fool, Fanny,' returned the Earl crushingly. 'Lady Sheldon will not turn away my friends.'

'Nor wish to, I assure you. It is nothing to me. Fanny, my dear, you must remember that I must not cheat your brother as to the terms of our marriage.'

Lucy's words were calmly spoken and caused the Earl some embarrassment, but he listened unmoved when his sister threatened, 'If that woman comes into this house, you know I must leave it Alex. If Lucy does not mind the riff raff you bring to Arunfold, I at least did not come to my old home to be insulted. I think my father would not have treated our mother so, and if you act differently I have little choice but to leave.'

'As you wish, of course,' replied her brother coolly, 'though naturally I hope you will reconsider.'

It took no more than a second for Fanny to take in all the implications behind his tranquilly uttered words, and straightening her shoulders, she declared, with awe-inspiring hauteur, 'I did not look for such an insult from you, but of course I shall go at once,' and walking majestically over to Lucy, kissed her on the cheek and left the room, her back rigid with disapproval. Her husband, casting one incredulous look at the Earl, strolled after her without a word.

By the time Fanny had reached her apartments, she was crying, fury at her brother overflowing into concern for the girl she had come to think of as her poor, dearest Lucy. All men were wretches, and her brother the worst!

By the time her husband had caught up with her, she had worked herself into a fine rage, her usually pale complexion ablaze, eyes spouting green fire behind tears, as she dragged from her wardrobe dresses and pelisses, and threw them into a heap on the bed, ignoring the frantic pleas of Pinner, her dresser.

Lord Oswaldeston came quietly into the room and seated himself on the chair set before Fanny's dressing table, watching with his habitual calm as his wife flounced here and there collecting up her personal belongings from where they had been previously placed on her arrival. Seeing her throw a particularly fine piece of porcelein which he had given her, onto the bed, without any regard as to its safety, he was moved to say, without raising his voice,

'That will do, Fanny. That is enough.'

'Enough!' she shrieked, glaring at him hotly. 'What do you mean that is enough. Are not you shocked? Can you be as lost to all sense of propriety as he? Ha! I need not ask! You are a man, aren't you and are bound to support him!'

'But I don't support him,' he replied gently, standing up and moving towards her in time to take from her hands another piece of china which was about to join the first on the bedcover, 'so do not include me in your fury. I agree with you that it is very terrible, but you have had your frenzy, and now it is time to stop,' and he took her into his arms, hugging her to his chest as if he were comforting a child, while her tears spoiled his cravat.

Over her head he gestured to Pinner to leave

them and when she had reluctantly closed the door behind her, gently persuaded his wife over to the bed, where he sat with her, one arm still around her shoulders as he reached for his handkerchief to wipe her face.

'Crying won't do, sweetheart,' he remonstrated. 'You know how you hate your eyes to swell.'

How well he knew his wife was immediately demonstrated when she blew her nose decidedly on hearing his words, and rushed over to her mirror to peer anxiously at the damage.

'Oh no! Just look at me, Piers,' she wailed tragically. 'How hideous of Alex, when he knows how sensitive my skin is! It is too bad of him. And now I must go back to London leaving that dreadful woman to crow at my expense. And with swollen eyes, too! I wish I had never come. Heaven knows how long it will take for these blotches to go, for I'm certain that Pinner said that all my Grape Lotion has gone and that is the only thing to get rid of blotches. I suppose I can try Dr. Withering's Lotion, but it is so messy! And you hate me wearing it in bed. I shall never speak to Alex again, for all that he is my brother, and everyone knows how I dote on him. It is too provoking!'

'Well, you may say that it is no concern of mine, Fanny,' said her husband reflectively, gazing abstractedly down at his fingers clasped before him, 'but yet I really should not have believed you would leave a prime article like Valentine D'Avergne to rule the roost—for such she will, of a surety. Lady Sheldon does amazingly well for one not born to it but she won't be able to depress her pretensions as you could.'

'I know it, I know it!' she cried, miserably, 'but you cannot think that I could stay after the way Alex has used me?'

'I suppose not. All the same, I cannot help worrying about Lady Sheldon. Madame D'Avergne could eat her for breakfast and still be hungry. She'll never manage to hold her own.'

'As always you are right, and yet how can I stay, dearest, when I have told Alex I am going? You will not ask me to beg my brother's pardon?' she cried, turning again to peer anxiously into her glass, her frown deepening as she noted how heavy and swollen were her eyelids.

Her husband reassured her on the point.

'I was only wondering, my love, whether you might be satisfied if I had a word with him for you,' he explained, 'and told him you had agreed to sink your very natural scruples. Remember, love, that it is all for Lady Sheldon. Madame D'Avergne has her precious brother in tow, and that makes me uneasy. If ever there was a schemer it is Léo Marechal. Devil take Sheldon! What a fool the man is, for all that he is your brother. I cannot understand how he could let them into the house, for I don't mind telling you that I had begun to be sure that he was not so indifferent to Lady Sheldon as he had us believe. Now I don't know what to think, but I'd as lief be here to keep an eye on the chit and try to see the pitfalls before she finds herself falling headlong into them.'

Fanny, who had already regretted her impulsive outburst and was more than a little curious as to why her brother's former mistress had arrived on his doorstep in flagrant breach of the rules governing the polite world, was willing to be persuaded. Having told her husband that she declined making an appearance downstairs until dinner, such a state as she was in, she turned her attention to her toilette for the evening.

Fanny was not alone in being affronted at the Earl's irregular behaviour. Tom, left behind in the drawing room when Alex and Samuel went out to welcome their guests, had no hesitation in condemning such smokey proceedings. Lucy had furnished Tom with enough of her suspicions regarding the precise nature of her lord's relationship with the lády so soon to be housed under her roof, to make him quick to jump to her defence. Seeing her obliged to swallow such an insult, his estimation of Lord Sheldon took an unwelcome plummeting.

'How dare he let them in the house when you are here, Luce!' he spluttered as His Lordship left the room. 'I am in a good mind to give him the cut direct for his insolence,' he said, striding manfully up and down on the rug before the fireplace, looking, Lucy thought, rather like a belligerent bulldog.

Even in her misery Lucy gurgled, 'Oh Tom dearest, how absurd you are to say so, for I'm persuaded you would make wretched work of it.'

'How can you laugh at a time like this?' he asked, equally furious at her giggling and at the fact that she was probably right.

'What point is there in indulging in a fit of the blue devils? And really, when all is said and done, it would be to make a fine piece of work about nothing. The Earl promised me nothing but his name. Which, if I am not much mistaken, you thought mightily fine of him at the time,' and here she lifted her chin higher, 'and, to be sure, his name is more than enough for me. I want nothing further. Lady D'Avergne is a friend of the Earl's. I promised to receive his friends graciously for him and that is what I mean to do.'

It was a pity that she ruined the effect of her clipped speech by adding venomously, 'Odious toad that he is!' but Tom was proud of her all the same.

They had time for little more, for in a few seconds, holding Mary by the hand, in sailed Lady

Valentine, perfection in royal blue; on her dusky curls a smart Waterloo hat reclining rakishly to one side.

'Lady Sheldon,' she cooed, as she came through the open doorway, stretching her free hand towards Lucy. 'How delightful to see you again so soon, and looking so blooming. But you, I fear, will not be so pleased to see me. It is naughty of me to descend on you so soon after your wedding. But I claim all the privileges of an old friend, for I pride myself on being quite the match-maker, as you may imagine!'

Lucy could only gape at such blatant self-misrepresentation, but found herself offering her hand as one in a trance. Glancing beyond Valentine she saw the satisfied expression on Monsieur Marechal's sallow face and recognised a force to be considered.

Valentine and Léo were not so foolish as to antagonise their hostess: it was their immediate intention to make themselves agreeable and few could be more charming when it suited them. Thus it came about that simple, uncomplicated Tom was entirely taken in by them.

At first, Lucy too found herself wondering if her suspicions were groundless, but then she remembered just how pleasant a welcome her husband had expected at *Ormaie* on his wedding night, nor could she believe that her sister-in-law would have reacted so violently to the lady did she not know and object to the true state of affairs. One or two warm glances thrown by the lady to the Earl only helped to confirm her suspicions.

She was relieved when Lord Oswaldeston came down with the sad news that his wife had the headache and would not be joining them until dinner, gratefully interpreting his message to mean that Fanny was willing to sink her scruples to lend Lucy support. But even Fanny was not quite enough. If her husband was to bring in the enemy she must call up her own reserves! As a consequence, she dispatched a messenger, begging Mr Thorne and his sister to join them at dinner that evening, though she chose not to inform her husband of this happy arrangement until long after she had received their acceptances. Indeed it was not until a quarter before the hour at which dinner had been set and Alex heard a carriage arriving in the forecourt outside, just as he met his wife coming down from her rooms, that she mentioned nonchalently, in answer to a quizzical uplifting of his eyebrow, 'Oh, did I forget to tell you, sir, that we are increasing our covers to include the Thornes. Not the Viscount, of course, but I felt certain that you would wish me to invite *some* of our neighbours.'

His lips twitched in appreciative amusement at the haughty unconcern with which his wife addressed him as they walked through to the drawing room, though Lucy's turning toward Charles Thorne at such a time he viewed with a certain alarm, which led him to say, tonelessly,

'I find myself wondering, my love, if everyone around here values the Thornes as you do. Others of our neighbours might have been glad to receive an invitation.'

'Even the most experienced hostess would find herself taxed in finding *suitable* dinner guests on such an occasion amongst *our* friends. I am not used to being the hostess in such an illustrious house as Arunfold, but I certainly feel fortunate to have such friends as Mr & Miss Thorne, ready to sink any natural disinclinations to be neighbourly. Gwendolyn is much admired and Mr Thorne generally liked, I believe, so I see no reason why our visitors should not find him pleasant!'

'You seem to find him so at all events, my dear,' he replied evenly.

'I *am* a woman, sir! I mention the matter only because you so often appear to forget it!'

Surprisingly, the Earl took her by the wrist and forced her to look at him. 'You were never more mistaken. Nobody seeing you this evening could forget it for a moment.'

Lucy, who knew she was looking her best in a gown of fine dove grey silk, had time for no more than a deep blush for, at that precise moment, Frensham opened the door and announced their dinner guests. Embarrassed at being found making love to his wife, the Earl let go his hand and stretched it instead towards Gwendolyn, who had appeared with her brother in the doorway. But he had not been quick enough, and Mr Thorne, witnessing all, could not prevent a gasp, which went some long way towards mollifying Lucy, annoyed with herself for her confused reactions to her husband's caressing words.

An interminable evening followed, enjoyed only by Léo, and by Samuel, as much smitten by Lady Valentine as ever and who took full opportunity of his cousin's impotency in the present circumstances, to ingratiate himself with her. Valentine for her part, encouraged his advances much as she might those of a playful puppy, while all the time keeping a watchful eye on the Earl. Alex's coolly amused way of regarding his cousin's antics was not designed to encourage the lady to hope that the Earl was regretting his hasty marriage, but she was too cautious to show disappointment and seemed content to spend the evening in pleasant dalliance. Her brother was more than happy! It had been he who had caught the rumour of the Earl's family gathering and had had the notion to join it. London at the height of the Season was never auspicious for Valentine, forced to move around the fringes of society. Brighton had been a bore and it had seemed an inspired idea to bring her instead to the Earl's doorstep to try her welcome. It was enough that the Earl had been coerced into allowing them within the presence of his family and close friends. At present he would ask no more. Lady Sheldon must be brought to accept their presence without question before it would be safe to attempt any further mischief.

Lady Fanny, who had spent hours on her own toilette and had sent lengthy advice through Pinner to Lucy, came down to dinner on her husband's arm, frostily prepared for battle. But Lady Valentine knew enough of Lady Oswaldeston not to fall into the error of attempting to outdress her and had appeared decorously arranged in a demure, high-necked gown of puce, a ploy which could not but put Fanny into the best of humours, dressed as she was herself in a diaphenous gown of silver and pink, which made her look as fragile as a camellia. Though Fanny could not like the situation, she found herself being less ungracious than she had intended.

Her husband was not at all taken in by Lady Valentine's tactics and spent the evening watching covertly as he tried to decide for himself which lady Alex favoured.

After some whispering from his love that Lucy had been perfectly correct in her fears that her husband had enjoyed a close intimacy with his new guests, even Miss Thorne's presence could not reconcile Tom to her presence. As a result, he spent most of the evening pugnaciously regarding the Earl from below lowered brows, Miss Thorne being scarcely able to coax him into a better frame of mind, though she succeeded rather better as time passed and no blatant insult was offered.

As for Miss Thorne's brother, he had been hardly

able to contain his indignation when he heard with whom he had been invited to dine, and, during the evening, made so obvious his intention to preserve Lady Sheldon's dignity by monopolising her for the entire evening, that the Earl's habitual coolness changed to angry watchfulness. He could not like the way Charles coolly assumed the part of champion to his wife, and found himself totally unable to damp down his annoyance.

Lucy, pretty certain of the feelings of the others, could not help but reflect on what a strange picture they must present. For herself, placed as she was between Tom and Mr Thorne, she felt rather like a bone being guarded by two terriers.

CHAPTER

15

When a large party is met together, even when it is formed of precisely the right mix of people to induce pleasure, some moments of unease are almost bound to occur, for a number of people in the confines of even so large a house as Arunfold provides just such a situation as is, perhaps, the most likely to create tensions. When the party is as ill-formed as the one now collected, such moments must be greatly multiplied and during the days which followed few were the hours in which some little matter did not occur to ruffle the atmosphere of calm resolutely created by Lucy. Her determination that Léo and Valentine's stay would be pleasant could not but fail with so many ranged on the other side. Not only did Charles Thorne (who had angled for and managed to catch from Fanny an invitation to remain during the whole of Lady Valentine's sojourn), but Tom also, not to mention Lord and Lady Oswaldeston, determinedly guarded Lucy from insult, real and imagined. Indeed, Tom and Fanny were so quick to jump to Lucy's aid that she began to feel embarrassed.

Fanny was always direct and the number of times she crossed swords with the lady were legion. One example will give the flavour of those skirmishes, which occurred with a monotonous regularity whenever one of them found the other alone.

The day after Lady Valentine had descended upon them, Fanny was seated in the drawing room unpacking some shoes which had just arrived from London. In her hand, she held a lady's evening slipper of deep pink ribbed silk, and she was looking doubtfully at its half inch wedge heel, wondering whether she had made the right decision in ordering a shoe with a heel. The fashion for flat shoes was so provoking when one was petite, she told herself crossly. It really was difficult to decide whether to remain in the latest mode or to take advantage of a little extra height.

Lady D'Avergne chose that very moment in her perambulations to walk in from the gardens through the open French window when, noticing Fanny, she gushed,

'My dear Lady Oswaldeston, what a delightful little shoe. Such a *delicious* shade of cherry. I have a pair of evening pumps in a very similar coloured spotted silk, but mine are lower, of course.'

'Lower?' said Fanny, correctly interpreting her sugared words to mean that Valentine considered herself the more fashionable. She replied kindly, 'Indeed? It must be a great comfort to *you* that lower heels are now in fashion, Madame, for when one gets to a certain age, heels must be so very trying. Mama used to say that feet *spread* so!'

Valentine purpled for no more than a second before returning the gentle words, 'I have always considered myself lucky to be tall. Being *squat* must be a sad trial. But perhaps you will be fortunate and styles will change.'

Having made her point she sauntered slowly past in search of better company, leaving Fanny smouldering.

So much for Fanny. Tom was little more polite

when he was around the lady, though fortunately he was often away from the house and Lucy was thus spared the necessity of keeping him in check.

Tom's absence is easily explained. Miss Thorne had felt herself quite unequal to accepting an invitation to remain with the company there. While Miss Thorne remained at home Lucy was assured some respite from Tom's guardianship, since he could not bear to let more than half a day go by out of her sight. It says much for his concern, however, that he often refused her dinner invitations and returned in time to ensure that that meal was as uncomfortable as he could make it, a task in which he was amply joined by Lady Fanny and Mr Thorne, who felt all the advantages of a third.

It might have been supposed that all this plotting would have discomposed Lady Valentine, but not so, an idiosyncracy explained by the fact that Tom's determination to annoy the lady appeared to the Earl so much in the light of criticism of his own behaviour that it was not to be borne! The more Tom tried to annoy his guest, the more the Earl felt it necessary to see that she enjoyed herself, this despite the fact that he knew that his behaviour must appear in a disgraceful light to his wife.

Moreover, Mr Thorne's attentions towards Lucy had become so patent that the Earl could scarcely look at him without feeling an overmastering desire to strangle him, though he was sophisticated enough to ensure that such harsh feelings were well hidden. A wish to show Lucy (who, or so he was convinced, encouraged Thorne unduly!) that he too could play dangerous games, made him adopt an attitude of careless unconcern at her behaviour, an attitude which entirely fooled his wife and led her to accept Mr Thorne's attentions far more warmly in her husband's presence than ever she had out of his sight. All this could only induce

Lady D'Avergne to hope. In the meantime she was content to be as pleasant as ever towards the Earl and, whenever Samuel was willing to let her out of his sight, found every opportunity to take Sheldon apart from the others, a form of behaviour which only confirmed Lucy in her determination that he must not be aware for as much as one moment how depressed she was.

Thus it came about, on the fourth day after her arrival, that Valentine found herself alone with the Earl strolling across the lawns behind the house and up towards the high woods, where a meandering path ran round the edge of the trees. Some of their party had gone out riding, leaving only, beside themselves, Lucy, Mary and Charles Thorne in possession. Mr Thorne, intercepting a warm look between Lady Valentine and his host, was quick to challenge Lucy to an archery contest, a sport to which they had all become much addicted in the past few days and in which Charles was coaching her. The Earl, seeing with intense annoyance the alacrity with which his wife sprang up to accept the challenge, sent Valentine a disarming smile and invited her to take a walk with him, which only encouraged his wife to cling rather more closely to Mr Thorne's arm as they made their way from the room, calling Mary to follow them.

Alex, who became less interested the moment his wife had gone, offered Lady D'Avergne his own arm in a way which made plain to the lady that he did not intend to indulge himself in any flirtation, so she did not make the mistake of offering him such, contenting herself instead with adopting the less exacting role of long-standing friend and talking of such everyday matters as must encourage him to think himself safe. In his relief, his lordship thawed noticeably and she soon had the satisfaction of recognising that he was enjoying her company much as he had once been used to.

They had reached the confines of the wood before she was ready to broach the matter which immediately concerned her, but once there she began to show such unmistakable signs of tiring that the Earl was constrained to ask if she needed to rest. She accepted and he found a convenient log for them to sit on, just to the edge of the trees by the lawns, from which they had a magnificent view of the house and lower woodland beyond. They had been seated only for a moment or two in companionable silence when Lady D'Avergne began expansively,

'How beautiful it is here, mon ami. It is little wonder that you love it so. I never see it without wondering that you can leave it so often as you do.'

His lordship made no reply and she tried again. 'But perhaps you do not find it so at present?'

Again the Earl deigned no reply. His companion persevered. 'These uncertainties must be a great sadness to you, Alex.'

This time the Earl could not allow her words to pass without comment and he turned to her, wondering dryly, 'Which uncertainties are these, my love? What mischief are you brewing up now?'

'Mischief, Alex? You mistake, I assure you.'

'Do I? I am relieved to hear it.'

She might have been warned as much by Alex's tone as his words not to continue, but could not resist going on to say, 'Yet you will not say that you are *not* concerned? You cannot fool so old a friend as me.'

'Nonsense, my love, you are not so old,' he said, wilfully misunderstanding her. 'But tell me what it is you wish me to be concerned about. Guessing games were never my forté. If it is important to you that I be upset I will do my best, but you must be more explicit.'

'Not I, Alex,' she said purringly. 'I want only your happiness.'

'You must then be very content, my dear,' averred his lordship, settling himself comfortably on the log again, 'since I *am* perfectly happy.'

'But you can't be!' she protested. 'No man likes seeing his wife making a spectacle of herself, does he?'

'He does not, my love, but what has that to do with me?'

'Oh, but Alex, if you haven't noticed I'd be the last person to mention it!'

'Then it seems I am to remain in ignorance, cherie,' he replied cheerfully, 'so there is nothing for it but for me to continue happy.'

This she could by no means allow.

'Nobody likes your wife as much as I do, that you know Alex, and I could never criticise her behaviour, or indeed, doubt her innocence. But others, you know, might not be so generous.'

'Then we must be grateful, must we not, that it is you and not they who are staying with us?'

'But, though I could not be brought to utter so much as a word of criticism elsewhere,' she pursued bravely. 'You will not mistake my motives when I mention to you that I fear a little, just a little, her behaviour with the charming Mr Thorne.'

'I must say that it is the greatest relief to me to know how reluctant you are to criticise Lady Sheldon's behaviour and I know it will be a great comfort to you when I tell you that nothing anyone could say to me of Lucy could make me doubt her innocence. You will be relieved, too, my love when I tell you that your motives could never be mistaken even by the least astute of men,' and with that he lifted her hand to his lips to mitigate the

170

sting of his words. She had the grace to blush, before they stood up, as if in mutual agreement, to continue their walk, the lady less content with her share in the conversation than had been her companion.

While the Earl was thus engaged, another conversation, equally interesting, was taking place on the West Lawn, whence had been set up, not far from the house, several archery targets. One target was placed apart for Mary, who had a small bow of her own and was practising her shots, rather erratically, paying small heed to her aunt and her companion.

Mr Thorne was in a quandary. The ticklish situation which had arisen between Lord and Lady Sheldon placed him most awkwardly, giving rise to all sort of problems. Just what *was* expected when the lady of one's choice was subjected to blatant insult? This was the question which most occupied his mind. He couldn't like the idea of making love to a married woman. He'd always been a trifle uneasy about tales of Sir Lancelot and the like, even as a boy. Not quite the gentlemanly thing! He tweaked his cravat uncomfortably at such a thought, squaring his shoulders. Surely this case was different? The Earl's behaviour almost made it compulsory for him to comfort Lady Sheldon. Every woman must have a champion. Thus, he could not resist saying, as he helped her with her bow, 'Really, my lady, I am amazed to see you take your husband's attentions to Madame D'Avergne so calmly. Why cannot you tell her to be gone?'

'You must know that I cannot,' she replied mildly, moving herself inside the arc of his arm to take the bow from him to herself now that he had positioned her properly. 'And anyway, so far as I can see, Alex's attentions to the lady have been most correct!'

They both watched as she let go the string and the arrow sped on its journey, satisfied when it landed just at the edge of the black ring.

'There, ma'am. I said you had a gift. Now try this one on your own.'

Lucy did so, with close concentration, tensing the bow and aiming carefully. Once again an arrow flew through the air, this time to land in the red band. Mr Thorne could not contain his delight, taking Lucy by the hands and swinging her round and round in his enthusiasm. Breathlessly Lucy begged him to let her go, but was shocked when he so far forgot himself as to pull her into his arms instead.

As soon as she could free herself, she wrenched herself away, turning her eyes swiftly in Mary's direction to make sure she hadn't seen the incident. She had not, but that didn't lessen Lucy's embarrassment.

Lucy's scarlet cheeks mortified Mr Thorne, but he could not resist trying to justify his behaviour, whispering so that Mary should not hear.

'No, Lucy! I'm dashed if I'll apologise, when I've been wanting to kiss you for weeks. It's no use trying to make me feel guilty. I'm not flirting. I love you. *He* doesn't kiss you, does he? Any man who leaves his woods full of pheasant is asking for poachers.'

Lucy was not at all gratified by his analogy and replied stiffly, 'You make your suit so attractive, Mr Thorne, that it is almost irresistable. You cannot think how flattering it is to be compared to a pheasant. And my name is Lady Sheldon!'

'No, I say! That's not at all what I meant,' he protested, pulling at his cravat distractedly. 'Loveliest woman in the world! Take my word for it! Not that you should have to, of course. Your husband should tell you, but there it is. He doesn't, does he, so it's up to me!'

'But that's just what it isn't,' pointed out Lucy reasonably. 'Just because he neglects me it doesn't give you the right to kiss me, or call me by my first name. *I* haven't given you the right. It's . . . it's insulting, Mr Thorne, that's what it is,' and to her horror she found tears springing to her eyes, less because she was shocked by his impulsive behaviour than at the realisation of just how miserable her husband's neglect made her.

Seeing her tears, Mr Thorne lost his head entirely and made another grab at Lucy. This time she saw red, and bringing back her foot, in its stylish Roman sandal, she kicked him as hard as she could in the shin, an action which caused her more pain than him, since he wore riding boots, but which dented his pride not a little.

'But, Lady Sheldon,' he cried frantically, pulling her back towards him, this time with more caution. 'I love you! Leave Sheldon. Come away with me. Nobody in the land would condemn you after his behaviour. Come with me. His pride will make him divorce you and then we can be married. I cannot do without you!'

'That, as they say, is your problem, sir,' she replied haughtily, fighting a wild desire to laugh as she pulled herself free of his grasp, adding gravely that they must return to the house, and showing him such an icy exterior that even he was not so foolhardy as to persist.

Her gravity lasted only until she chanced to see her husband, with Lady D'Avergne leaning heavily on his arm, walking slowly across the lawns to meet them, at which time Lucy instinctively felt for Mr Thorne's arm to support her, sending the confused man such a winning smile as to make him more her slave than ever.

While these interesting tête-a-têtes were in progress, the rest of the party had used the morning to

173

call on Viscount Thorne. Fanny was a good horse-woman, but no intrepid taker of fences, which meant that a ride with her was quite a pedestrian affair. For neck-or-nothing riders, like Tom and Monsieur Marechal, the pace she set was so irksome that they galloped off together as an advance party. Lord Oswaldeston preferred to remain with his wife, and Samuel stayed with them, giving them a first opportunity to discuss in the privacy of family, the state of affairs at Arunfold.

Samuel did not at all like the present situation, though his view of things differed essentially from Fanny's.

'I don't like this Thorne business coz, do you?' he said, as soon as the others had ridden out of earshot. 'It seems to me that Shel had better watch that little affair. I shouldn't like a wife of mine to make sheep's eyes at another fellow. Next thing you know she'll be squeezing in a Thorne on the wrong side of the blanket.'

Fanny was indignant.

'I should have thought rather that it is Lucy who should object when her husband brings his light-skirt to Arunfold,' she declared hotly.

'Lady Sheldon? What can she possibly find to object to? It's not every girl who becomes a Countess overnight. Alex did more than his duty in marrying her and now she repays him by flirting with Thorne. It's outside enough.'

'Isn't that just like a man? And I suppose Alex is a saint bringing dearest Valentine and the charming Léo to the party.'

'He didn't exactly bring 'em,' Samuel pointed out fairly. 'And anyway, I flatter myself that the lady is looking elsewhere than Sheldon for her entertainment at present.'

'Then you're a bigger fool than I took you for,' interposed Lord Oswaldeston, who had appeared to be paying only cursory attention. 'If Valentine D'Avergne has changed her quarry by so much as a hair's breadth I'll be very surprised.'

'I don't see that it matters much either way,' replied Samuel, manfully trying to hide his indignation at this light dismissal, 'since Alex and Lady Sheldon married for convenience. Why should Lady Sheldon care if he has a liaison? He doesn't share his chambers with her, it isn't that sort of match. Told me so himself.'

'It may interest you to know that before Lady D'Avergne showed herself here Alex was in a fair way to falling in love with Lucy,' said his cousin witheringly.

'What makes you think so?' asked Samuel, in a tone which suggested that his reading of the matter was entirely dissimilar. 'I've been here as long as you and it didn't seem so to me.'

'But you must have noticed how his face softened when he looked at her, Sam,' she said incredulously. 'What about when they sang together? Can you deny that he had begun to like her?'

'Making it all up, m'girl. It's my belief that Shel is making the best of a bad job. He's not going to ill treat the woman he's made Countess is he, but that's no reason to suspect him of wishing a closer relationship with her. Treated her handsomely if you ask me and now she repays him by dropping the handkerchief for Thorne.'

'If you think that the Countess is in love with Thorne then you *have* been taken in,' interrupted Lord Oswaldeston calmly. 'She's only interested in one man and that's not Charles. If Alex's little light o'love hadn't shown herself it could have ended well. But now! Who knows?'

'I shouldn't think there's the least doubt about the outcome,' said Samuel pugnaciously. 'If you're asking me to believe that Shel could fall for a girl like Lady Sheldon after all the women he's known I'd say you were doing it rather too brown, old fellow. Not saying that Lady Shel isn't a charming girl. She is. Like her very well as my cousin, assure you. But it stands to reason that someone who's been friends with the Lady D'Avergnes of the world aint going to want to settle for a Lucy.'

'Not everyone has your tastes, Samuel,' declared Fanny frostily.

'Ask ninety nine men in a hundred and you'll see who they'd choose,' he stated provokingly.

'Then they'd be fools,' cut in Fanny's husband.

At this most unsatisfactory point they perceived that, having already made their way through the lodge-gates which led to the Viscount's home, Tom and Léo were cantering back to escort the rest of the party. With Léo close by all talk on the subject was suspended and the three spurred on their horses, each left with his own thoughts.

CHAPTER

16

Lucy awoke next day with the headache, which she accounted for by the distinct change in the weather, for, though it was still warm, the sun was hidden by banked cloud and the air lay oppressive and still.

As usual, she breakfasted alone, the other ladies preferring the leisurely inactivity of the boudoir to being up and about, and the men long since gone to join a small bank of local landowners determined to thin out a colony of rooks.

The breakfast table was laid as generously as usual and Smudge waited, not without hope, by Lucy's chair, rubbing his head compellingly against her skirts. For once the little creature met with no response and instead of bringing him up on to her lap, she gently pushed him away with one hand, while she stretched the other towards a table nearby to pick up the latest copy of Ackermann's lying there. The serving maid having poured her coffee, Lucy dismissed her so that she could indulge herself heartily in a fit of the dismals. Indifferently flicking over the pages of the journal and shaking her head briefly over a remarkably ugly evening dress described as being "of pale blush-coloured gauze over a white slip and ornamented with an intermixture of white satin and moss roses, surmounting a new and most fanciful trimming," she was moved to protest morosely,

'Fanciful indeed! It's the most hideous thing I've ever seen, and the Gloucester turban she has on with it is worse!'

She pushed the journal from her in disgust and rested her elbows on the table, holding her chin cupped in her hands and looking at nothing in particular as she remembered the previous evening. 'Everything's gone wrong!' she admitted to herself wildly. 'Just when Alex and I were beginning to rub along together. If he hadn't brought *that woman* here, why we might have lived here quite comfortably.' Perfectly content to inhabit separate rooms, she was still the Countess, and it was not only too bad of him to have subjected her to the despicable events last evening, it seemed unlike him too.

Just for a moment she wondered if her husband had seen her in Mr Thorne's arms. Brow wrinkled, she focused her mind on the scene, but when she held it in her mind, she was certain that even when she had first noticed him coming across the lawns Alexander had been totally engrossed with Valentine. Only a simpleton could suspect him of pique!

She wanted to bang on the table in her vexation, remembering that when she had come down to dinner last evening he had given her not so much as a glance, even though she was wearing the evening gown which he most admired. She had not realised until that moment how she had come to rely on his nod of approval. But last night there was none. His eyes had been only for Valentine, who, after dressing so circumspectly since her arrival, was now confident enough to show herself in a daringly decolleté gown of ice blue, stunningly complimented by a magnificent sapphire necklace, which flashed against her pale skin. Small wonder her husband

178

was captivated, thought Lucy miserably. And he wasn't alone. Samuel couldn't take his eyes from her, and even Tom found it hard to ignore such a vision. Lord Oswaldeston was wise enough to concentrate his attentions on his pettishly pouting wife, for she was appalled at the ease with which the creature had stolen her limelight, but the sympathetic glance Mr Thorne had sent Lucy was enough to make *her* abandon all hope. Why, even Mary had called Valentine a fairy princess! It was too much!

The evening had been one of unmitigated misery and, as she remembered it now, she could not help but wonder how she had come to be so mistaken in Alex. Before last night she had begun to develop a certain admiration, even fondness for him, which made their present way of going on possible. She would have sworn that his own sense of fitness would have prevented him from abandoning so entirely the behaviour of a gentleman. Not so! Not the most determined flirt could have bettered his performance: singing with Lady D'Avergne; accompanying her on the piano; listening as if fascinated, to reminiscences which poured from her lips in the devastatingly attractive accent, while her eyes held his captive. He asked no other lady to entertain them, and was assiduous in his attentions only to her. Every movement Alexander made was designed to prove to anyone in doubt that he had indeed brought his mistress into his home, and the company could only look on speechless in wonder.

Léo alone was gratified, and his ugly, monkey face gleamed with good humour in the candle light.

Lucy and Fanny retired early in high dudgeon, but as the evening wore on and Lucy still caught the strains of a pianoforte from below, it became clear that Lady D'Avergne had no intention of giving up the advantage and following their example.

Reclining in her bed, reading fretfully, Lucy had furiously watched the clock reach and then pass the hour of twelve, and still she had heard music. She *would* not look at the clock again and resolutely blew out her candle, but by the time sleep had claimed her no footsteps had passed her door. Small wonder that this morning she felt so low!

Reaching unconsciously towards her coffee cup, she was about to pour in some cream when she noticed the coffee in it had gone cold with all her musings. She felt the coffee pot, realised that that too was no longer hot, and rang the little hand bell for her serving maid, who came bustling in in an instant. While she was waiting for more coffee, the demands of the kitten on the floor became more pressing and she felt his claws catching in the fine muslin of her dress.

'Do be good, Smudge!' she said sharply, patting him heavily away. But then, at the reproachful look he threw her, she was ashamed of her bad temper.

'Poor kitty. I shouldn't blame you, should I?' and she picked up a saucer to pour him some cream, which she placed on the floor nearby.

All was immediately forgiven, as the kitten bent his head towards the creamy pool, leaving Lucy to her journal and her doldrums. She was still morosely staring at nothing when the girl brought in fresh coffee and a fresh jug of cream. Noticing her cap was crooked, she was just about to scold her pettishly when a strange retching sound caught her ear. Glancing down, she saw that the sound emanated from Smudge, lying stretched on the carpet, his face and body contorted agonisingly as he tried unsuccessfully to vomit. She watched horrified for some seconds, expecting every moment for him to dislodge from his throat whatever was troubling him, thinking it must be a fur ball or perhaps a small bone. But as the seconds went by, the animal continued to writhe and she knew that more drastic action was required.

The serving maid was flapping uselessly around the room until Lucy gathered her wits and cried out sharply,

'Quickly girl! Salt and water—lots of it. We must make him sick.'

The girl continued to stare blankly unmoving until Lucy pushed her firmly from the room. As soon as she had gone Lucy turned her attention to the suffering kitten, whose eyes by now were starting from his head, as his back arched and fell with his retchings. Lucy sat on the floor beside him, took hold of the fur at the back of his neck and put a finger into his mouth to try to make him sick, but without success. Only a moment later, Mrs Perry came bustling into the room with a jug and a bowl of salt in her hands, the girl at her heels.

'Quickly,' called Lucy urgently, jumping up with the cat in her arms. 'Bring it outside, Mrs Perry.'

Lucy went before her, carrying the wretched creature and placed him on the ground, where he continued his contortions. Mrs Perry mixed a strong solution of salt water and, motioning to Lucy to hold the kitten still, she pulled his mouth open and ruthlessly poured the noxious liquid down his throat. Smudge pulled his head frantically away from her and some of the salt water was spilt on Lucy's dress, but the two women had done the trick. In only a few seconds the kitten began vomiting and didn't stop again until he lay in a heap exhausted.

'What could have caused such a thing, Ma'am?' asked Mrs Perry anxiously, when they had cleaned him and made him more comfortable. 'There's been no rat-catching going on for months, so he can't have picked up anything in the barns—and anyway, he's almost never away from the house. It's queer as a hatband.'

'He probably swallowed a fish bone or something.'

'Where could he get fishbones at *your* table, Your Ladyship? He couldn't. Not at breakfast. It's a rare mystery.'

'You know what a greedy little thing he is,' replied her mistress, with typical unconcern. 'Who knows what he has been eating? I don't think it's so mysterious. Only think how he manages to look half-starved even when he's just eaten an enormous meal. I can imagine how he must grovel for food in the kitchens, and everyone quite convinced that he is fading away.'

'That's as may be, Ma'am,' said Mrs Perry, refusing to be quieted. 'But I still say it's a queer thing!'

CHAPTER

17

The storm which had threatened all that day burst forth finally and spectacularly during the night, to leave the world on the morrow fresh and green.

When Lucy, smart and pretty in a house dress of lemon spotted muslin, entered the breakfasting parlour, she was surprised to find the Earl there, seated alone at the table, hidden behind his newspaper. He did not look up at her entry, and bristling at his lack of courtesy, she joined him without a word, pausing only to pick up the journal she had been reading on the previous day, which she propped up before her in emulation of his manner.

She had almost finished her breakfast and had fully satisfied herself that it was to be a silent one, when the Earl put down his newspaper, let fall his quizzing glass, leaned back in his chair so that only its two back legs rested on the floor, and asked abruptly,

'So, Lady Sheldon. How much longer are we to enjoy Mr Thorne's company?'

Lucy looked up in surprise.

'How long are Lady D'Avergne and her brother to remain at Arunfold?' she returned shortly. 'Mr Thorne is Lady Fanny's house guest, not mine, and since she invited him to remain for the duration of Lady D'Avergne's stay, I don't know how you can possibly expect *me* to tell you when Mr Thorne is going. Your information must be better than mine.'

And she returned to her journal, turning its page briskly.

If she expected a scene, she was disappointed, since, with no more than an angry glare, her husband picked up his paper again and returned to his reading. For a time the room was silent, apart from rustlings from Smudge, now fully recovered and playing with a skein of wool, which he had teased out of Lucy's workbox and strung in knots around the legs of a footstool.

Lucy was about to get up from the table to disentangle it, when her husband once more lifted his head from his newspaper and said, a fraction less frostily,

'This houseparty: since it seems to be going on for ever, what think you to giving our guests some better entertainment? We're all as dull as ditchwater. What do you say to an archery contest? We could invite all the families from roundabout and make a thing of it. Prince Regent's rules; prizes; you know the style of thing. And to end up with, a ball in the evening. Do it on a grand scale. Haven't had anything like it here for years.'

'Now I wonder who could have put such an idea into your head,' remarked Lucy mildly, for she had overheard Valentine only the evening before suggest the scheme to the Earl. Indeed, remembering with what elegant ease the lady was able to hit the target, apparently whenever she wished, Lucy could hardly blame her for wanting a chance to show off.

His lordship reddened. 'What does it matter who thought of it? You've spent quite enough time these past few days being coached by Mr Thorne to like the idea. And if you are worried about the arrangements, Fanny will assist you. Lady D'Avergne would be only too pleased to give you the benefit of her experience, or, if you prefer, I could send to London for my secretary. He is extraordinarily good at that sort of thing. I shouldn't expect you to deal with the arrangements for the shooting, of course. Just the refreshments and the ball. If you ask for advice you should be able to manage quite well.'

Now it was Lucy's turn to redden. She did not need three guesses to decide from which corner had come the idea that she might be incompetent.

'I think you need not trouble yourself, my lord,' she replied coolly. 'I will naturally see to any arrangements in my own house. And certainly, I do not envisage too many problems in arranging for a ball. I have not Lady D'Avergne's experience, of course—how should I when I have not nearly so many years—but yet I am not completely a novice. It has been known for my Aunt to offer refreshments, and we have even given parties, though I think it will come as a severe shock to you to hear it! No—my only fear is to wonder how many of our neighbours will agree to come to the house when Lady D'Avergne is staying here.'

The Earl said icily, 'But Ma'am, you have just pointed out that this is *your* house, and I think that none will care to insult you by refusing your invitation.'

It was settled between them that the contest should be held the following week, giving all those fortunate enough to receive such an invitation a full seven days to arrange for costumes and to practise their archery.

When their guests were informed of their plans they could speak of little else, immediately taking down for assistance Mr Waring's excellent little handbook from its place on the library shelf, and noting among the multiplicity of other useful facts set out on its well-thumbed pages that "care should be taken that every member's coat be cut from the same cloth." Since Fanny could by no means share the author's enthusiasm for such an idea, Samuel quickly expressed it as his opinion that the rule applied only to regular clubs and need not concern them. Perhaps they should all wear green, he thought, just to keep to the spirit of the venture, but nothing more.

There was some disagreement as to prizes, Fanny being determined that nothing shabby should be given, but vetoing all the admirable suggestions put forward by Lady Valentine. Lucy kept well out of it and finally it was agreed by the others to award a gold bugle to the gentleman champion, in the spirit of Robin Hood, and to the lady champion, a gold hair slide in the shape of an arrow, appropriately studded with pearls and emeralds to imitate feathers.

Samuel agreed, good-naturedly, to oversee all the outdoor arrangements for the contest, since he was the most enthusiastic sportsman among them and, as a result, little was seen of him all week. To him fell the appointment of all officials with special duties for the day—standard bearers; markers to signal each shot; officials to set up targets and ensure that the Prince Regent's lengths were strictly adhered to, and everyone else without whom the day would be a failure. All took time, and he was seen scurrying to and from the estates early and late in his efforts to select good men from among the tenantry to see that nothing was left undone.

Lucy too was well occupied, but she was a born organiser and found it no very arduous task, rather enjoying seeing all her arrangements gradually slot into place.

During the afternoon on the day before the contest she was sitting at the table in her favourite salon, ticking off items from a long list of reminders for the morrow, when her husband, who had left the others riding in the grounds, came through the

186

French windows to catch her there. Since her back was towards the windows, she did not immediately perceive him and he was able to come up silently behind her, to see what she was doing, before she felt his presence in the room. She started up in surprise as his shadow fell onto her papers.

'Gracious, what a start you gave me, sir,' she exclaimed breathlessly, standing up quickly and holding a hand to her bodice. 'I thought you were riding with the others.'

'I was, but I began to wonder what mischief you were up to. But I can see that I've maligned you. I'd no idea that you had so much to do for this wretched ball. Let me look at that list. "Numbers of card tables; Cards; Fresh Packs for each; Candles; Spare supplies for all rooms; Flowers; Lists of music; Intended order of dances; Dance cards for ladies." Good heavens, woman. You must have wished me at the Devil a thousand times. Certainly you will wish you had sent for my secretary as I suggested.'

'Nonsense. I like it!'

'Is there no end to your talents, Lady Sheldon? Languages, music, geography, and now, clever hostess. Anyone who did not know the true state of our relationship must certainly think me the luckiest of men.'

'Even I don't know the true nature of our relationship, my lord,' she replied tartly, remembering his recent transgressions. 'And as for clever hostess,' she went on before he could say another word, 'Perhaps you should wait to find out. I might make an awful mess of it. Though I must say that I don't think I will, for to be able to do it in style is most agreeable. Not to have to contrive little economies is very pleasant, though I couldn't expect you to know that.'

'I haven't always had *everything* I've wanted,' he returned sharply, stung by her words.

'Yes, yes! I am sure you have been used most wickedly,' she replied sweetly, a gleam of mischief in her eye. 'It must be hard indeed to do without life's little necessities.'

'You are determined to despise me, aren't you Lucy?' he said, taking her by the shoulders and pulling her towards him so that she had to look at him.

'The word "determined" suggests that I have laboured at it, sir,' she replied with deceptive meekness, 'but yours has been all the work. Why, you have tried so hard to give me reasons to despise you recently that there has been very little for me to do.'

She tried to keep her voice steady and to pull away from him as she spoke, but he would not release her. She was forced to raise her eyes and face him again.

'Tell me then, won't you, just what you fancy I have done,' said the Earl quietly.

'I don't *fancy* anything, Sheldon. Indeed, nothing I have seen here since Lady D'Avergne's arrival has been to my fancy.'

'Trust you to have a clever retort, my dear. I would be disappointed if you didn't. But punning won't help sort out this mess. Tell me instead if I may expect never to receive a more friendly answer from you. Do you *really* despise me. Certainly you enjoy telling me how much you dislike me, but this dislike—has it become a habit with you, or do you indeed hate me so much? You mustn't, you know. I never meant you to.'

His words were entirely unexpected and, furious at her weakness, she felt tears stinging her eyes. 'Hate you? No . . . I . . . Indeed I . . .' She broke off in confusion, looking down at her hands so he should not know how he affected her.

But he *had* seen. She heard his sudden intake of breath and then the words,

'Lucy. Lucy, my dear . . .' as the pressure on her shoulders increased. He leaned towards her as if to kiss her, and to her surprise, Lucy found herself moving forward to receive him.

Before their lips touched, they heard simultaneously a thud of hooves coming across the lawns towards the house. The mood was broken, Lucy released, and blushing violently they both moved towards the French windows in confusion, only to see a riderless horse thundering past outside, from the direction of the West Lawns where Alexander had left the remainder of the party.

'It's Brigg!' cried Alexander, as the horse bolted round the side of the house towards the stables. 'Something's happened to Sam! I'm getting saddled up again.'

Before he had a chance to run more than a few steps, Lucy had glimpsed in the distance a small band of horsemen coming out of the woodland below, one of whom was being led. As the group got closer, Alexander and Lucy could see that it was Sam, on Lord Oswaldeston's horse, and being led by him. Sam's arm was wrapped in a rough sling fashioned from his cravat, and he was looking decidedly pale.

As soon as the riders were near enough to the house, their host ran forward to meet them, an anxious crease between his brows.

'Sam, old fellow. What happened? Just saw Brigg, bolting past in a lather, racing for the stables.'

'Merest piece of bad luck, old man,' replied his cousin with a wry grin. 'Took a toss.'

'A toss? You? You're roasting me,' exclaimed the Earl incredulously, as he helped him down. Best horseman I know.'

'Kind of you, coz, but we all take a toss now and again, don't you know.'

'Really Alex. You'd be better occupied in seeing that no harm has come to Brigg than with all your questions. Poor Samuel fell on his wrist. It needs a cold compress if he's to have any chance of entering the contest tomorrow.'

'Of course he will enter,' returned her brother. 'He's the best of all of us. I'll not hear of you crying off, old fellow.'

'Not a chance. But I'll have to do something about my wrist right away.'

The Earl was soon demanding the full story of his cousin's accident from Lord Oswaldeston.

'How came he to do such a stupid thing, Piers? I've seen him ride any time this last fifteen years and he's never been thrown. How did it happen?'

'Can't tell you, old man,' replied his brother-in-law, not particularly interested. 'Wasn't paying much attention. Shouldn't let it worry you. If I know Sam, he'll be there with the rest of us tomorrow. He won't let a little thing like a fall ruin his chances. Once he sets his mind on something he never gives it up.'

Lord Oswaldeston was wrong. When Samuel came down to breakfast next day, his arm was still in a sling, and he declared his wrist to be too swollen to enter the day's proceedings. Not only that, but his man was of the opinion that it would take at least a week to heal, and perhaps even two!

Samuel wouldn't hear of anyone taking over his arrangements, and was soon seeing to all the final details outside, while Lucy completed those indoors.

By one o'clock, all had been made ready, and favoured guests were beginning to arrive just as their own party assembled on the lawns in front of the house to compare costumes.

Lucy's heart sank when she saw Valentine. In bright green velvet, which clung to every curve and with a roguish cap, from which hung a saucy green feather, she was a sight to behold. Green, on the other hand, had never been Lucy's colour, a fact which she had come to admit, if only to herself, since the Earl had interested himself in her wardrobe, and she had had to come to terms with the knowledge that, on this all-important day, she could hardly hope to be in her best looks. But she had asked Mrs Gardiner's advice on the matter anyway.

Mrs Gardiner had by no means considered the case hopeless, and had applied herself to the problem with vigour, bending the rules on colour only slightly and producing a charming round dress of grey-green zephyrine silk, cut tight to the bosom and ornamented with tiny arrow-shapes in velvet at the hem of the skirt. Until she saw Valentine, Lucy thought it answered very well, but one glimpse of Madame showed her that she had wasted Mrs Gardiner's time.

Among the lower sorts of people only the Earl's tenants and their families had been admitted to Arunfold for the day. As for the Earl's more aristocratic neighbours, their presence was restricted by invitation so as to ensure that the number attending remained within the limits of convenience for the dinner and ball to be held later. As a result the merry band of archers was a very select one, most of whom were already known to Lucy, but who now treated her with a new respect more in keeping with her exalted state. As she stood by the Earl's side to greet them and they took trouble to be courteous to her, she reflected on how pleasant her life might be if only hers had been a conventional marriage.

Predictably, among the early arrivals were the Thornes. Charles had ridden over to his home on the previous evening to provide an escort for his father and sister, and they arrived in good time in the travelling chaise which had been adapted to convey the Viscount in comfort.

As she descended from her father's chaise, it became clear to those who watched that the lovely Gwendolyn was set fair to rival Lady D'Avergne, for her gown had been cut into a boyish style which, on her, quite took the breath away, and made Lady Fanny, who was herself determined to be the most admired lady of the day, pout prettily.

Fanny had cheated shamefully, being the only lady to wear white, albeit lavishly trimmed with green and silver acorns, confiding to the others ingenuously that green was the most trying colour to wear, wasn't it, and she could hardly be scolded, could she, since it was their contest?

The Earl himself went forward to help Viscount Thorne down the steps from his chaise. To ensure that his old friend and neighbour would find as much comfort at Arunfold as he could at home, one of the downstairs rooms in the house had been especially prepared for him, where a cheerful fire had been lit so he would not feel any damp, books left out for his entertainment and a cold collation to satisfy his appetite. Done with the best of intentions, it seemed not to please the Viscount, who said irascibly,

'There you go again, m'boy. Trying to get me buried before I'm dead.'

'Nothing of the sort, Father,' said Gwendolyn embarrassed, 'Lord Sheldon is being neighbourly, if you will let him, and I shall certainly thank him if you do not have the grace for it, for if you don't need to rest later, I am certain I shall.'

The Viscount was immediately contrite.

'Of course I'm grateful, my boy, really I am,' he said, turning to the Earl and clasping him on the shoulder in apology. 'But it's deuced hard to be reminded how feeble you are on such a glorious day— as you'll know to your cost when you're my age. Let me tell you, my lad, twenty years ago nothing would have stopped me from running off with your prizes.'

'So I've heard, Sir,' replied the Earl smiling. 'I well remember my father telling me that you were the best archer in these parts. Seen some of your trophies too. Maybe you'll even feel like trying a few shots today. Show us whippersnappers a thing or two.'

The Viscount looked down ruefully at his gnarled hands. 'Much I could do with these, m'boy. Still I'm interested to see how Charles fares. We'll go down, shall we, and meet you later? You'll be stuck here a while doing the pretty if I'm not mistaken.'

'Are you *quite* sure you feel up to it, Father,' said Charles, eager to take his place in the lists, but considerate as always for his father's comfort.

'Don't you start, Charles,' he replied tetchily. Then more gently, 'Come on, boy, before it's all over. Let's see if you can't win something.'

Charles took his father's arm and threaded it through his.

'Can I tempt you to take my other arm, Lady Sheldon?' Charles asked Lucy, for Gwendolyn had already been claimed by Tom, and along with Lady D'Avergne and her brother, was already saunter-ing down towards the enclosure.

The Earl was not pleased to notice the silent en-treaty in Mr Thorne's eyes, but, in the event, Lucy knew her duty too well and remained by her hus-band's side.

Swallowing his disappointment, Charles walked away from the house, his father leaning heavily on his arm as they followed the others.

CHAPTER

18

A few of their most respected neighbours were so tardy in making an appearance that it was some while before the Earl and his wife were freed from the receiving line. Eventually, Sheldon decided that they had been patient long enough and, drawing his wife's arm through his in a picture of agreeable domesticity, he led her from the front of the house towards the West Lawn, today a riot of colour in the sunlight.

At the Earl's suggestion, Samuel had arranged to have several marquees erected, which surrounded the northern end of the archery enclosure in a semi-circle, to provide shade and hold refreshments for the gathering. Every marquee was coloured differently, and from the top of each flew multi-coloured banners, exotically reminiscent of ancient jousting tournaments. The enclosure itself was festooned with more banners, interrupted by massive baskets of flowers, and just by its entrance was sited a bandstand, from which wafted the insistent strains of a waltz.

'How well your cousin has organised everything, my lord,' said Lucy, determined to be pleasant, and eager to avoid any gaps in their conversation after their encounter of the previous day. 'Really I cannot think how it would have been managed without him.'

'Oh Sam's a Trojan,' he replied at once, quite at his ease. 'It's deuced bad luck that he cannot shoot today, for he's an exceptional shot. I'd have liked you to see him.'

Though the group of archers was a select one, it was yet large enough to mean that a good deal of shooting must be completed if all were to be accommodated and no time had been lost in starting. By the time the Earl and Countess neared the enclosure things were well under way, and they could hear the dull thud of arrows interspersed with polite applause. It was a perfect day for archery: the sun warm, but not excessively so; a suggestion of a breeze, cool enough to calm burning cheeks, yet not windy enough to despoil any careful coiffure or send an arrow off course. Looking around her Lucy felt all the charm of the moment. For a few hours at least she would try to ignore Lady Valentine, just then being attentively escorted by Samuel toward the spectators' seats. Everywhere she looked joyful young people were preparing for play, while their elders looked on indulgently from the stands, or helped themselves to the delicacies Mrs Perry had had prepared for their luncheon. Lucy's face beamed in the afternoon sunshine only to think that she had helped to arrange such pleasant activity and she was so engrossed in the scene around her that she didn't notice the long, thoughtful look the Earl gave her.

Presently she shook herself from her happy thoughts and prepared to follow the stream of those going into the enclosure itself, when her husband put a hand on her arm to prevent her. Surprised, she turned enquiringly to him, as he pulled her to one side.

'I've had no chance to tell you how smart you

look today, Lady Sheldon,' he said, smiling in a way which made her heart leap.

Lucy blushed, but she could not prevent her tongue.

'Now then Sir,' she said pertly, placing a finger to one side of her mouth, 'is it written in our marriage contract that you must say pretty things to me? I've forgotten.'

'Lucy, you vixen,' replied her lord, between amusement and annoyance. 'Won't you ever cry truce with me?'

'Oh today I am in charity with everyone, sir,' taking up his smile.

'Even me?'

'Oh yes. For I am not at all nice. Ask anyone.'

'No, you are *not*' he said, tucking her hand firmly under his arm. 'But I won't quarrel with you today, and especially when you are looking so well. Mrs Gardiner's notion of grey-green was an inspired one.'

'What makes you think it was *her* idea?'

'It could not possibly be yours, could it? Had you allowed yourself to have your head you would be in rainbow-coloured silk or something just as hideous,' replied her husband, unperturbed by signs of a growing storm.

'Oh, you are impossible!' she cried, snatching her hand away.

'So I understand, my love. But may I anyway be allowed to wish you luck?' he asked, grinning now with more confidence.

Before she had a chance to realise what he was about, he calmly pulled her back towards him with one hand, while with his free one he tilted back her chin and kissed her firmly on the mouth, holding her until he chose to release her.

Lucy, infuriated by his impudence, would have protested, but noticed several amused faces around them who had seen the incident and taken it to be husbandly ardour, quite permissible in a new bride-groom. She knew she would only look foolish if she made a fuss and was forced to assume a smile, while whispering indignantly under her breath.

'Don't you have any shame, sir?'

'Very little, I'm afraid,' he replied, smiling broadly. 'But it is not so bad, after all. I am only picking up where we left off yesterday.'

'I suppose I need not have expected you to behave properly after all that has occurred in this house recently.'

'If,' said her lord, the smile hardening on his lips, 'You refer to Lady D'Avergne's continued presence in our home, perhaps I might suggest that your own behaviour with a certain party might bear a little examination.'

As if on cue, from among the crowd, Mr Thorne's massive presence strolled toward Lucy with a pro-prietory air.

'My dear Lady Sheldon, we are all waiting for you,' he called when he saw her. 'Come now, or I shall miss the pleasure of seeing you win.'

Never had Lucy been less pleased to see anyone, for she would have liked to pursue this very interesting conversation with her husband. She was considering what excuse she could offer for refusing to go with him when, to her intense annoyance, the Earl had the effrontery to say to Mr Thorne,

'Lucy win? Flying kites aren't you, old chap. Lady Sheldon may have improved, under your expert tuition (and so much of it, to be sure), but she hasn't a hope against Lady D'Avergne. Valentine has the strongest wrist of any woman I know. I've never seen her lose. Lucky if the Countess manages to do half as well.'

Mr Thorne could not allow this challenge to his favourite to pass unheeded. 'I don't know why you

197

should wish to humiliate your wife, Sheldon,' he said heatedly, 'and I daresay you'll say it's no business of mine. But I'll lay you twenty guineas that she wins.'

'I'm not surprised you'll only wager such a paltry sum,' replied Lord Sheldon maddeningly. 'No point in throwing good money after bad. Lady D'Avergne is named "Diana the Huntress" by those who have seen her shoot, which speaks for itself.'

'Oh, is that because of her archery?' asked Lucy sweetly.

'Naughty!' replied her husband appreciatively, thoroughly enjoying himself. 'But what say you, Charles, to raising our wager to fifty guineas?'

'Fifty: a hundred: what you will! You will eat your words when Lady Sheldon wins the prize.'

'Oh, I think not, old man. But a hundred guineas will do nicely.'

'Don't be foolish, Mr Thorne,' cried Lucy frantically. 'Sheldon is right. I could not possibly beat Lady D'Avergne.'

'I have the greatest faith in all that you do, Ma'am,' said Mr Thorne staunchly, adding disconcertingly, 'and if you don't win, I'd rather lose a hundred guineas on you than bet on any other lady.'

'Magnanimous Charles, but foolish nonetheless,' declared the Earl, heartily amused at his confusion.

'It will give me the greatest pleasure to see you eat your words, sir!' he replied frostily, taking Lucy's arm and leading her into the enclosure, while her husband followed behind, a gleam of mischief in his eye.

Taking her place with the other ladies in her heat, Lucy was put out to discover that, as well as a Miss Darnley and a Miss Hooper, both of whom were slightly known to her, she had been drawn against Lady D'Avergne.

Miss Darnley, an athletic Amazon of a girl was

to shoot first. She looked, to Lucy, as if she would be a competent archer, but her shooting did not match her appearance and she managed only to hit the target with the last of her four arrows, and even then only managed to get into the blue. She retired quickly to polite applause.

Miss Hooper, a tiny blonde, was rather better and managed two arrows in the blue and one in the black, while only one went wide of the mark.

With a highest score of only thirteen to beat, Lady D'Avergne seemed quietly confident as she took her place, looking to the marker for his signal to begin. She took her time to prepare her shots, for her figure was never displayed to quite such advantage as when she was shooting with the long bow. Her first shot was magnificent and landed in the Red circle. She looked into the crowd and smiled triumphantly at her brother nearby, her catlike face sharp with pleasure. Her other three shots were less impressive, but still she completed her round with a score of eighteen, to enthusiastic applause, especially from the men.

Now it was Lucy's turn, and she viewed the target with increasing trepidation. Somehow it looked much further away than sixty yards, and surely the day seemed to have suddenly become much warmer? Her hands were moist in her leather gloves as she took the first of her arrows from her quiver and placed it to her bow. The spectators disappeared in a blur as she forced herself to concentrate, tensing the string with all her strength to release the arrow. It went wide, missing the target by a full foot: not only that, but it was the worst shot of the heat! Lucy was mortified. From the corner of her eye she saw Miss Darnley looking suddenly more cheerful, and she panicked. Nearby Mr Thorne chewed on his lip.

Taking her second arrow, Lucy put it to her bow.

Her forehead shone wet, and she was forced to put her arrow down again so that she could wipe it, wishing all the time that the ground would swallow her up. Just then she happened to catch sight of her husband in the crowd: in the next seat, and in animated conversation with him, was Lady D'Avergne. Heads together they both had their eyes fixed on Lucy and they were laughing.

With renewed determination Lucy drew back her bow. This time she made no mistake, and the arrow landed in the Red band, to huge applause. Satisfied, she looked for Mr Thorne and returned his warm smile. Her third arrow gained her a respectable black, but still gave her an aggregate score of only ten. She had done well, but certainly it looked as if she must resign herself to defeat.

Again she prepared to fire, but just as she pulled back the string she heard a light laugh from the audience, which she recognised as issuing from Lady D'Avergne. It was just too loud for politeness, and several spectators turned to hush her, one or two going so far as to hint to their neighbours that Lady Valentine was trying to distract Lucy. There were murmurs of "shame", intended to show disapproval, for many of the Earl's neighbours, though forced through Lucy's presence to accept Lady D'Avergne, could not be pleased to have her among them and were glad of any opportunity to voice their annoyance. Unfortunately, their murmurs had little effect on the Frenchwoman, but disconcerted Lucy instead. She lowered her arrow, her eyes scanning the audience to rest once more on her husband: on his face was an expression which stated so plainly that she had no chance that Lucy was again filled with grim purpose, necessary purpose, since nothing less than a shot in the Gold would give her points enough to win.

Placing her arrow for the last time, she pulled

back the string and fired. She had made a perfect winning shot and, to tumultuous applause, Lady D'Avergne was displaced from the contest.

The first person to congratulate Lucy was Fanny, who ran up and threw her arms round her in ecstasy.

'My dear girl,' she crowed. 'How perfectly splendid of you to beat that odious woman. Not that I had any doubts, of course, as you may guess, but I kept my fingers and toes crossed just in case. I should have loathed her even more than I do already had she won.'

Lucy returned her hug with relief, beginning to enjoy herself at last, until she suddenly caught sight of Lady D'Avergne's brother standing just behind Fanny. He had heard Fanny's unguarded words, and for a moment he looked as though he could cheerfully kill them both. Noticing that Lucy had seen him too, however, his expression switched immediately to one of complaisance, and he raised his hat in compliment. She could do nothing but nod back at him, though she knew how nonsensical it was. His dark looks had unsettled her. More than ever his ugly face reminded her that she had enemies about her. But she would not let him see that she was perturbed. Turning back to Fanny, who had not noticed him, she asked her saucily, though she already knew what her answer would be,

'Well, Fanny, and when are we to have the pleasure of seeing you shooting, dearest?'

'I? Shoot? Good heavens, my love. What an idea! *I* don't shoot! If I wished to have arms like a costermonger, why I am sure I could think of dozens of less exhausting ways to secure them.'

Lucy choked in appreciation, and Fanny began to giggle with her, her laughter so infectious that others around them could not resist joining her. Their high spirits soon led Tom and Gwendolyn in their direction eager to add their congratulations to Fanny's. As if she had won the whole contest rather than a single heat, she was toasted in champagne, grandly ordered by the Earl's sister for the occasion. Amidst all the extravagant compliments showered upon her, the Earl's absence went unnoticed by the others. Only Lucy realised that he had not moved from his seat next to Lady D'Avergne and she was nettled enough not to be able to resist mentioning the wager he had struck with Mr Thorne, for she knew that they would all be on her side.

Fanny was, if anything, more disgusted at this than the others.

'I simply do not understand the man,' she cried vexedly. 'If he was odious to everyone perhaps I could understand it, but it is so unlike.'

She pouted crossly as she found him in the crowd and noticed his neighbour. 'Well, for all that he is my brother, I think him a brute and a bore. And it is all that woman's fault. Thank heaven Charles put him in his place.'

'I think it was Lucy who put him in his place,' said Gwendolyn smilingly. 'Even if she doesn't win the final round she has still beaten his champion and, incidentally, won my brother's wager for him. He won't like that much.'

They were all much struck by the thought: delighted that Lord Sheldon had for once proved less shrewd than Mr Thorne, whose own absence was explained by the fact that his heat was, at that very moment, being announced.

Gwendolyn wanted to watch her brother and drew Lucy along with her towards the stands, but as soon as Lucy noticed that in order to reach an empty place she must pass her husband, she remembered several things left undone for the evening ball, and excused herself with alacrity, promising to return to the enclosure in plenty of time for the final heat of her own contest. Refusing Fanny's offer of assistance, she drew away from them, noticing as she did so that her husband too was now standing up, for he had been drawn against Mr Thorne. She was half-inclined to watch, for she was curious to know who was the better man, but wouldn't give Sheldon the satisfaction of appearing interested.

Lucy had put down her parasol somewhere and she now found the day too warm to relish crossing the lawns to the house in the full glare of the sun without. She decided, instead, to go by way of the track of woodland which skirted the west lawns in a continuous stretch to the gravel walkway fronting the house.

After her exertions it was refreshing to walk amidst the sheltering trees and she dawdled along, reliving in her mind the triumphant moment of her recent victory.

Since that part of the woodland was normally little used the path was thickly overgrown and strewn with half-rotted leaves and tree debris. As she walked she felt little pieces being trapped among the thongs of her Roman sandals and scolded herself for being so foolish as to try to walk through the wood in them. She lifted the hem of her dress and clucked to see the dust which had dirtied her feet and ankles. She would have to change her stockings when she got back, she thought, as she let down her skirts. Every moment her sandals became more uncomfortable until eventually she felt she could walk no further. Bowing to the inevitable Lucy put down her bow and quiver and leaned down towards her sandal. As she bent to untie it her ear caught a slight noise. Something had moved in a bush nearby. For an instant she was uneasy then, with a little shake of the head, she laughed to herself. Of course there would be people in the wood on such a day. She brushed her foot, retied her sandal and moved towards the house. She had gone only a few steps, before she remembered her bow and arrow, and she turned back in order to retrieve it. As she turned she felt a burning sensation at the top of her arm and felt herself being propelled backwards against a tree. In astonishment she looked down at her sleeve, now pinned to the tree by an elaborately decorated arrow, and for the first time in her life she felt herself fainting quietly away. As her senses ebbed, she felt her sleeve rip and saw, amidst swirls of vagueness, her husband, bow in hand, coming towards her. She turned her head away from him in sudden fear and saw, not twenty yards from him, half hidden in the shadow of a fir tree, the dark figure of Miss Mincham: her face a picture of satisfaction.

CHAPTER

19

As Lucy found her wits returning, she felt herself being lifted. She did not need to open her eyes to know that it was her husband who had taken her up and was prey to a confusion of emotions.

She fought the lassitude and managed to open her eyes, to find herself looking straight into her husband's dark, troubled ones, searching her face with concern.

She heard herself saying weakly. 'There really is no need to carry me, sir. I can walk very well.'

'Of course you can. And you shall do so if you really think it worth making the effort. But we are very nearly at the house, you know, and it hardly seems worth it since I have you.'

This sounded so much like commonsense that she remained where she was and further obeyed his wishes by closing her eyes again.

She heard her voice, as if from a great distance, and even to her her words sounded incredibly childish.

'You won't let me fall, will you?'

'No, I won't let you fall,' he replied calmly. 'You are quite safe, for I have you.'

She was comforted and allowed herself to rest easily in his arms.

Even with her eyes closed she knew when they reached the gravelled courtyard in front of the house, for when the Earl stepped onto firmer ground, a shuddering pain shot through her arm, proving more than she could bear. She fell once more through the darkness . . .

She was lying on the bed in her room when she awoke, to an insistent voice. The curtains of her fourposter were pulled partly around and the blinds at the window let down. A dimly lit lamp glowed just out of her vision. In the background hovered Miss Havering, hurrying to collect a bowl and cloths while the Earl sat on the bed beside Lucy, peering anxiously into his wife's face saying her name over in a calm, steady voice.

When Lucy's eyes flickered open he gave a satisfied nod and reached to take the tray from Miss Havering, wasting no words of thanks, but saying briefly,

'Downstairs, if you please, Miss Havering. Some brandy.'

Miss Havering clearly felt that no better courtesy was required for she went at once.

Lucy heard her husband's voice again,

'Now Lucy, we must take a look at your arm and I think, my dear, that you may need to "bite on the bullet", as your Papa might have said.'

Lucy was intrigued at once,

'I think I never heard such an expression, my lord. What does it mean?'

'It means, my dear, that you must prepare for a little pain.'

Lucy was not the daughter of a Major for nothing and gritted her teeth determinedly as her husband cut away the sleeve of her dress with the scissors Miss Havering had provided. It needed all her resolution for the material had already begun to stick to the wound, but she was determined that the Earl would find no fault with her courage and, though she felt nauseous as he eased the silk from her flesh, she remarked with a shaky laugh,

'My poor dress. How cross Mrs Gardiner and her young ladies will be.'

'Oh I think not,' replied her husband, without taking his eyes from the wound. 'While I am more than willing to admit that Mrs Gardiner did very well in the circumstances and made you look quite presentable, she would be the first to agree that you should never wear green if it is at all to be avoided. Grey; peach; white; they all look perfectly well on you. Leave green to those who can wear it to effect.'

'Meaning Lady D'Avergne, I suppose,' she replied, her brows drawing together.

'Not only her, though I must admit that she does look stunning in green. But then, she looks marvellous in anything, doesn't she!'

Lucy felt her bosom swell.

'Even now you cannot help but be disagreeable, can you.'

'No,' he agreed pleasantly, washing the wound carefully with some warm water and cotton. 'But then, I am a monster, don't you remember? You have been at pains to tell me so on more than one occasion.'

'Then it is gratifying to know that I did not exaggerate. I know of no other man who would sit here and compare me unfavourably with other women at a time like this.'

'Indeed I should hope not, Lady Sheldon, for I should certainly have something to say to any man I found on your bed, whatever he was saying to you. I've said it before, but your indelicacy shocks me at times!'

Lucy tried hard not to giggle: she was determined to be cross, but was so unsuccessful that she could only be pleased that he was still examining her arm.

By the time Miss Havering had returned with the brandy, the wound, which had been found to be not so deep as the Earl had feared, had been cleansed and bound, Lucy lying back on her pillows, pale but stoical.

When she heard Miss Havering re-enter, Lucy looked towards the door and eyed uneasily the tray she was carrying on which stood a glass and decanter.

'Oh not brandy,' she protested faintly. 'That really would be the last straw.'

Miss Havering made to remove the tray, but the Earl prevented her, taking it from her and placing it firmly on the bedside before dismissing her. When she had gone from the room, Sheldon returned to his wife with a grin.

'But my love, I am persuaded it will do you good,' he said provokingly, pouring a glass.

'You always are! And I suppose you will force it down my throat as you did before.'

'No,' he said disarmingly, as he moved the glass towards her lips and lifted her head from the pillow, 'but I really do wish you would take it.'

Lucy's eyes met her husband's, wondering at his gentleness. She sipped at the glass without a murmur.

The brandy began immediately to exercise its usual effect on Lucy and the Earl watched amused as her colour heightened and her eyes began to shine mistily. He knew her reserve was down when she admitted, some few moments later,

'I saw you in the wood ... Just after I had been hit. You had your bow with you.'

'And?'

'And ... well, I wondered what you were doing there ...'

208

'What do you think I was doing there?' he asked, staring at her so hard that had she not been sustained by the brandy she would have been afraid. As it was, she only returned his stare and waited.

'As you are too well-mannered to voice your suspicions, I suppose I must tell you—though since you are determined to think the worst of me I doubt you'll believe me . . . I saw you leave the enclosure just as it was my turn to shoot and, if you must know, I was pretty annoyed that you could not even be bothered to stay and watch me! Surely keeping up appearances was part of our bargain?'

'*I* keep up appearances?' she replied hotly. 'That is rich when you did not even leave Lady D'Avergne for long enough to congratulate me on wining my heat. I leave you to judge what our guests made of that!'

'So *that's* why you went off in a huff,' he laughed. 'Lucy, you *goose*! Surely you realised that I could not come to you then? It was my turn to shoot next. I didn't have *time!*'

'You certainly did not appear to be in a hurry, sir,' she said primly. 'And I did not go off in a huff. I had matters to attend to.'

'And I remained where I was only because it was my turn to shoot next,' he insisted.

'You always have an answer, but you still have not explained why you were in the wood.'

'I took my shots and then came after you. I wanted to congratulate you on your win,' he replied promptly.

'Do you really expect me to believe that? You didn't want me to win, else why would you back Valentine?'

'I wasn't sure how good you had become, you see. I suspected that if I backed Lady D'Avergne it might give you the edge. After all, aren't you the most obstinate woman I know?'

'If you expect me to believe that tale you must think me half-witted!'

'I said you wouldn't believe me.'

'And did you really follow me to congratulate me?' she asked wistfully.

'Not only that,' he had to admit. 'I wanted to give you a good scolding as well, for not waiting around long enough to see me beat that half-wit, Thorne. I thought very likely the wood would be the only place where we could be private enough for a good quarrel. And you know how we always enjoy them. It was a whim, nothing more. Certainly I did not go into the wood to shoot at you! I admit to being cross, but that would be going a little far even for me!'

'Then who was it? You were there so quickly that you *must* have seen someone.'

'That's what so damnable. I didn't see anyone. I was so worried when you fell that I didn't get a chance to see who had shot at you. I was a little way from you and by the time I had reached you there wasn't a soul to be seen.'

'Not even Mincham?'

'Mincham? What a strange thing to say. Why should she be there?'

'She *was* there! I saw her!'

'You're imagining it. I must have seen her had she been there.'

'That's just what I was thinking.'

'I see,' he said thoughtfully. 'And have you really convinced yourself that either I shot at you or I am in league with Mincham to dispose of you? You read too many of Mrs Radcliffe's tales. Don't you think it more likely that someone was practising in the wood and hit you by mistake? Only think how frightened they would be to see they'd hit someone. Surely anyone might run away in fright on the spur of the moment.'

'I don't know what to think. But I *know* I saw Mincham and I saw her in the wood. I didn't tell you, but she was there once before. She frightened me!'

'You are overwrought and tired or you would not be so foolish,' he said, pushing the hair from her eyes. 'Get some rest now and I will come up to see you later.'

'I haven't time to rest,' she said pettishly, raising herself on the pillows. 'I've the ball to prepare for.'

'You will prepare for nothing,' he said firmly, pressing her down again. 'You are to get into bed like a good girl. I shall tell our guests what has occurred and Fanny can take your place as hostess. You are not well enough to go to the ball.'

'But my new dress! I've had it specially made.'

'Indeed? Let me guess,' he said, lightly running a finger along her chin. 'Bright green and yellow stripes?'

She flushed furiously and sat up. 'No it is not! Mrs Gardiner designed it for me.'

'Then I am sure it is most becoming and I promise to have another ball very soon so that you may wear it,' he replied, pushing her firmly back on her pillows. 'For now you must remain quietly here.'

'Impossible, Alex. Who will get everything finished?'

'Give me your precious list and I promise to see that all is as you would like.'

'You will not ask Lady D'Avergne to do it?'

He laughed indulgently, took her list and promised that Lady D'Avergne would not so much as arrange a flower.

CHAPTER

20

Lucy's fever worsened during the evening and Miss Havering was sufficiently concerned to send a message to the ballroom to fetch Lord Sheldon. He came at once and seeing Lucy's hectic colour, immediately sent his man for the doctor.

Lucy protested weakly.

The Earl ignored her protests and busied himself with bathing her forehead with lavender water.

'Havering can do that, Alex,' said Lucy, her eyes unnaturally bright in her flushed face. 'Lady D'Avergne will be missing you.'

'Vixen! Don't think of that now. Only close your eyes. Dr Marston will soon be here.'

He was too sanguine, for the doctor was dining from home and it was two hours before he reached the Hall, by which time Lucy had lapsed into semi consciousness.

Dr Marston crossed the threshold and came briskly into the room with all the confidence of one who knows his business. But on seeing Alex sitting at his wife's bedside, he stopped short. He knew the Earl well and would never have called him unfeeling, but certainly he would have considered him a man well able to conceal his fears. He was unprepared for the haggard look he saw on his face.

'Well, my lord,' he said heartily, in an effort to hide his surprise. 'What's to do?'

His matter of fact voice went some way to restoring Alexander to his usual sang-froid, but he watched intently while Dr Marston examined the wound.

'She's lost some blood,' said the doctor briefly, while he was rebinding it. 'But she'll soon be well. Feverish, but I'll give you some cordial for when she wakes and that'll soon improve her.'

Fastening the bag from which he had extracted the cordial, he gave the Earl a searching look.

'Suppose it's no use asking you to take something, my lord? You look a bit on edge yourself.'

'Don't be absurd, man. It's my wife I'm afraid for!'

'Afraid? Yes.' The doctor hesitated. 'You'll tell me if I'm sticking my nose where it's not wanted, but I've heard a tale about some cream.'

The Earl looked up sharply.

'Where did you pick that up?'

'You know how these things fly about,' he said with a shrug. 'Maid's sister works in the kitchens here. Anything you want to tell me?'

'That's the devil of it, Marston. Lucy didn't even bother to tell *me* about that. I only found out because Mrs Perry made sure I knew. Said she thought there might be someone spiteful around trying to hurt Lucy. When I mentioned it to Lucy she laughed, and when nothing else happened, I wrote the incident off as imagination. Now, I don't know what to think.'

'But *could* anyone want to hurt her ladyship?'

The Earl was thoughtful. 'Oh I fear so,' he said quietly. 'I very much fear so.'

Lady Oswaldeston came bustling into Lucy's salon, closely followed by her maid, who was carrying a number of intricately wrapped parcels. It was two days since Lucy's accident and she was now to be found seated on a small sofa by the window, a shawl draped over her legs and a marble-covered book lying neglected in her lap while she looked fretfully through the window onto a perfect summer's day.

Outside, a pair of wagtails bobbed to each other as they enjoyed the heat, while in the flowerbeds beyond, Mary's bright head could just be glimpsed over a tall lupin as she chased Smudge through the undergrowth. Lucy was so engrossed that she started in surprise at her sister-in-law's voice.

'Lucy, my love,' said Fanny contritely, waving her hand to direct her maid to place her parcels on a table by the sofa. 'I know you won't forgive me for not coming to see you before, but Alex will tell you I am the worst person in the world when it comes to sick-rooms.'

Lucy's eyes creased.

'He already *has*, goose,' she replied, holding out her hands to her.

Fanny clasped them both and sat on a stool, peering intently into Lucy's face.

'I can see you are better, though still a trifle pale. Piers sends his best love and asks if he may come to see you later, but I've sent him out riding this morning, so we can have a nice comfy coze.' She barely paused for breath before explaining, 'I did peep in on you on the night of the accident, but Alex said that if I couldn't do anything but cry, I was no use!'

'He would!' said Lucy, giving Fanny's hand a sympathetic squeeze. 'But I am so pleased to see you. Tell me all that has happened. Who won the archery contest? I wouldn't give Sheldon the satisfaction of asking. Who won from among the ladies?'

'Whom do you think?' said Fanny grimly. 'When you could not shoot in the final round, dear Valentine was persuaded, with how much reluctance I give you leave to guess, to take your place and she beat the others hands down. And how she strutted about afterwards.'

'She is still here then,' said Lucy in gloom. 'I had hoped it would be too dull with the household being taken up with nursing me.'

'Dull, my dear? She is too busy to be dull!' Which Lucy interpreted as meaning that Lady D'Avergne was still monopolising the menfolk.

'Who won the men's contest?'

'Valentine's odious brother, I'm afraid. I hoped it would be Piers, but he made a bad shot at the last. And if ever a day was a waste of time that one was, for here you are injured, and Sam's hand is still paining him, and all so that that pair can lord it over the rest of us. Valentine wears the hairslide wherever she goes to remind us all how clever she is! I wish we had never had the contest!'

'But you must have enjoyed the ball?'

'Enjoy it? It was a fiasco. I ask you, my dear, to imagine the scene. *You* are not there! Alex tells me that *I* must greet the guests in your place when they come down from changing, not telling me until later what had occurred, and me thinking you had the headache or something. But, of course, I'd do anything for you and Alex, so I hurried to dress—in my white lace with the rose knots—you know the gown I mean. The dress that the Regent said made me look like Titania. Not that I cared for that at such a time, of course, but appearances *are* important, as you will be the first to admit! And a wreath of flowers in my hair, which Piers thought just the right touch. So I came downstairs to take my place with Alex—I decided to wear the pink shoes with the little heel after all. I do *detest* that woman leering down at me. I came downstairs and who should I find but Valentine D'Avergne, standing beside

215

Alex as impudently as you please, for all the world as if she had a right to be there! And there she stayed, my dear, until Alex had seen the last guest in. I leave you to decide how much I enjoyed the ball after that.'

'You have forgotten to tell Lucy that you were more than half an hour late in coming down, Fanny, and since Lady D'Avergne was rather more punctual it would have been impolite of me not to ask her to take your place,' said a deep voice from the doorway.

At the sound of it Lucy's head jerked up and she stared across at the figure silhouetted in the doorway by the morning sunshine. Satisfying herself that it was indeed her husband, she immediately became too busy untying parcels to greet him, her cheeks on fire.

Fanny was now in full flow.

'Of course I was late, goosecap! You wouldn't have wished me to look anyhow, would you? Though had I known that you would allow Arunfold's guests to be greeted by a woman in a scarlet dress! Yes, Lucy, Scarlet! Had I known that *my brother* cared so little what people thought of us, I probably wouldn't have bothered to change at all!'

'What a pity that would have been, Fan. I don't know when I've seen you paid so many compliments.'

Fanny was straightway restored to her sunniest humour. 'Yes, I rather think I must have been in my best looks,' she said complacently, patting at her curls. 'So absurd for an old married woman, but I had any number of gentlemen begging me for every dance, and my card was filled before the dancing began.'

Peace regained, Alexander turned his attention to his wife, still steadfastly ignoring him, though there was a trace of a smile on her lips, which confirmed her appreciation of his easy handling of Fanny.

'No need to ask how you are today, Lady Sheldon,' he said, placing his hand briefly on her forehead, while she kept her eyes rigidly on the parcel she had in her lap. 'You are looking positively blooming, isn't she Fan?'

'Oh I'm well enough, sir,' she replied, to save his sister the trouble of a reply, but she found she could not be at her ease with him.

Lucy was in a quandary: her mind could not rid itself of a damning vision of him close by in the forest, bow in hand, when she had been shot. But opposed to that, she could not but remember his very real care of her while she had been ill. Alexander it had been who was there when she awoke hot and thirsty, who held her close to his shoulder while he gave her the barley water she craved and made her take the cordial which helped her fever to abate. She wanted to be able to trust him, but was nagged by fear.

Now, just to think of their enforced intimacy was to be embarrassed, yet his manner was so matter-of-fact as to suggest that it had been nothing to him at all.

She was afraid that they would be left alone together. But Fanny did not consider herself *de trop* and chattered on with all the confidence of a person who knew she was welcome. Seeing how well Lucy seemed, she cajoled her brother into agreeing to her taking a short walk. Lucy was enthusiastic and the Earl eager to oblige her, but, parasols and pelisses sent for, Fanny rejected Alexander's company, determined not to allow him to spoil their confidences. Promising not to let Lucy walk too far, she and her sister-in-law walked out through the French windows and across the lawns, the Earl deep in thought, watching them from the house.

Once out of earshot, Lucy rejected out of hand the idea of a gentle walk around the formal gardens and insisted on making for the high woodland. Fanny protested, afraid that Lucy would overtax her returning strength, but even she was not proof against Lucy's disappointed pout, and finally agreed to it, though she made her promise not to stride along as she usually did. And so, with Lucy slipping a hand through Fanny's arm, the two ladies made their ascent up the gradual incline towards the high wood. It was wonderful to Lucy to be outside again. She hated being confined to the house and only wanted to be allowed to enjoy the peaceful scene around her. Fanny had other ideas. Intrigued by the happenings of the previous few days, she was curious to know just how things stood between Lucy and the Earl. She hoped that Lucy would bring up the matter, which in a roundabout way, she did.

'What has become of the others, Fan?' asked Lucy, as Fanny paused for breath and turned to look back at the house below. 'I'm not complaining at not having to entertain Lady D'Avergne, but do you think we should have left like this? Won't she think me a strange hostess?'

'My dear girl! Of course, you don't know, do you? How very remiss of me not to keep you up with all the news, to be sure. You won't find yourself bothered with our dear Valentine at present. It is just as I predicted. Now that Alex has foisted them onto all the neighbours, she has been using the time of your illness most usefully, and entirely to her advantage. Every day she has made a positive *tour*, my love. Imagine the scene, every morning. "Dearest Lady Oswaldeston"—for I *won't* let her call me Fanny!—"Dearest Lady Oswaldeston, I do hope that you won't think me a bore, but at the ball Lady Hargety *begged* me not to stand on ceremony with them. It will appear oh so rude if I don't pay my respects!" (Her voice was in perfect mimicry of Valentine's). ' "And Mrs. Pargeter, too, made me *promise* not to leave without paying a call on them first! You do see how it is, don't you?" I certainly *do* see how it is! Those poor dears have been forced into appearing complaisant so as not to risk offending Alexander, and Valentine is laying up her store of acquaintances like a farmer's wife lays up her hams for winter. But at least it means that she is not forever around *us*.'

Lucy longed to ask if Alexander accompanied the lady on her travels, but instead asked about Tom.

'When she knew you were ill, Gwen took Mary to stay with her for a week or so, so Tom spends his time with them. It seemed best, my dear, for Tom seems as useless in the sickroom as me.'

'Oh Tom has never been any good with invalids.'

'Charles, of course, was in agonies for you, as you may imagine, and every day he has ridden over to make his enquiries. But his presence seems to offend Alexander—you will know why more than I—and Alexander is barely civil to him. Charles brought you the prettiest posy the first day you were ill, but Alexander told him that he does not like flowers in a sickroom and made him take it away. When Charles brought peaches, Alexander said that the doctor had forbidden them, though, to be sure, *I* never heard him.'

'Poor Charles,' was all that Lucy replied, but her heart fluttered, not for his flowers, but for Alexander's response to them.

Fanny hoped that Lucy would be more forthcoming as to how things stood, but when she remained silent was too much intrigued to leave such a promising subject.

'Alex would not let anyone come near you while you were ill, my dear,' she persevered. 'I cannot remember when I've seen him so distressed by an accident.'

'If it *was* an accident!' said Lucy, before she could stop herself.

'If it was. . . ? What on earth do you mean?'

It was clear from her expression that Fanny had accepted without question the Earl's explanation of an accident and this new possibility horrified her. She begged Lucy for her reasons for thinking herself a target and listened intently as she told of the afternoon's events on the day of the archery contest. Unlike the Earl, Fanny was perfectly ready to think the worst of Mincham and, when Lucy told her that she had seen her loitering in the wood, she considered the matter settled. She could not go so far as to think that Mincham meant to hit Lucy, but certainly it would be like the dreadful creature to try to frighten her.

But when Lucy hesitantly told Fanny of her fears that Sheldon might be involved, Fanny absolutely refused to listen any further, saying only that Lucy's accident must have been worse than they had suspected and had left her unhinged. Lucy wished she shared her confidence, but during her illness she had found her mind focussing with increasing clarity on the incident with Smudge. Much as she tried to put it from her mind, she could not help remembering that Mrs Perry had found the matter suspicious. And if Mrs Perry's suspicions should prove correct, dreadful new possibilities opened up before her. Since it was difficult to believe that Mincham could possibly have found her way into the house without being seen, it seemed to Lucy that she must have an accomplice. But *that* incident could not be viewed in isolation and, since as far as she could tell, only Alex had been close to her when she had been shot at in the wood, everything pointed to him. He *must* be in league with

Mincham! Though, Heaven knew what he had to gain by it!

She did not feel up to explaining all this to Fanny, but the hint had been more than enough, and an ominous silence fell between them, Fanny's lips pressed together indignantly. Lucy could not bear the silence and searched around desperately for something to say. On hearing a tapping noise in the wood, she drew it to Fanny's attention, hoping to get her to speak to her.

'Listen. Is not that a woodpecker?' she asked, brightly.

Fanny was not to be placated.

Lucy tried again.

'No, but listen how loud it is!' she said, looking all about her trying to see it.

The two ladies were at the time just passing a large expanse of felled tree trunks, cut down and piled side-on on ready to be removed before the hill was replanted with new trees. A vast number of trees denuded of branches were stacked up in piles one above the other, high on the hillside, each pile held by wooden stakes driven into the ground to keep them in place.

Fanny walked across the clearing still angry, trying to decide whether she should deign to reply to Lucy's half-expressed conviction of Sheldon's guilt. Lucy made to follow her, but once again the tapping noise diverted her.

'Listen Fanny, won't you. I am sure it is a woodpecker. What else could it be?'

'It's too slow for a woodpecker,' said Fanny, without interest, too cross with Lucy to pretend politeness.

Without warning a rumbling came from above. Fanny was still ambling along at her usual pace, telling Lucy in her mind what she could not say to her face. But it took Lucy only a moment to realise what was happening and she rushed forward, unceremoniously pushing Fanny before her, to escape from the path of a tumbling mass of logs hurtling towards them.

Fanny protested only momentarily before she too realised the danger. Throwing down parasols and picking up their skirts with scant regard for elegance, they dashed for the edge of the clearing and flung themselves behind a stout tree, not daring to move, until the terrifying thunder had ceased. Dust flew everywhere, but when it finally settled and they were able to survey the scene around them, they were horrified to see amidst the tangle of logs now blocking the lower reaches, the smashed handle of Fanny's parasol.

CHAPTER

21

Lord Sheldon's investigations revealed that the retaining stakes on the uppermost pile of timber had been knocked away, probably by a large stone found at the scene. The force of the logs tumbling down the hillside had been enough to smash the retaining stakes on the lower two piles as the whole mass of tree trunks had plunged down the hillside towards the unsuspecting ladies.

There could be no possibility of an accident and the household drew together in its fear. The Earl gave immediate instructions to have servants posted in the grounds with orders to report anything suspicious, and there was a general understanding among the men that Lucy and Fanny were not to be left alone until the culprit could be discovered.

Samuel tried to insist that both ladies remain safely in the house, but Lucy reminded him how she had not been safe even in her own breakfast room and continued her daily exercise in the gardens and around her succession houses, though prudently staying away from the wood. Fanny would have been more than happy to remain indoors, but Lucy laughed away her fears and she unwillingly joined her on her walks.

Considering her conviction that *she* was the intended victim, Lucy felt strangely happy. Someone was trying to be rid of her, to be sure, but at least it could not be her husband, since he would never hurt Fanny. He must be innocent. And each time she remembered it, the colour flooded her face in her pleasure at the thought.

But still, *someone* was attempting to harm her, and trying to decide on the most likely suspect was the subject of endless hours.

'What have *we* done to anyone?' said Samuel, sweeping the salon expansively with his hand to include them all. 'Who could possibly wish to harm one of *us*?'

'How can we tell what is behind it?' replied the Earl grimly. 'All we can be certain of is that it is someone entirely ruthless. Entirely without honour.'

Samuel was shaken by the possibility. It seemed impossible to him that *their* family could be acquainted with such a person.

'We suddenly seem to be acquainted with all *sorts* of people!' said Fanny seriously. Then, looking at her brother and seeing that she had gone too far even with such a guarded reference to their foreign visitors, she went on hastily, 'And then there is this business with Mincham! I know not what to think!'

'Ar you sure, Fanny?' flashed the Earl with annoyance. 'It appears to me you have already made up your mind who is to blame.'

'It seems to *me*,' interrupted Tom, 'that Mincham would have to be deuced strong to have started those logs rolling.'

He shared Fanny's suspicions and had, on more than one occasion, and without success, demanded of the Earl the Lady D'Avergne and Monsieur be sent from the house. A distinct coolness had, as a result, arisen to temper what had once been a promising friendship.

It was a relief to them all that the Frenchwoman and her brother were still indulging themselves with the round of morning and afternoon calls begun from the day of the archery contest, aggressively visiting anyone and everyone they considered could be of use to them in future. Their neighbours could not welcome such attentions, but at least during the day the party at Arunfold was select. As long as the ladies remained within their charmed circle they felt themselves safe.

And their circle was indeed select. Not even Charles Thorne visited the house during this anxious time. In terror for Lucy, for once he was in agreement with the Earl and submissively endorsed Alexander's judgement that she would be safest among her own. But given their present rivalry it was impossible that they should agree on much else and, like Tom, he too had quarrelled with Alexander on the subject of Lady D'Avergne. There was so much aggravation between them already that the Earl had chosen to take Mr Thorne's remarks as a criticism of his own behaviour. The resultant frostiness between them made Mr Thorne unwelcome at Arunfold, so he whiled his time away at home as best he could, writing Lucy endless letters of support, which she barely read.

Thus did matters stand at Arunfold and with the reduction in their domestic circle Lucy found herself thrown more and more into her husband's company. She was unsure how she should behave, and so that she should not expose herself to any disadvantage, remained at all times coolly pleasant. His eye was often on her, but whether this was in order to store up faults for criticism or in sympathy she could not tell. Now that Lucy was almost fully restored to health he was content to leave the small ministrations to her shoulder to her maid. Lucy could only think that his previous assistance must have been a bore to him and resolved to show nothing but acquiescence with these new arrangements.

The unvarying nature of their company threw a stultifying lethargy over them all, which a period of warm, settled, heavy weather did nothing to dispel. They were all living on their nerves. Every moment expecting that *something* would happen, and every moment determined to make sure that it did not. The gentlemen had at least some release, for they could go out riding, as long as one of their number remained behind with the ladies, and even Samuel, whose arm still prevented him from riding, took long walks to rid himself of the lethargy engendered by high walls.

The ladies wanted neither to play or sing, to paint or to sew. It was too hot: too oppressive: and invariably they sat together in the drawing room in dull sympathy, reading or chatting in a desultory manner, while they languidly wafted their fans to and fro to stir the air.

On the third day of such enforced stupidity Lucy could bear it no longer. Yawning vigorously and throwing down her book, she said to her companion,

'Come, my love, let us take a ride for pity's sake.'

Fanny looked up in alarm.

'You know we cannot.'

'I am more like to die here of the mopes than if I go riding!'

'You are always such a tease, my sweet,' said Fanny, reassured by her smile, and relaxing back into her chair, 'but Alexander would *never* let you go!'

It needed only that, and Lucy was halfway upstairs to change before Fanny could comprehend her intention. As soon as she realised that Lucy was indeed going riding, she rushed towards the billiard room, where her husband and brother were playing a match.

It is not altogether surprising, therefore, that some minutes later the Earl entered Lucy's chamber and found her already attired in her grey Kerseymere riding habit and just collecting up her whip. The obstinate line to her mouth told the Earl what to expect. He dismissed her woman.

'So, my lady! What is all this?' were his first words to his wife.

'I'm bored, sir. I have decided to go for a ride. My mare is being saddled up for me!'

'No, my dear,' he replied gently. 'She is not!'

She pulled herself up to her full height.

'I do assure you, sir, she is! I gave my orders on my way up!'

'Which was foolish of you, since it made it necessary for me to countermand them!'

Incensed by the implacability of his demeanour and forgetting that she had her whip in her hand, Lucy raised her hand to strike him. He was too quick for her and caught at her wrist with one hand, wresting the whip from her with the other.

'My dear girl! Must you for ever be trying to strike me? You really are the most spirited woman of my acquaintance. I am married to a shrew!'

'You are not!' said Lucy vexed, rubbing her wrist, 'But why must you always have your own way?'

'I? Have my own way? I think few *husbands* can have had their way less than I, Lucy. Have I ever gone back on my word to you? Have I not kept to the *letter* of our agreement?'

They seemed once again to be approaching interesting matters. Lucy was determined to goad him into going further.

'It cannot have been so difficult, my lord. Lady D'Avergne must certainly have reconciled you. No-one seeing you together would consider you depressed.'

'Lady D'Avergne? What? I thought you too sensible to listen to my sister.'

'If it were only your sister, perhaps I should not, but your *friendship* with the lady is a matter of wider knowledge, I think.'

He had the grace to blush, but would have defended himself had not Fanny chosen that inauspicious moment to knock.

'You will be angry with me for telling him, Lucy, but after all I have only one sister-in-law and I refuse to allow you to put yourself in peril,' said Fanny, barging in, unaware that she had interrupted such a promising tête-a-tête and concerned only with her own defence.

Lucy was not prepared to argue, and she was furious to find tears welling when she explained to Fanny,

'It is just that I am so bored!'

Surprised by her show of weakness Fanny appealed to her brother. It was so unlike Lucy to be miserable.

As much surprised by her tears as Fanny, Sheldon conceded that they could not go on without some form of diversion.

To cheer them up, he suggested inviting some of their most trusted neighbours to dine with them on the following evening. Lucy could only be gratified by his consideration and readily agreed, and by six on the following evening the large dining room was laid out ready, china, glass and silverware gleaming in the mellow evening sunlight.

At Lucy's insistence the Thornes headed the guest list, and they were first to arrive. Charles nodded curtly to Alexander and passed determinedly to Lucy, but after her husband's consideration on her behalf, Lucy had decided to keep

Charles at a distance and received him with calm friendliness. More specifically she had placed him at dinner at quite the other end of the table.

The old Viscount, meanwhile, engaged the Earl in conversation.

'Nasty business this, my lord,' he said grimly as he shook hands. 'Hope you've got it under control. Sweet girl, the Countess. Shouldn't like to see anything happen to her.'

'I shall keep her safe, never you fear.'

Casually the Viscount said, 'Your fine French lady and her brother seem to have been doing some visiting. Are they in the house tonight?'

The Earl stiffened. 'You will have the pleasure of renewing your acquaintance with Lady D'Avergne and her brother at dinner.'

The Viscount flushed.

'Don't get on your high ropes with me, Alex. Known you too long. Remember you in skirts!'

Alexander smiled charmingly. 'It is impossible to be on one's dignity with anyone who can say as much, sir.'

Mollified, the Viscount clasped his hands again.

'Just remember to be on your guard while they are in the house, that is all I ask! You may think me an old fool if you wish, but such a lot has happened since they arrived.'

They were interrupted by the vision of Lady D'Avergne descending the grand staircase. All conversation was halted, but for once, she did not preen herself. She had overheard the old Viscount's words and her face mirrored her shock at his suspicions.

Tonight Lucy was not alarmed by Valentine's beauty, for in her ears still echoed the congratulatory phrases her husband had spoken earlier when he had first seen her in her new gown. It was the dress she would have worn at the ball: a gown of white gauze over a maiden-blush slip, with satin rollio and flowered hem. On catching a glimpse of herself in the mirror, Lucy knew how well she looked. Her husband's words and the way he caught his breath when he saw her, made her feel that she need not fear Valentine in her flamboyant gold satin.

Country hours were kept at Arunfold, so dinner commenced early and her guests were soon enjoying the feast Lucy had provided. The Earl's idea of a small dinner party was rather different to that which Lucy had been used and the dining room seated more than forty, but her neighbours no longer had the power to unnerve her. Helping herself to a piece of a particularly appetising looking venison pasty, she prepared to listen to a racy anecdote from her dinner partner, an elderly Baronet who, with his family, were familiar guests at Arunfold and who remembered just in time that one did not repeat such stories to ladies. He blushed a fiery red, but Lucy kindly filled the breech by drawing attention to his empty glass. She had just beckoned to a footman when she was aware of a weird constriction in her throat. Next moment the room seemed to close in on her. The candles in the chandelier appeared very close, as if they had been lowered by the servants, and she was suddenly very warm.

'What a singularly warm evening,' she said faintly to her companion, but she had no time for another word since nausea now threatened to overtake her. She wondered fleetingly if the Earl would disown her should she be ill in front of his guests, and, to the astonishment of all present, without a word of apology, fled from the room.

But she was not the only person in the room to be taken ill and the Earl's dinner party shortly floundered in disarray as one after another of their guests politely excused himself. Arunfold rapidly took on the appearance of a battle ground as maids and footmen ran to and fro to assist their discomforted guests, while Lord Sheldon lost no time in sending for Dr Marston. The good doctor confirmed that the party was suffering from some kind of food poisoning and, while the stricken were being ministered to, it was speedily established that the only thing commonly eaten among them was the venison pasty. The Earl enquired minutely into the catering arrangements for the evening, while his sister whispered pointedly to her husband that neither Valentine nor that lady's brother was affected.

Mrs Perry was mortified. Such a thing had never happened in all the years she had been in charge of his lordship's kitchens and she gathered her staff, determined to get to the bottom of the matter. In the event, the countenance she exhibited was so forbidding that extensive enquiry was unnecessary. One of the kitchenmaids had that day seen Jenkins, Miss Mincham's old confidante, in the kitchens, "where she'd no right to be". Having been summoned to the Earl's study, Jenkins tearfully admitted that she had been bribed by Mincham not only to tamper with the food for dinner that evening, but that she, too, had tainted the cream which had made the kitten ill.

'I'd never have done anything which would really have hurt anyone, whatever she said,' mumbled the girl tearfully. 'I only replaced some of the mushrooms in the pie with pieces of fungus she picked in the wood, just like she asked me. Nothing poisonous. Just enough to make you sick. And that other time I put some dissolved emetic tartar in with the cream. It doesn't hurt you. Not really. Just makes you a bit anyhow for a day or two. Miss Mincham, she said as how it was wrong of My Lady to dismiss her like that, without a character. Staying with my mum is where she's been since leaving the house, and paying good money too!'

The strange matter of Miss Mincham was swiftly dealt with. Brought to the house and questioned closely by the local magistrate, she summarily refused to admit any of the charges against her, closing her lips tightly when Lord Sheldon tried to get her to admit that she had loosed an arrow at Lucy or had sent the logs sliding downhill onto her. Since there was little in the way of positive proof to submit, the Earl could do nothing by accept the magistrate's plea for leniency, and, with only a stern warning, she was released, on condition that she left the district at once, the Earl sending two of his men with her to see that she obeyed.

In the kitchens, Mrs Perry held her own court. Nobody cared to gainsay her when she remarked enigmatically,

'It's like Mincham to have thought of making them suffer in that way. Sickness: queasiness: anything in that line, to make them look foolish. But all this business with logs and arrows—well I don't know about that! That's out of character if you ask me. The other is spiteful. Murder's different!'

CHAPTER

22

With the sudden release of tension, things were free to return to normal, though normality encouraged change. For one thing, Lady Valentine felt she had stayed long enough. Shocked that she could have awakened such emnity, Valentine had finally given up trying to woo the Earl. It was time for new pastures, new targets. Her visit had not lacked its pleasure, nor its usefulness. None of those who had entertained her in recent days would ever be allowed to let the acquaintance drop. It could only bring Almacks closer. But Valentine had had too little encouragement from the Earl to make her waste any more time on him and had regretfully decided to venture on. That her departure coincided with that of Lady Pargeter to Brighton was true, but it would be a harsh critic who connected the two events, even though it was clearly understood that Lady Valentine's destination too was Brighton.

In any case, she had remained so long at Arunfold that, as long as she went, nobody much cared why. They could only sigh with relief to see her travelling coach, piled high with luggage, drive away from the front portico, the lady's handkerchief waving from the window of the coach in regretful farewell.

Though Lucy and Fanny rejoiced in the freedom gained from her absence the Earl remained aloof. Lucy could only imagine that, unlike the others, he intended to miss Madame D'Avergne.

When the family came down to dinner it was clear that Fanny and Lucy were ready to enjoy themselves. Prepared to renew all former local acquaintances now that danger was past they talked over their plans with a great deal of animation.

But it was the Earl who made the first suggestion for change. Rumour had reached him that, on the following day, two champion pugilists, Jack Scroggins and Ned Turner, were to meet not thirty miles away for a return match. The ladies were pleased to retire to the music room, while the men, an unconscionably long time over the port, talked over with great enthusiasm, the bloody details of the previous encounter at which the press of thirty thousand spectators had broken into the ring, knocking down posts, treading ropes under foot, and the whole affair had turned into a street brawl. It seemed too good an opportunity to miss enjoying themselves in similar fashion once again and it was enthusiastically agreed that the Earl and his friends should leave the ladies to themselves as early as possible next morning, to ensure that they obtained a good position from which to view this splendid spectacle.

Only Samuel would not accompany them, and this through no disinclination to see the fight, since he was the keenest sportsman of them all. He too, was to leave early and would certainly join the men for breakfast, but London must be his destination, he said, as he had received a letter from his man of business concerning some affairs to which he must attend.

'Too smokey by half, old man,' said the Earl, tapping the side of his nose. 'It's Brighton, not London that draws you away. Only Lady D'Avergne would be enough to keep you from a mill.'

Reluctant at first to admit it, he was finally persuaded to confess that, the lady had given him more than a hint that he might step into his cousin's shoes, should he care to follow her to Brighton. He *did* care, and had determined to leave next day.

The Earl stared hard at him.

'My dear boy, I beg you to think hard before you do anything foolish. Much better come to the fight with us!'

But Samuel was not to be dissuaded and before the noisy party broke up that evening Samuel had made his farewells to the ladies, promising to come down to see Lucy before too many months had passed.

Lucy had grown so fond of Samuel while he had been staying with them that she thought of him as her own cousin and wished he might stay. But men must make their own mistakes, and Lucy kept her own counsel, wishing only that he might not be too hurt when the Lady found a larger purse to amuse her.

By the time Lucy had come down to breakfast next day, the men were already some hours on their way and she looked forward to an undisturbed morning pottering around the succession houses, which were her pride and joy and in which she had been helping the head gardener to nurture some luscious peaches.

Since Fanny was not yet to be expected down for some while, she decided to go down to the glass houses early, before the heat of the day made them uncomfortable, and she carried a basket over her arm to collect fruit for the house. Early as she was, Peckworth the gardener had been there before her, watering the fruits, and she caught him on his way back to his cottage for a late breakfast. Lucy was very fond of the old man and he returned her affection, delighted to have a mistress whose interest in his work extended further than her dish at luncheon.

She stayed some few minutes with him while he warned her which of the fruits looked ripe but were not quite ready to be eaten, adding kindly, as though he and not she owned the house,

'If you go to the far end, my lady, you may pick

as many peaches as you like, for there's a goodly number ripe up there. But don't pick any by the eastern door, will you. Nasty and hard they'll be for a day or two yet.'

Lucy giggled to herself at his unconscious presumption, but none of the family would have dreamt of trying to put Peckworth in his place.

She continued down the path, pushed open a door and entered into the humid atmosphere. The houses had been built against a high brick wall and peaches trained to cover its length. She walked along minutely inspecting the downy harvest, pleased that Peckworth had warned her against picking those closest to the eastern entrance, for to her untrained eye they looked sumptuously ripe. The building was perhaps a hundred feet in length and she had neared the western entrance before she began to basket the fruit. Warm and firm in her hand, she could not resist trying one, the juice running through her fingers as she bit through to the flesh. She had not brought her reticule and looked around for something on which to wipe her fingers.

'Would you like to borrow this?' asked a well known voice from the doorway. She looked up sharply. 'Samuel! Good heavens, what a fright you gave me!'

'What you? Afraid of me? Never!' he said laughingly, handing her his handkerchief. 'Nobody is afraid of me.'

'Well *I* was!' snapped Lucy. 'Really Samuel, you should not creep up on people like that! And anyway, what are you doing here? Shouldn't you be on your way to Brighton?'

'Oh, but it was never my intention to go to Brighton, dear coz. It was good of you all to find a reason why I *should* be there, but I am afraid the lady could never take *me* seriously until my fortunes were more promising.' His voice was bitter.

Lucy had never considered Samuel as anything but

content with his situation in life and it came as something of a shock to realize that she had misjudged him.

'Poor Samuel. Do you indeed admire her so much?'

'Admire?' His voice altered to a new harshness. 'No, I don't "admire" her at all. I *want* her. Can you understand that? All my life I have heard Alex scorn such women as Valentine D'Avergne and yet he lifts his finger and they are his. I despise them, but I want that power.'

'But women find you just as attractive as they do Alex, Samuel,' said Lucy kindly. 'I'm sure they do.'

'You would be surprised how many *would* find me quite as attractive if I inherited the title. It makes my head spin to think how many.'

Lucy felt she was being dragged into something she did not comprehend.

'What do you mean, Sam? Why did you say you were going to Brighton if you weren't? And why are you speaking like this? And all this about the title,' she said faintly. 'You cannot have lived on hopes of that, surely?' You must always have known that it might not pass to you. It is not that important, is it?'

'Oh, but you are wrong, Lucy my dear. Quite wrong. It is of the greatest importance to me. Not only that, but I mean to make quite certain that it *will* pass to me.'

As Lucy watched, he slipped his right hand from the sling, which he took from around his neck and began deliberately to unknot it.

'There is nothing wrong with your arm,' whispered Lucy unnecessarily.

'No, nothing. There never was,' he said, matter-of-factly. 'But I could not take a chance on Alex suspecting me, could I?'

'Suspecting you?'

'Of murder, my dear, of course! With my arm in a sling how could I aim a bow? How could I manage to start a log-slide?'

237

'It was you! You tried to kill me!'

As this realisation dawned on her, so did the dreadful probability that he would do so again, and with it the absolute necessity of getting away from him. She took a few stumbling steps back the way she had come, dropping her basket in her haste, only to find herself further from the door as he reached her and took hold of her arm.

Lucy was not one who would give in without a struggle and, with her free hand, began to beat his shoulders and head to try to escape him, as he tried to get the sling around her throat. Fear made her desperate. She scratched at his face in her terror, which gave him the determination he needed to slip the sling around her neck.

Lucy was almost as tall as he, but Samuel was heavy. She didn't stand a chance against his strength and every moment found the sling tightening, though she had managed to slip her hand between her neck and the material and was determinedly preventing it from biting into her.

'That is enough, Samuel,' sounded a cool voice from a few feet away.

Samuel raised his head in disbelief. As if refusing to heed his senses he continued to struggle with Lucy.

'I said that is enough, Samuel,' the Earl said again, and in his hand he now held a pistol. 'You will release my wife, *now*!'

Holding Lucy before him, Samuel backed away from Alexander, his face a mask of fury, but he had gone no more than a few steps before a noise behind him made him look over his shoulder. Piers and Tom barred his way, and he was forced to recognise defeat. He dropped the sling and leaned away from his prisoner.

'Come Lucy,' said her husband quietly, holding out his hand.

She went to him gratefully, and he held her against him for a moment, rubbing his hand gently on her neck. 'It is alright my love. You are safe now,' he said, murmuring into her hair.

'Will somebody please tell me what is going on?' she said faintly. 'I don't understand any of this.'

'It was for you, Alex, and for the family,' blurted out Samuel, incensed by the sight of Lucy in his cousin's arms. He looked toward Piers for confirmation, but Piers looked away as if it was too painful to meet his eyes.

'Not *now*, Samuel!' said the Earl curtly. 'Don't make me more ashamed for you than I am already.'

Samuel made to reply, but bit his lip and was quiet.

The Earl turned again to Lucy.

'Now, my love, I am going to ask Tom and Piers to escort you up to the house, since it is necessary for me to talk to Samuel. Go with them and I will explain all to you later.'

She looked at him, startled, holding onto his arm. 'You will not . . . You will not *argue*,' she said anxiously. 'You will promise me that you will not *argue*?' She could not bear to put her fear into any stronger words.

'I promise you that we will not. What could be served by it? But you will see that it must be spoken of.'

For once Lucy submitted without question. The events of the morning had overset her mind too much for argument and she found that she needed to lean heavily on Tom's arm as he led her away.

The Earl waited until the others were out of earshot before he said another word. His face was set and his lip curled, but whether in derision or from hurt would have been impossible to determine.

The heat inside the glass building was oppressive: Alexander could not bear it.

'For God's sake let's get out of here,' broke from his lips as if he didn't know what he said, and he led the way outside, making for the shade of a

239

nearby oak, so old that their grandfather had entertained both of them with tales of his own boyhood around and in its branches. Its massive presence was part of their shared experience: the Earl turned toward it for reassurance, but Samuel felt outlawed from its comfort. He stood away as Alex leaned against one of the lower branches. Surprisingly the Earl's first words were,

'Poor Samuel. How sorry you must be feeling for yourself.'

For a moment Samuel was relieved. 'Then you *do* understand, Alex,' he said eagerly. 'You do see that I had no choice!'

'No choice? No choice but to choose dishonour? There is always a choice. We both know that!'

Samuel flushed before he spoke.

'What made you suspect me? What made you turn back today?'

'Turn back? From where? I made no journey, neither did the others.'

'But you said . . .'

'You see, it was necessary,' said the Earl flatly. 'You had to be stopped. I was foolish enough to want to give you another chance if only you had been prepared to take it. After the affair with Mincham I hoped that would be enough. I hoped you would consider yourself fortunate in getting away with the other attempts—that her small crimes could cover up your greater ones. That's why I had her let off so lightly. If only I could have been certain that you would not try again to hurt Lucy I'd have let the matter rest! When I pleaded with you yesterday to come with us it was because I knew that if you had given up this business nothing would have kept you from a prize fight—not Valentine D'Avergne, no, not the Queen of Sheba! It was a test. Remember I've known you man and boy, Samuel. I know you as well as I knew my own brother. How often have you and I gone off to a fight when we were wanted elsewhere. As if I could be taken in by such a tale.'

'You are so clever, Alex, aren't you.'

'Apparently not. I'd have sworn you would never do me any hurt—that's how clever I've been!'

'Hurt you? But of course I'd never hurt you! Quite the opposite. All this was done to save you, not to hurt you!'

'Coming it too strong, Sam!'

'You're wrong! When I came down here I never had any blacker intention than to enjoy myself— you must believe me. But almost as soon as I arrived I could see how things stood between Lucy and Thorne and then Fanny started to say that you'd become fond of Lucy! At first I didn't believe it, but when I started to watch you, it seemed to me you *were* fond of the girl! Lord, if it had only been a matter of you falling for Lucy and her loving you in return all would have been well—nothing better! But any fool could see she was fonder of Thorne than of you. The outcome was obvious. Nothing simpler than for her to foist a child of Thorne's onto you when she'd got you hooked. Good God, man, the estate would have passed out of the family—to a Thorne bastard! You must see I couldn't allow that!'

'My very dear Sam,' replied the Earl quietly. 'Do you take me for a flat? You'd have tried to get rid of Lucy even if there had never been a Charles Thorne! She was not safe after you realised that I loved her. That's the most difficult thing in all this to come to terms with. And, the devil of it is that it is probably my fault! After my brother's death I should never have promised that you would be my heir. I should have realised that a situation might arise where it might not happen. It must have been a cruel blow. But you see, Sam, I've only just realised how you wanted the title! One or two things lately have opened my eyes to it but before that I had no idea. When you told Viscount Thorne that "when" you were Earl he could have his land I should have been alerted. Instead, I was only surprised to think that you had ever so much as considered the matter. When you spoke of the day that Arunfold *would* be yours, not that it *might*, the next question must be to ask how long after Lucy's death would you have found a way to rid yourself of me?'

'I'd never have tried to kill you, Alex, never!' replied his cousin shrilly. 'You have no right to say so!'

'Of course you would, Sam! You told Viscount Thorne that he should have his land! That must at most only have given me a few years.'

Samuel flushed. 'I never meant . . . I would never have . . .'

He could not continue and they were both silent for several minutes until Samuel said grudgingly,

'What made you suspect me, Alex? You still haven't said. I was sure that you thought it was Léo—and then when Mincham was caught I thought I must indeed be safe from suspicion!'

'If it's any consolation to you, it took me some time before I was even certain that someone *was* trying to hurt Lucy. And with all this business with Mincham it was even more confusing. When Lucy was shot at I didn't know what to think! It could so easily have been just an accident that it seemed foolish to think of it as anything else. After the logfall it seemed it had to be attempted murder, but the cream business still confused me, and the mushroom affair even more so. Once I knew that Mincham had persuaded Jenkins to tamper with the cream and the pasty it all became crystal clear. Obviously we were dealing with two people. Mincham was trying to cause unpleasantness, not more than that, but someone else was a killer!'

'That still doesn't explain why you should suspect me!'

'It wasn't too difficult. Once I faced the fact that we were dealing with murder it was easy for me to think back over what had happened and work it all out. *You* had everything to gain. No other was really in the running.'

'What about Léo Marechal and Valentine? Why shouldn't it be them?'

'Too much of a long shot, old fellow. Only someone with much more cause to be sure I cared for her than Valentine would have risked it. We're not speaking of some paltry crime, Sam. We are speaking of killing someone! No! It had to be you. And your accident. It really was quite clumsy, you know. Falling from a horse? You? Far too obvious. And then you were the only person whose whereabouts at the time of the shooting I didn't know! Léo was with his sister. And there was really nobody else I could remotely suspect. And I know how good you are with a bow. If Lucy hadn't turned back to pick up her own bow and put you off your aim, you'd have killed her without compunction! And I've no doubt that you'd have finished off the job if I hadn't been in the wood that day.'

'But it was for you, Alex. Don't you see. I'd never have hurt *you*!'

'Do you expect me to believe you when you might so easily have killed Fanny with that logfall? Good God, man, you grew *up* with her. No, my boy, none of us were safe! But enough of this. Let's have an end to it. It's done with: in the past. Discussion futile.'

'What will you do, Alex?' Samuel asked, looking anxiously at his cousin. His voice sounded quite calm, but a pulse at his throat showed how much he depended on his answer.

'It is necessary to ensure that nothing ever gives you a reason, or indeed a chance to hurt me or mine again. I am sure that you will understand that. I've talked it over with Piers . . .'

Samuel caught his breath.

'Yes, with Piers,' said the Earl evenly. 'He guessed more or less at the same time that you were behind all this, so we've had time to make our plans. I have had to decide to remove you from the succession.'

The Earl was shocked at the agonised look on Samuel's face. He seemed like an animal hunted.

'It cannot be any other way, Sam,' said the Earl. 'For your own good. You must see that I must remove all temptation from you. For your own and the family good! I have already sent instructions to my solicitors and I shall expect you to voluntarily withdraw from the entail!'

'I shall not do so!'

'Oh but I think you will. I shall lodge letters with my solicitors, along with statements from Piers and Tom, to explain how you tried to murder my wife. If you do not withdraw from the entail these will be made public.'

'Nobody would believe you. You can prove nothing.'

'It wouldn't matter. You would be ruined anyway.'

'You would not do it!'

'You are wrong! To protect my family I would do whatever was needful! And that includes denying the house to you! Never set foot on my lands again, Sam. Never come to Grosvenor Square. Never expect me or mine to acknowledge you.'

Samuel Carne let out a cry of pain . . .

CHAPTER

23

Samuel was gone from Arunfold before luncheon, without being allowed an audience with the rest of his family. Lord Sheldon busied himself with making sure that Samuel's rooms were closed up and all trace of him removed before the family met for dinner.

When Fanny heard that the menfolk had suspected Samuel for days without telling her or Lucy she was furious, but the facts of the case upset her so much that she had not spirits enough to complain.

Lucy was deeply depressed to have been the cause of so much enmity and wished aloud that she had never answered Lord Sheldon's advertisement for a governess.

Her husband looked at her intently.

'And do you *really* wish that, Lucy?' he asked her, forcing her to meet his eye. 'That would be a pity indeed.'

Lucy blushed and lowered her gaze to her plate. Her voice shook,

'None of this would have happened but for me.'

'But I have explained it all to you,' said the Earl patiently. 'Samuel would have tried to hurt anyone

I married. The fault was mine. I gave him too much to hope for. Mine must be the responsibility.'

'Alex is right, my love,' said Fanny, squeezing Lucy's hand in sympathy. 'You cannot be held to blame. Nobody who was not already bad could have been led to such things—and I am sure that none of us could have guessed at what was going on in Samuel's head, Alex, so it is nonsense of you to shoulder the responsibility as well. Now just both listen to me! Mary shall come home from the Thornes tomorrow and we must all try to get back to normal as best we can. Self-recrimination cannot help us and it must stop!'

'I agree with Fanny,' said Lord Oswaldeston. 'Tom shall go over to Gwendolyn's tomorrow and bring Mary home. And Fanny and I must think of returning to London. We have been idle for too long, my love,' he said, turning towards his wife. 'It is time we left Alex and Lucy in peace.'

His look was so pregnant that it was not only Fanny who caught his meaning. Lucy turned a furious scarlet and even Tom was moved to remark casually,

'Thinking of going home myself, Luce old girl. Like to tip Papa the wink about Gwendolyn and me. Don't want them thinking there's anything sly going on.'

'What an excellent notion, Tom,' said the Earl, appearing not to notice any undercurrents. 'And you must take a letter from me to invite your parents to spend some time here with us, mustn't he my dear?'

He looked at his wife, who was now beginning to feel trapped by her friends' patent machinations to leave her alone with her husband.

'I wish you will not *all* leave us,' she said faintly. 'Perhaps we should come to town with you, Fanny? We shall be quite moped on our own.'

'Nonsense my love,' returned her husband in a flash. 'Did not you once tell me that there is so much more to do in the country than in Town? And with your music, and your drawing and sewing, how can you possibly be moped? And if all that flags, I shall let you give me another geography lesson!'

'Of course you won't be moped, love,' insisted Fanny. 'Charles Thorne and Gwendolyn will be sure to come over. And as Alex says, you have too many resources ever to be bored! You must play for us tonight, mustn't she Piers?'

Later in the drawing room when she had been persuaded to play she stopped suddenly, remembering that, when she had last played in that room, there had been an extra guest, one who would never be among them again. It brought home to her, as nothing else had, the full horror of the day's events. She tried to explain herself, but her halting words were unnecessary. They had all shared the same thought and had been made aware of how much they would miss their cousin.

'This is not a very auspicious start to our resolution, is it?' said the Earl, sweeping Lucy from the piano stool and beginning to play, not very expertly, the rousing introduction to a jolly song they all knew. 'Let us be more cheerful!'

A kind of desperation to enjoy themselves, in spite of all, reigned. Tom and Piers drank too much: Fanny enjoyed scolding them for it: the Earl and Lucy played and sang with them, all the time aware of each other.

Before it seemed possible it could be time, the tea tray appeared. Lucy looked enquiringly towards the clock on the mantelpiece and saw that it was not yet ten.

'You have brought tea too early, Frensham,' she said, surprised that this most perfect of all servants could make a mistake.

'I asked Frensham to bring the tray in early, my dear,' said the Earl. 'You are looking tired. An early night will do you good.'

'Oh, but I am not at all tired,' protested Lucy. 'I never felt less like going to bed.'

'But *I* think it will do you good,' repeated her husband, with meaning. With rather too much deliberation, Fanny yawned.

'Lord, yes! An early night is just the thing. I'm feeling positively hagged, aren't you Piers!'

Her husband, always co-operative, agreed, and Tom, who not five minutes earlier had challenged Piers to a game of billiards, professed himself suddenly exhausted.

With so many ranged against her, Lucy soon found herself in her room, being helped into her delicate muslin nightgown and cap by the ever-faithful Miss Havering.

Lucy climbed into the large fourposter and reached toward the side cabinet for her book, "Pamela", bringing her candle closer so that she could read its small print. It was a ridiculous time to go to bed, she thought crossly, as she watched Miss Havering close the heavy curtains against the warm summer evening. Certainly it was too early to sleep, especially in that heat. She plumped up her pillows and sat primly, trying to concentrate her mind on the exploits of Richardson's silly heroine in her attempts to defy the attentions of the sinister Mr B . . . !

'Foolish, ridiculous girl!' cried Lucy to herself, as she read of Pamela's ill-treatment at the hands of the unholy Mrs Jewkes. 'I should never allow myself to be put upon like that!'

Her indignation got the better of her and her desultory reading soon changed to gripped attention as Pamela awaited in fear her would-be seducer.

"Though I dread to see him," she read, with in-

creased indignation, "yet I wonder I have not ...
And then I heard his voice on the stairs, as he was
coming up to me."

Lucy was jerked from her book on hearing her
husband's voice on the stairs, giving Frensham his
instructions for the morning. It was just as in her
book! Intently she listened to his footsteps, berat-
ing herself, since she knew full well that he never
entered her room at night. For sure he would pass
by her door as usual.

The steps did not go past. They halted, and there
came a knock at the door. Lucy swallowed nervously and called her permission to enter.

'Reading my dear? How very domesticated,' said
her husband, as he came through the doorway.

'You *would* insist that I came to bed, sir, but it
is too hot to sleep!'

'How very strange! That's exactly what I thought
myself,' he said, walking over and seating himself
on the bed beside her.

Lucy found her heart thudding painfully. She was
sure that he must hear it, and hurried to say,

'Are the others all gone up, sir?'

'Yes all. Even Tom. Now you will admit that it
was magnanimous of him on such a night!'

'Magnanimous?'

'Very,' said her lord, casually removing her
nightcap, so that her hair tumbled around her
shoulders. 'What a very pretty cap,' he said admiringly, dropping it to the floor without a glance.

'I am surprised that you've taken it off then, sir,
since you hate my hair so much!'

'Hate your hair? Oh no,' he replied, smiling in a
way which made her catch her breath, and taking
one of her curls between his fingers. 'It *is* abominable when I am trying to make a Countess of you,
of course, but quite delightful in a wife!'

'I shouldn't think it mattered very much in *our* case!'

'Oh, but you are wrong,' he said caressingly, twisting a curl around his finger. 'It matters very much to me.'

'Why should it?' whispered Lucy, not daring to look at him.

'I think you know very well,' he murmured, before their lips met and his arms closed around her.

Some few moments later she spoke again. 'When did you realise you loved me?' she asked shyly.

'Loved you? Who said anything about love? Why, I am as much as ever of the opinion that you are the veriest brat!'

She pulled away from him, ready to be cross, but he took both her hands and would not let her go.

'Ask me instead when I first realised you were the only woman in the world I could ever care for.'

Made nervous by the dark expression she saw in his eyes, Lucy could only whisper, 'When?'

'It is difficult to fix the exact time,' said his lordship, gazing intently at her hands, 'but I rather think it must have been from the moment in the barn when you became absurdly aware that your silhouette was being thrown onto the wall!'

Lucy pulled her hands away indignantly. 'You did not *look*? You did not *look*? But you *assured* me that you were not interested in watching me!'

'Ah my sweet,' replied the Earl, regaining her hands with some difficulty, as he strove to check his amusement, 'so I believe I did.'

'Why you . . . you . . . fibster! You promised me!' she cried, tugging her hands again.

'But who told you I was *not* a fibster? The provocation was irresistible, believe me! And you could have taken advantage of the same privilege.'

'What do you mean, sir?' replied Lucy with awe-inspiring dignity, pulling herself straight up against her pillows.

'Well, I promise you, my love,' he said, unable to prevent the corners of his mouth from lifting at the memory, 'your determination not to move your head so much as an inch in case you should catch sight of me was quite as entertaining as your embarrassment over your own predicament just before. I think the effort I made to reassure you that I had seen nothing was *admirable*!'

'But it was a lie!'

'Yes, wasn't it?' he replied agreeably, sliding himself closer to the middle of the bed.

Seeing this tactical manoeuvre, Lucy swallowed hard and said breathlessly, 'But you couldn't have begun to like me then, else why were you so horrid to me after we were married. You went straight back to Valentine. Admit it. You did not want me!'

'What purpose could have been served by my staying, sweet?' he asked reasonably, reaching towards her shoulder and allowing his finger just to touch the disappearing mark of her arrow wound. 'You told me I was the last person in the world you wanted to marry, don't you remember?'

'But you married me anyway.'

'Of course,' he agreed pleasantly, his lips moving to find a spot just below her ear. 'Have I not already told you that the sight of you in the barn, limited as it was, gave me an appetite for more?'

'But you told me you were marrying me to save my reputation!'

'Yes, I believe I did. I really am a dreadful manipulator you know.'

He moved to settle himself beside his wife, both arms now around her, to his considerable satisfaction. 'And especially where my own comfort is concerned.'

'Do you *really* think I shall be necessary to your

251

comfort, my lord?' she asked wistfully, gazing intently into his face.

'My dearest sweet,' replied her husband warmly, kissing her cheek and then her lips. 'It is simply aeons since my comfort depended entirely on seeing you in my home every day. And,' he added, having moved his lips in the general direction of her throat, 'you really must stop calling me "my lord", as though I am a stranger. It will look most particular if you persist in calling me "my lord" by the time we have been married a decade. Almost as if I have been your ravisher rather than your husband!'

'Oh no, Alex,' gurgled Lucy, reaching her hand behind his dark head to bring his eyes back on a level with her own. 'You could never be that!'

'Oh I think, my darling, that in all honesty I should confess that the possibility exists . . .'